Afallon

The Year Of The Rabbit

Ken Dancer

New Generation Publishing

About the Author

Ken Dancer was born in Hillingdon, Middlesex, in 1951. He studied for his BA Degree and graduated with Honours from Liverpool University. Ken's profession was primarily in the field of Adult Teaching. This gave him the opportunity to travel extensively in later years.

He and his wife Allyson and their family live in Wales and have done so for many years. Ken and Ally are now residing in the beautiful market town of Usk.

Much of this landscape and character of Monmouth is included in this suspense thriller *Afallon*. Ken says, "I am really thrilled with this novel and hope it will intrigue and excite its readers."

He is now writing a sequel to this book entitled *The Dog and Drum Killings*. It is a complex crime thriller based on a psychotic killer loose on the streets of London.

Ken has a trilogy of children's books. The second is about to be published shortly. These all include the lovable character of 'Willit the Sprokwobble' and the mysteries he has to solve. Check out – www.authorkendancer.co.uk.

I would like to thank my family and friends for their encouragement and patience while I have devoted much of my time and effort to these ventures.

Ken Dancer

CHAPTER 1

Afallon Cottage, Llancayo, Monmouthshire –
Date: Wednesday 27th April 2011

It was her first night's stay in the sparsely furnished, two up two down, bedraggled country rental. Carrie-Anne shuffled uneasily beneath the frayed sheets of a time-worn king-size. Her solicitous mind was fused with an intrinsic sense of foreboding, and a hunger for answers. She listened intensely for any curious sounds, anything that might announce impending danger. So far, her morning ensemble consisted of a rowdy cockerel, the internal clunking of the antiquated heating system, and the faint, unnerving howl of an agitated dog.

"Oh, for a relaxing and quiet life in the country, that's a bloody joke for a start!" Carrie-Anne had a quick wit, mostly sarcastic, extremely to the point and satisfying. However, she failed to raise a smile this morning. Bed had always brought her a sense of warmth, security and calm, that in the womb feeling. This occasion was different.

She needed to shower; her body was markedly clammy. During the night she had perspired profusely. She had slept little, if at all, feeling drained, vulnerable, and alone.

1

Her stinging eyes, dry and sore, begged for sleep. She yelled heatedly, "How does he get away with this?"

The tired mattress had seen better days. Its wayward springs were sprouting through the remains of the fabric, like virgin shoots reaching for the sun. She glanced with an air of disbelief at the vintage Teasmade on the bedside cabinet. "No expense spared. What a tight-fisted, bloodsucker." She sharply refocused, abandoning her venomous snipe of the cheapskate landlord. Clearly, there were more disturbing things on her mind this morning.

It was 7.50am. Against the trend of waiting until the hour, she tossed the faded floral quilt to the side of the bed, and briskly tiptoed across the cold linoleum floor to the shower. Slowly she brushed the silken straps off her freckled shoulders, stepping out of her Betty Boop nightie as it fell to the floor. She tugged the grubby knob of the light chord. There was light, all forty watts worth. Her small hand found it difficult to rotate the encrusted shower tap. Eventually, with both hands and gritted teeth, she succeeded. It let out a torturous screech and obligingly spat into life. She stared despairingly at the perished rubber hose with its blocked shower head. True to form, out dripped the lukewarm water like a reluctant participant at a swingers' party.

In the bathroom cabinet above, there were exhibits that laid tribute to a foregone era. Realistically, they were just a ragbag of derelict products. A modest bar of unyielding blue soap sat moulded to its enamel tray. She stared at the uninviting soap, and as she bent forward to sniff the fragrance she wondered whose armpits it had previously surveyed before she arrived.

The smell lingered, giving her that sickly feeling, reminiscent of an old peoples' home she had the misfortune to visit a few years ago. "I'd have more chance of getting laid by Brad Pitt than trying to extract any suds from that."

Hanging shabbily by the chipped washbasin, was a dark blue, bath towel, embroidered with the words, *Royal Caribbean Cruises.* "I wish, I bloody wish."

Her mind took flight, or should I say cruise? She had entered fantasyland. Her troubled mind eased. Suddenly, she was lazing on the sun-drenched deck of some magnificent ocean liner, seductively sipping a Malibu cocktail. Bronzed young men in their pristine white uniforms paraded around the deck pandering to her every whim.

Just then, a loud shattering thud jolted her back to reality. Like a knife piercing her heart. Fear returned and hit hard. She instinctively held her breath, straining her ears and widening her eyes. Her toes curled downwards as if to grip the cubicle tray. Then, with her heart pounding, she stepped out of the shower, stretching out to grab the towel, slowly pulling it from its rail.

She sidled her naked body against the dank bathroom tiles, clutching the towel to her goose bumped flesh with a vice like grip that turned her knuckles white. She intuitively shielded her nakedness from any would-be intruder. Now on the verge of panic, her hands started to shake uncontrollably. Fear and cold were unwelcome guests. "Come on Carrie-Anne; pull yourself together; deep breath, that's the girl." She scanned the shower room for a viable weapon. What a choice; it could not have been worse; a lavatory brush, wet sponge, or the hard soap. She whispered despairingly, "Oh God, this can't be happening."

A few minutes passed; there were no more unsettling noises from upstairs or downstairs. Perhaps it was all in her mind. She hesitantly edged out of the washroom and peaked around the wall into her bedroom – nothing! She quickened, walking to the edge of her bed, glancing across to the brown chest of draws nestling in the corner of the room. Her scant belongings were present and correct.

She turned her head. Her eyes suddenly alighted onto some broken shards of wafer thin glass on the bed sheet. "It looks like parts of a light bulb." Looking upwards, all she could see hanging above was a brown twisted flex and the remnants of a shattered light. All that remained was the brass bayonet fitting and a whisper of filament.

The sash window was a little open at the top, and the smell of the recent muck spreading infiltrated the room,

4

leaving that love it or hate it country aroma. "I didn't think I left that open." She berated herself loudly. "You daft bitch, get a grip!"

Beyond that, she rested with the conclusion that it was simply a faulty light bulb or a power surge. She regained her composure, cleaned the debris from her bed and floor, sighed, and got on with her dressing. The bed creaked as she sat on the edge shivering, putting on her skimpy knickers. Then standing up, she took a deep breath before tugging up her snug fitting denims, wiggling her hips to accommodate. Before the final thrust to pull the zip fast, she slumped heavily back on the bed and began weeping. Swaying from side to side as an emotional jumble of shock, fear, loneliness, and regret cascaded out of her like a doleful requiem. She wrenched the charger out of her mobile, wiped the tears from her eyes, and tried to make a call, only to find that her phone was out of credit. "Oh Shit, would you believe it?" In utter frustration, she threw her mobile so hard towards the bed it somersaulted off, and ended up on the floor with its back adrift, and the battery several feet from the phone. How did it come to this and why?

CHAPTER 2

Destination Malaga, Costa del Sol, Southern Spain –
Date: Sunday 11th April 2010

Carrie-Anne had decided to crash out of Bristol University approximately seven months after enrolment. She was disillusioned, frustrated and struggling to muster up any enthusiasm for study. In truth, university gave her a legitimate reason to leave the troubled home-life that was becoming simply unbearable. Such was her impetuous nature, that in no time and with little thought she planned to cut loose, and follow the dream of sun, sand and sangria on the Costa del Sol. Pursuing a degree in commercial art had lost its allure.

Avoiding a lengthy and highly charged tête-a-tête with Mam, she crammed her personal belongings into her bright yellow backpack, and with 500 Euros, an economy flight to Spain, and a pipe full of dreams, she departed on a windswept, rain sodden afternoon from Bristol airport. This inclement weather added even more to the allure of Andalusia. She arrived two hours and twenty minutes later at her eagerly awaited destination, Aeropuerto de Malaga.

The heavy cabin door opened. The raven-haired, curvy, thirty something stewardess, wearing a big smile, heavy black mascara, ruby red lipstick on lips and teeth, stood on sentry duty at the front of the aircraft. "We do hope you have enjoyed your flight today, and we look forward to seeing you again soon; from all of us here, have a great holiday. The Save the Whale charity box is by your exit. Any loose change…" etc, etc.

Of course, what she really wanted to say was, "Come on, shift your backsides, you irritating bunch of sun seekers. We've got forty-five minutes for a fag and a coffee before flying this cattle tube back to Bristol."

After years in this industry, her initial goodwill had dissipated. Now, she came fully equipped with a mean, sardonic streak. Her perfunctory view of Brits abroad, when they board the plane they leave their brains at the airport. Carrie-Anne's actions did not convey her cynical thoughts either; she smiled, nodded, and walked forward inhaling the warm Spanish air.

"Fresh air, fresh start," she mused. Then gingerly holding the scorching handrail, descended the aircraft stairs and on to the blistering tarmac.

In true *mañana* custom, she was transported to an entrance leading to a series of long gleaming corridors, and entered the fray with an eager procession of tourists in carnival mood, racing towards the arrival lounge as if first

7

to the carousel wins the cigar. Illuminated signs bedecked the long corridors, displaying a mixture of prime locations along the Spanish coastline and Mediterranean Sea life. Carrie-Anne was jolted back to earth from gazing at the roomy scene of a sea bream swimming around a dusky grouper, when she caught the toe of her trainer in the end of the walking escalator. Slightly embarrassed and hoping nobody noticed, she hastened her stride. A disguised trot would do perfectly.

A bulky, middle-aged, bottle blonde, parading a fake tan the colour of burnt orange, bustled along wheeling her oversized hand baggage at a fair rate of knots. Wearing an extra large Welsh rugby shirt, a white and green sequinned cowboy hat, heavy black tights, and fluorescent pink trainers, she was the quintessential Brit tourist. How apt, Carrie-Anne thought, demonstrating a neat Merve the Swerve manoeuvre that would have impressed the Welsh rugby legend himself.

Carrie-Anne arrived with a rather smug feeling of victory at the finishing line. She added an hour to her Swatch watch, resisting the urge to burst out with *We are the Champions.* "Good old Freddie Mercury," she muttered under her breath.

Instinctively she raised her fist in a victory salute as an unusually tall, lean, snappily dressed Chinese man, who seemed to appear out of nowhere, interrupted her. "Hey, hello there, sorry to bother you young lady, I think this belongs to you?"

She turned quickly, smiled awkwardly, and sheepishly took the card from the man's outstretched hand. She glimpsed into his piercing dark eyes and quickly averted her gaze. He was handsome but unnerving. "Oh! My God, thank you, that's my Student I.D; must have dropped to the floor when I pulled my passport from my backpack. I'd lose my head if it weren't screwed on. You are very kind." Once again, she reiterated her gratefulness.

"Maybe you should thank your little travelling companion?" he said, touching the fluffy toy rabbit that was fixed to her bag to explain his point. "He's brought you luck today." He spoke gently. "Forget the favours given, remember those received." Then as swiftly as he came, he dispersed, integrating into the crowd.

With her passport aloft, after the swiftest of glances from passport control, she was waved through customs. With no luggage on the carousel to collect, she passed quickly on, ignoring the gauntlet of Spanish property agents armed with an array of glossy leaflets. "Villas and golf courses; if only. What do you think my name is? J.K.Rowling?" She proceeded through the large glass doors of the Picasso Lounge, promptly boarding the airport bus to Estacion Malaga.

She entered the station café, El Barco (The Ship), which smelt of cigarettes, old beer, prawns and chorizo. The café boss wiped his hands on a stained chequered tea towel, then without looking behind him, lobbed it like a pro basketball player into the awaiting sink. He had done this before, many times. *"Hola señora, ¿listos para ordenar?"* he asked.

Armed only with a smattering of Spanish, like the few pebbles in a young shepherd boy's pouch, she placed one in her sling, faced her Goliath and fired, *"Café sombre y un bocadillo de queso, por favor."*

She was reassured when out of his black moustache-covered mouth came the reply, in true Manuelian, "You would like a milky coffee and a cheese sandwich?" Then with a broad grin on his large swarthy face, *"Me llamo Miguel; encantado. La cuenta es tres euro."*

She laughed timidly, paid and responded with a gentle, *"Gracias Miguel."*

She placed her backpack down within easy reach, as she tried inconspicuously to stamp on an escaping cockroach *(la cucaracha)*. Carrie-Anne was far too slow for the scurrying invader, who nestled quickly under a cracked floor tile. How she hated those crawlies. She sat down at the crumb laden table awaiting the coach to Nerja. The sandwich was dry, probably two days old and filled with tasteless sheep cheese; it was discarded after only five bites. The coffee was agreeable.

The station loudspeaker confirmed her coach was waiting in bay 81, (*ochenta uno*). In no time at all, she tossed twenty centimos on to the café table, then with backpack in hand, alighted the *autobús* to her place in the sun.

CHAPTER 3

Playa Burriana, Nerja, Spain –

Date: April 2010

In contrast to the dream, the stark reality was quick to learn and hard to swallow. Renting a small villa or *apartamento* overlooking the sun-drenched beach of the Playa Burriana, was a bridge too far. Hired bar staff on low income and irregular hours, were always going to struggle.

British teenage girls, trying to live the Spanish adventure, constantly blitzed the restaurants and bars with their promising CV's and fluttering eyelashes, desperate for work. The following, inevitable merry-go-round for most of these, involved frequenting small dusky tapas bars and frenetic dazzling night clubs. You would dance to the early hours, indulging in a whatever- your-fancy variety of cocktails, wines or alcopops, with the added supply of recreational drugs for the experimental or needy, whilst searching for that illusive Antonio Banderos or Jennifer Lopez lookalike.

Eventually this heady lifestyle took its sapping toll on the physical well-being of even the most energetic. Carrie-Anne finally grasped that without money the good life would soon grind to a serious halt. She'd be left behind in the cruel lay-by of disenchantment as the seductive Ferrari sped on.

Working the bars was hard, tedious, and physically demanding. An early morning stream of aged ex-pats, crusaders with sun-baked skin resembling jacket potatoes, fought for the comfy terraces. Their daily quests, to seek, find and chart the latest café bar. That dream watering-hole that serves the largest free-pour of spirit for the smallest possible price. The expert way that Carrie-Anne hid her seething intolerance of the constant loud-mouthed entourages, gave her much credit and splitting migraines. The lager fuelled lads on the lash, donned in their tribal shirts, chasing happy hours and televised football. Parents that would invade the bars like the marauding hordes of Genghis Khan, with their screaming offspring running amok with dripping ice-creams, ketchup seeping hotdogs and huge inflatables.

Tourists or terrorists?

What could compare to the beer bellied, middle-aged men, who parading up and down the strip with their ill-fitting Speedo trunks, hairy chests and big egos? Wearing white socks and Jesus sandals complete with compulsory bum bag. Carrie-Anne often thought the ten plagues of Egypt would be easier to cope with.

She ploughed through the long hot sweaty days owning her philosophical mantra, 'When things can only get worse, they generally do.' Somehow, that relieved her disappointment.

Little pay and scant loyalty followed from the bar owners. Work generally was seasonal. To pay a rent regularly she had to share a tacky apartment with numerous drifters who moved on as quickly as they came. The demand on her time was generally excessive; you complied, or you were yesterday's news. The owners and the life of the bars were as transient as the staff who worked in them. It really was here today and gone tomorrow.

Soon melancholic, discontent, behind with the rent and increasingly tired of the continual harassment, it was time for a quick and decisive exit from Andalusia. Anyway, it was November, getting colder, and the darker nights were setting in. There was no heating in the apartment, work and money were drying up simultaneously. Carrie-Anne left the Café Del Mar before she was deigned surplus to requirements, or how she used to think of it, ceremoniously dumped like the many that had gone before her.

She laughed nervously as she remembered that cheesy chart hit, *Y Viva España.* "Long live Spain," she giggled, "but not with me in it. Whatever happened to 'fresh air, fresh start'? More like, 'better the devil you know'."

It had been a hard and rude awakening to the nuts and bolts of life. The bubble had burst, and Wales didn't seem that bad after all. She shrugged her shoulders in a 'what the heck' fashion; bravado mainly, but it helped. Then she made hasty provision to return to the Land of my Fathers. "Oh God," she mused; "I'll soon be singing, *The Green Green Grass of Home.*"

She couldn't help laughing aloud, recalling her parting words to her café employer. After all, she had nothing to lose. She fired an impressive broadside of expletives, fuelled by her pent up fury at the injustice of it all, startling the boss, who, besieged by such a verbal barrage became speechless, retreating hastily into the men's toilet.

Her 'she who laughs last, last longer' amusement spilled over, rubbernecking the heads of those sitting in the same aisle on the aircraft with mild curiosity. Then, opening up her backpack, she reached inside for her favourite fruit jellies. Tilting up the head of her little stuffed travelling companion she attempted a Humphrey Bogart impression. "Well Dandy, here's looking at you kid. Looks like it's you and me against the world."

Just then, an irate, bumptious, spectacled, bank clerk of a man, trying to insert some rather large baggage into the smallest of spaces cried out for all to hear, "These bloody overhead lockers!"

"Hurry up Doogie, don't be so peevish; the sooner you do that, the sooner the plane can take off."

Douglas's face changed colour as the fuse on his irascible temper got shorter. He yelled explosively, "I've told you before Maggie, you can't get a pint in a half pint pot. Now shut up, or do it your bloody self, and don't call me Doogie!"

Carrie-Anne amongst others seated ahead of the commotion turned around nosily. The leggy flight attendant hastened to the all too familiar fracas. She tripped on a large white trainer that belonged to the foot of a sweaty, clinically obese man, wearing a multi-coloured, Hawaiian short sleeved shirt and matching shorts. Somehow, he had managed to wedge himself into his seat, looking about as comfortable as a man with haemorrhoids sitting on sandpaper. She turned and looked at him with dagger eyes and a company smile. "Sir, could you kindly fasten your seatbelt, tuck any extra hand luggage under your seat and any protruding feet out of the aisle please, ready for take-off." She turned away whispering under her breath, "That useless leviathan is going to need another five yards of seatbelt before we can strap him down."

Then just for a moment, as Carrie-Anne began to face the front in response to the call, "Please, fasten your seat belts," out of the corner of her eye, she thought she spotted the tall Chinaman. "No it can't be. It can't be," she whispered.

Then pursing her lips and emitting an enquiring hmm sound, she resumed her ready for flight position, and relaxed. She picked up the complimentary magazine, unstuck its tea stained pages, and began to read.

"Chair up straight ready for take-off." A broad showbiz smile emanated from the immaculately dressed, skinny, flight attendant name tagged Tristan. Carrie-Anne thought he would have been more at home in the theatre. Then laughed as she mused, "Yes, probably the backside of the pantomime cow in Jack and the Beanstalk." She chuckled audibly, and then went back to reading the flight deals on the duty free.

CHAPTER 4

Cardiff Airport, Wales –

Date: Saturday 27th November 2010

Carrie-Anne was just 20 years of age when she alighted back on British soil at Cardiff Airport. She had no misgivings about herself. She was not overly bright, no model like figure, pretty rather than attractive. Five foot six on tiptoe, cropped ginger hair, obligatory freckles, green eyes and generous full lips (which, she attributed as a desirable asset giving her that sexy feeling). With her indisputable outgoing nature and inner confidence, she would achieve well. Not particularly dressy, she was quite happy wearing coloured short-sleeved tops, tight denim jeans and trainers, no socks. She loved bangles and beads, costume jewellery, mostly bought in Spain and made in Morocco. The more enduring features obtained from her brief life abroad, amounted to a small tattoo on her right ankle, (bearing a Celtic Eternal Knot) and a right ear full of piercing, housing five earrings. What would Taid and Nain (Grandfather and Grandmother) say if they were still alive? Carrie-Anne smiled like a naughty schoolchild; she knew the answer to that.

She was no longer a virgin thanks to Spain, but no ecstatic memories of the encounters. It seemed easier to lose her inhibitions and indulge into liberating sexual experiences after several glasses of red wine. This coupled with the long hot sultry nights, somehow, that being in the moment, made it more lust driven and exciting. In truth, she felt deep regret; it seemed so incredibly tacky now, although candidly, she was the first to admit her compliance into those passionate liaisons.

She had returned to Wales with more street cred and had downsized to a size 8, but was not sure it was all worth the effort. The brevity of her stay in Spain was extremely disconcerting. She was relieved to be home, but still embraced that tail between the legs feeling. Yes, Carrie-Anne had toughened up by the experiences, and had unquestionably learned to fight her corner.

The harsh learning curve made her long for the safety, innocence, and naivety of her childhood, if only for a while she could be taken back in time. She recalled with affection helping Mam in the kitchen, sneakily eating the uncooked cake mix. The fun of gathering fresh eggs from the makeshift chicken coup. Mam's cwtches (cuddles), bubblegum, beans on toast, collecting conkers, bedtime stories, hot water bottles. "Oh to be seven again," she sighed longingly. To wear her pink fleecy jim-jams, nestling under her Girls Aloud quilt, warm and snug, nuzzling her small teddy bear, sharing secrets under the bedclothes with her make believe friend until falling asleep.

This is the home where Carrie-Anne Siân Lewis was born on the 28th March 1990. A small detached cottage, in Nant-y-derry.

CHAPTER 5

Pendine Sands Caravan Park, Pembrokeshire –

Date: 15th - 22nd July 1989

It was a warm and muggy July night, the intense, sweet fragrance of jasmine filled the air. At the leisure park club, the house D.J going by the name of Wayne Prince, who incidentally was last night's bingo caller and resident comedian, was just beginning to get into full swing. His introduction into this next song was befitting of any club D.J.

Wayne Prince, whose real name, that of Timothy Smalling, was a good looking, charismatic individual, and at just twenty-one years of age he was definitely destined for better things.

"Grab a partner, you gorgeous people; come on, monitors and janitors. It's the legendary Hollies, with their chart busting 67 hit, *Hey, Carrie-Anne.* Is there a Carrie-Anne in the house? Because if there is, what's your game now, can anybody play?"

The song was thumping out of the two giant Vox speakers located on either side of the stage. It was the 'Sixties Night' session and this is when a shy, but determined Rhian, first met and danced with Terry. She had never forgotten that dreamy summer night of 89. She was just 18 years old. That evening she fell hook, line and sinker in love with him, and if the truth were known, years, and tears later, she still loved him, or at least the memory of him.

Rhian's only daughter was the unexpected, but truly loved product of this swift and hot-blooded holiday romance at the caravan park. Naming her baby daughter Carrie-Anne seemed the obvious thing to do, after all, it was that song, the catalyst for her unforgettable liaison with the only true love of her life.

Just one look at Rhian's soft body, the way she walked, laughed or smiled aroused Terry. He was fun, and his firm grip around her small waist, his sense of daring, made her well up with excitement; this was young love.

Making love seemed the most natural and exciting way to culminate their young passions. Their minds were on intimacy and their hearts were pounding to that beat. No thought for safe sex this week, the danger and thrill of the moment transported them. Friday came too soon; if they could only halt time, or the flow of the tide.

Terry sat on the beach, put his arms around his knees and drew them up to his chest. He turned to Rhian and shared his thoughts with such ease; it was as if he had known her all his life. "You know, I've always wanted to visit these sands. The Welsh TT motorcycle event had been held here

22

for years, but even more fantastic than that, on this very beach Sir Malcolm Campbell in his Sunbeam 350HP named Blue Bird set the world land speed record. The event was cancelled in 1927, after one of his competitors in a car called Babs lost control and was tragically killed. I think his name was…" He took a pause to recall, after all he'd done brilliantly up until now.

Rhian looked and listened with intense pretend interest whilst gazing into his celadon eyes. In truth, she knew precious little about the subject of motor racing. Oh, please wont you just kiss me, she pleaded inwardly. In all fairness, she was extremely impressed at the way Terry conveyed the data, recognising his passion for motor sport and how it brought him truly alive when he spoke about it.

"Thomas, that's it, Parry Thomas," Terry concluded.

As they huddled together, under their towels for warmth, Terry resumed by singing *Waterloo Sunset.* He changed the words: *"Terry meets Rhian, down by the seaside every Friday night, and they don't feel afraid, as long as they gaze on Pendine at sunset they are in paradise,"* Terry sang flatter than a squashed hedgehog. It was hilarious. "I'm not sure the Kinks would approve," Rhian commented giggling.

That last night, they kissed and hugged each other tightly as the full moon started to rise over the charcoal sea.

During that week, young Terry in a moment of wild impetuosity had purchased a little silver locket for Rhian.

His holiday spending power took a considerable economic downturn, but when he saw her wide smile and appreciative eyes, he just knew it was appropriate.

Saturday morning came; campers had to vacate by 10am. All that remained was the briefest of encounters. Terry held both her hands manfully. "Rhian," he began, but halted as the screeching seagulls fought over a morsel left by the departing holiday makers. "Before you go, I have a little memento for you. It is special; my parents received it on their wedding anniversary. It was a gift from close friends, something to do with 1987 being the Year of the Rabbit. Mum has since passed away, and Dad wanted me to have it. He told me to keep it safe. I'd really love you to have this, Mum loved it, and somehow, I know you'll look after it."

She looked into his eyes; and caught a breath; there was no reply just a gentle nod. "Thank you Terry isn't he a cutie?" She kissed him and the rabbit on the cheek delicately. "I promise I will always treasure this."

She clutched the fluffy rabbit with the long floppy ears and patchwork tummy drawing it to her chest. Rhian wanted to tell Terry she loved him, but it came out of her trembling lips as, "You know, I had a really special time this week and I shall never forget it."

"Me too babe, I'll be in touch soon. Anyway, I need to make sure you're looking after Bunny."

Then with a few rapid exchanges and farewell glances, they parted.

CHAPTER 6

Arnant, Nant-y-derry, Monmouthshire –

Date: May 2004

Tad (dad) was rarely spoken of in their small cottage home. Even now it was still painful and an extremely sensitive area for Mam. Carrie-Anne, although just a young teenager, tried diligently to piece together any vague snippets of information, any clue that filtered through over the years. She was never told his surname. It was always just Terry.

There were holiday snaps that Mam had given to her some time ago, but they gave little insight into what her tad might look like at present. Carrie-Anne had deduced that Terry must be at least 35 years old by now. In her possession were three of four holiday photos. The first snap showed Terry and Mam side by side, heads tilted together smiling for the automated camera. The second, kissing each other sweetly rather than passionately. The third, facing the camera, poking their tongues out, with their thumbs placed on either side of their head, waving their fingers at the lens. It clearly displayed Terry's mop of thick ginger curly hair. Emblazoned on the front of his white t-shirt was the faded words, FRANKIE SAYS RELAX. He radiated vitality of youth.

Then there was Rhian, her smile, young and starry eyed, with long wavy brunette hair, tied back in a ponytail and held with a red scrunchie. Carrie-Anne could just make out the top of a stylish, red party dress from the snap. A silver heart-shaped pendant sat demurely above the cleavage of her breasts. She looked gorgeous.

She thought how intense that romance must have been. How meaningful to Mam. That same dress was still hanging in her wardrobe, along with the scrunchie and white pointy toed stilettos. The silver heart-shaped pendant still embraced her neck. Rhian often clasped it tightly with warm affection.

So, she knew that her tad was an Englishman, ginger hair and lean of build. A working class Londoner, he was fun-loving, generous, strong minded and witty.

She recalled the evening; her mother was relaxing on the frazzled, fireside chair by the open hearth reading a romantic paperback. She gently raised her head up from her book, stared at the ceiling and into her memories, and with a knowing smile sighed, "He was a real charmer you know." Then, she would hum to herself quietly the tune from *Waterloo Sunset.* This reflective appraisal was hardly directed towards Carrie-Anne, but she held on to it tenaciously. It was like a lifeline to her past; this was her tad. She was fourteen.

CHAPTER 7

Arnant, Nant-y-derry, Monmouthshire –

Date: November 2008

Rhian was 37 years of age. She raised the village gossip level to fever pitch by suddenly announcing her intention to marry Afon Llewellyn… It caused a great stir; he was a much older man, abrupt in speech and churlish in manner. After the predictable furore, it was deemed an unreasonable, but reluctantly acceptable partnership by the locals. They tied the knot in November 2008 at the Holy Trinity Church in Abergavenny.

Time passed on, old habits didn't die hard, in fact, they resurfaced with gusto, it became increasingly obvious the relationship would bring nothing but heartache, tears and regrets.

She had married a bullish son of a dairy farmer. He had promised the earth but delivered incarceration, becoming nothing more than a manipulative control freak. He became increasingly dominant, verbally abusive, questioning constantly what Rhian's daily routine would entail, a jealous man.

Afon came from a generation of Welsh farming stock, and could not shake off his strict disciplinarian upbringing. He became a product of his past, could not quell the need to be ruling the roost. His abusiveness soon turned to violence. Over a short period of time, poor Rhian lost all confidence and self worth. She indulged more and more in the need for alcohol, escaping into the world of gin and vodka. She became a shaking, skinny, pathetic figure of her former self. Unkempt hair, pink stained dressing gown and tatty carpet slippers, she looked a pitiful site. These days she was hardly ever coherent, with no sense of purpose, rarely venturing outside the home. Her inner self was crying out for help, and when nothing came, gin was her best friend.

Carrie-Anne hated him. Afon held her in total contempt. He could not dominate her like he could her Mam, and it angered him greatly. She had witnessed firsthand what he was doing to her. It was painful to watch.

Vivid in her memory was the time he arrived home late from work. She recalled the blood soaked bandage wrapped around his left hand. "That damn sheepdog of Dai Thomas bit my bloody hand this afternoon. I've told him, if he doesn't keep it under control I'll shoot the mangy thing with both barrels."

"Are you alright Afon? Have you put any antiseptic on it? Will it need stitches?"

"Get off me woman. Don't fuss. Where's my supper?"

He sat down at the table. After taking a mouthful of shepherd's pie, he yelled, "What the bloody hell do you call this?" He pointed angrily at his evening meal. "Come here, you useless bitch. You're pathetic. That's what you are, bloody pathetic. It's stone cold." He exaggerated. "Would you like to eat this dished up slop?" He grabbed her hair and dragged her to the table. "Would you?" Then louder, "Would you?" Now bellowing, "Then go on, eat it all up!"

He then rammed her face violently into the food, as if he was wiping the plate with it. He let go. She stood up mournfully, and whimpered like a scolded puppy dog. With her face covered in mess and her nose bleeding from the impact, she began to apologise. "I'm sorry Afon, it won't happen again, I promise."

It was then that an infuriated Carrie-Anne leapt upon Afon's back. She began to pummel his broad shoulders with her clenched fists. "You fat pig! I hate you, I hate you, I hate you!"

She was beside herself with rage and fear. At that point, Afon slapped her powerfully with the back of his brawny hand, marking instantly her young cheek, sending her spinning until she connected with the kitchen door. "You'll get more of the same, if you ever try to do that to me again girl. Now get up those stairs."

The next minute the front door slammed. Afon was gone. Seeing the erosion of the one she loved, Carrie-Anne began to lose all sense of pride and respect for her mam, who surrendered without a fight to his forceful will.

Carrie-Anne could not wait to leave home and was glad to accept a placement offered at Bristol University. It was kindly paid for by Elwyn, her loving taid (grandfather). Sadly, he had passed away about three months ago. In truth, Granddad always longed to be reunited with his wife. Myreg had died the previous year, and frankly, he was an empty man without his soul mate. He met Myreg at the local Methodist chapel and she would become his one and only. They would share their lives together, till death us do part. Faith was a strength and inspiration for the pair of them. Death had no sting and graves no victory as far as Elwyn and Myreg were concerned.

Elwyn had placed money into trust for Carrie-Anne's eighteenth birthday. He knew his daughter Rhian would succumb, squandering it away in the local off-license or giving it to that bully Afon, to feed his obnoxious gambling habit.

Carrie-Anne was not convinced about her future studies, or where it would lead her, but used this opportunity to her best advantage, to escape from the suffocating circumstances surrounding her.

As soon as the opportunity was confirmed of a placement at Bristol University, she hastily accepted. It was Sept 2009.

CHAPTER 8

Queen Charlotte's Hospital, Hammersmith –

Date: 4th October 1967

Terry was born some two weeks before schedule at Queen Charlotte's Hospital, Hammersmith, in the October of 1967. He was the only son of Harry and Jenny Mead. They resided on the sixth floor of a council owned tower block in Shepherds Bush; 41, Charecroft Road, Busch Court. They were married on the 7th March 1963. Their relationship was not without the highs and lows of a cut and thrust partnership. Both gave a little and took a little. Intrinsically their love allowed immense tolerance of each other's shortcomings. It was charged with emotion, volatile at times and genuinely passionate.

They were a working class family, trying to rise above the status quo, endeavouring to create a better future. Harry was a taxi driver, whose hours were long and tedious. He loved to get the occasional Saturday afternoon off to watch his beloved Queens Park Rangers at Loftus Road. With his beer and piped tobacco he was a happy and uncomplicated man.

Harry was not tall in stature and walked with a distinct limp (due to a bad collision with a mini-bus that had jumped the lights by Euston Station). He was a chirpy, stereotypical London cabbie, full of wit and a forthright opinion on any situation.

Jenny was an engaging woman, of a pale complexion with pointed features; she was tall and gangly with rather large feet. Terry laughed when he heard his dad's endearing cry of, "Yoo-hoo Olive, can I have a cup of Rosie Lee?" followed by a Popeye-like chuckle. She was motherly, no gossip, could keep a secret better than most and extremely loyal.

This meticulous, pernickety lady could always find something to do. Harry often shook his head, recognising the sheer futility of attempting to halt her indefatigable nature. Often alluding, "What's the point of that? Sit down girl, for goodness sake; talk about wear yourself out."

What seemed of no consequence to Harry became of great importance; a stubborn quest, worthy of her time and energy. She hardly ever sat down and fidgeted if she did. It was almost as if the world would stop turning if she stopped for one moment. Harry in his angry times called it an illness, Jenny's dogged syndrome.

Jenny loved being busy and really enjoyed her outside work, employed as a part-time dinner lady at the local secondary modern school. She felt that it kept her sprightly and young at heart; together with the added perk, the occasional helping of rhubarb crumble with lashings of lumpy school custard, it was worth it all.

All in all, they were content with their lot. Their only offspring Terry was loved and cared for. He was showered with abundant affection and generosity. In turn, Terry's love was reciprocal. He loved Mum and Dad deeply.

CHAPTER 9

Macmillan Hospice –

Date: September 1987

Sadly, tragedy struck in the family. Jenny, who had been concerned about her well being, eventually visited the doctors. What followed was a horrific, devastating X-ray revelation. She was diagnosed with breast cancer in 1986. Despite all efforts made by the consultants at the Hammersmith General, nothing more could be done except to prolong her life as long as possible. Jenny fought with dignity and courage; however the aggressive spread of the cancer continued its insatiable hold. Jenny's health diminished rapidly.

She was barely recognizable in September 1987. Wedding and engagement rings on the bedside locker, now being far too large for her frail fingers, and then, even at this stage of her life, her insistent list of 'Don't Forgets' given to Harry would stay with Terry forever.

Finally succumbing to this heartless disease, she passed away in the presence of Harry and Terry at the Macmillan Hospice. It was at times like this that Terry longed to have a sibling or two, even if the notorious rivalry was part of the inevitable consequence. He was nineteen years of age and motherless.

Harry was never the same man again. Months of depression, drink and anger followed. His slovenly appearance and his loss of esteem grew by the month. Terry tried to help, to be there for him. He could never replace Jenny; it became an uphill fight to keep Dad above giving up altogether. Harry began to stay out much later at night. It became more frequent. He hated facing the home without Jenny.

Terry never really knew the whereabouts of Harry, who increasingly became distant from his own son. He mentioned something to Terry about giving up the taxi business for some new line of work, chauffeuring and couriering. The details were vague, Terry did not pursue it.

Harry dressed for work in a baggy pinned striped suit with turn-ups and large lapels. The white creased shirt with curled up collars, no tie, and unpolished brogue shoes, amplified his, 'what's the point?' attitude. He was often unshaven, bleary eyed, smelt of stale sweat and tobacco, becoming less and less a father. His frustration and depression intensified. He loved his son, but the light had gone out in his life. The black tunnel seemed eternal.

Jenny was his life, he had never imagined a time without her. Her smile, her warmth, her humour, her care, that unselfish dedication and commitment to family, truly characterized her life. He tried to recreate in his memory the inviting smell of baked cakes that often greeted his arrival home from work; somehow it seemed to epitomize everything about her. She adored making pastries, jams, chutneys, and her spicy pickled onions were the bee's knees.

How she would delight in decking the house out with her favourite flowers, gerberas and roses. Modest and content with her life, apart from her secret dream to have a small garden all of her own someday, how she would have loved that.

It was her domestic skills, and caring insistence that kept Harry presentable, clean and tidy. She gave so much until the very end. How utterly helpless he felt. He could never forget. Now she was gone and he was alone.

CHAPTER 10

Griffin Autos, Uxbridge Road W12 –

Date: Monday 8th February 1988

In the wake of this background, Terry tried to fashion his own way in life. This was the age of Adam Ant, Acid House, Dirty Dancing, and Roland Rat. He was all too aware of his own developing manhood. His mind was filled with girls, music and flashy cars, in that order.

Terry found employment thanks to a friend of a friend. He was relatively content in his occupation as a trainee car mechanic. Working in a small, privately owned garage just off the Uxbridge Road was convenient. It was cold, greasy, labour intensive, and poorly paid, but with good prospects for the knuckle-downs. It was his passion for cars that kept him interested. The tedium was often relieved by the daily ritual of fetching the sausage or bacon sarnies from the local bakery. Endless teas and coffees (that only just passed the Trades Description Act) flowed out of the vending machine. Serving your apprenticeship very much required the art of holding and sipping from these piping hot plastic cups. This resulted in gaining finger-skinning blisters and numb furry tongues.

The entertainment was a diet of zany Radio One DJ's. Their popular music played out of the battery powered Roberts radio. This had clearly seen better days. Cream and maroon in colour, with a broken plastic tuner, wire coat hanger for the aerial and carrying dents that any stock car racer would have been duly proud of. In miraculous fashion, with the odd violent shake and change of angle on the workbench, Lazarus burst into life again.

The workbenches were another story, covered in spanners, socket sets, feeler gauges, and discarded car parts. There were empty brake and steering fluid bottles everywhere. Old newspapers, crushed pop cans, crumpled cigarette boxes and a plethora of plastic cups filled with mouldy tea strewn everywhere. There undoubtedly was some method in their madness, but for sure, no-one in the garage suffered from Obsessive Compulsive Disorder.

The garage boss, Lenny Riley, used to laugh as he shouted across the floor to Terry, "Give the old jukebox the kiss of life, you idle grease monkey."

His boss took over the family business four years ago, and ran a very tight ship. He was mid-forties in age, and firmly time-locked into the late 50s early 60s, which he just loved. He had hazel eyes, stick out ears, Ringo Star nose and heavily greased, dyed black hair. As the rock and roll song by the Poni Tails suggests, he was 'born too late' for that era. Nevertheless that did not deter Lenny. A Teddy boy, he was forever preening his hair with his stainless steel comb as if in some vintage rock and roll movie.

Terry only ever saw him in his navy blue work overalls, smothered in grease and grime, with a faded Castrol Oil cloth badge on the right upper pocket. That is where Lenny kept his fags, lighter, and a clutch of ballpoint pens. The other pocket was for his precious steel comb and car keys. His strong hands where almost the colour of coal. His fingernails always caked with congealed dirt. Swarfega and Lenny went hand in hand, literally. His footwear consisted of a pair of black winkle-picker boots. He was affable, and yet sarcastic, but there was no malice in him. Of all the remaining mechanics and trainees working for him, he had a lot of time for Terry and Terry new it.

CHAPTER 11

Beijing, China to Great Britain –

Date: Friday 14th April 1972

Shanyuan and his wife Lijuan arrived in Britain in the early 70s from mainland China. Shanyuan spent his early years in Beijing, perfecting his craft as an artisan locksmith. The poverty ridden back streets of Beijing made it a boiling point for opportunists of all descriptions. Thieves, drug dealers' and heartless thugs all dodged the police patrols, wreaking havoc and terror in their neighbourhoods. These were hungry, desperate people with nothing to lose. Extortion and murders were common.

Against this background, Shanyuan decided to make his way to the UK. This was a new chapter in their lives; they wanted to start a family in a different country, with prospects and opportunities for the hard working. They worked industriously, with an ambition and indefatigable resolve to establish their own eating house in London.

Fortune favoured the brave, and after years of scrimping and saving, in 1979 they were able to afford the rent on what was to become the catalyst of their future prosperity. The small Happy Garden Take-away shop appeared on the

Fulham Palace Road. Within six years, relocation was essential. They had outgrown the Happy Garden and their well earned reputation for fine Chinese cuisine had projected them into a constant pursuit for more capacious premises. 1985, and The Golden Dragon Chinese restaurant was proudly standing along the Palace Road. Their joint assiduousness had paid dividends. They were now employing consummate staff along with family members.

Inside was a complete oriental experience. It boasted plush velvet scrolled wall hangings, Chinese garden paintings and fancy ornate mirrors. There were delicate, silky, festival lanterns with dangling golden tassels and finely carved statues of golden dragons sitting proudly on emerald coloured columns. The tables were immaculately covered with red tablecloths and white linen napkins. On them stood table candles set in box surrounds depicting lotus blossoms, and spotless wine glasses shimmering under the subtle lighting. Together with an atmosphere of traditional eastern music and authentic, quality food, you had a success story.

Harry began to form his friendship with Shanyuan in the Happy Garden years. On his late night taxi runs he picked up customers from the small take-away several times a week. Consequently he and Shanyuan progressed from mere acquaintances to firm friends. After his tedious shift had finished, he would often enjoy a Chinese meal after closing time with Shanyuan and family. He referred to the family affectionately and humorously as the Clan. He got to know them extremely well.

One of the things that always used to amuse and eventually infuriate Harry was Shanyuan's party piece. He would present three Chinese tumblers upside down on the table, place a bean under one of them and shuffle the tumblers in figures of eight. Harry would always choose the tumbler that did not enclose the bean. Time and time again he racked his mind as to how Shanyuan did this. He even guessed at random, using no logic at all to what he had just observed, but always - nothing. Shanyuan loved to tease; it made him laugh heartedly, as he watched his friend's frustration.

"It's a good job you're not a betting man, not everything is at it seems Harry, remember that. How easily the eye and mind can be deceived."

"One day, Shanyuan, one day; just you see!"

Harry enjoyed spending those leisurely nights, often indulging in his growing passion for the game of Mahjong. They would sit till the early hours around a little square table sipping a warm glass of Huangiu (yellow liquor). Harry longed to win just the once, to achieve a complete hand - four sets of three and a pair with his tiles in hand.

CHAPTER 12

Arnant, Nant-y-derry –

Date: 27th November 2010

Carrie-Anne returned from her vexatious escapades in Andalusia to her cottage home in Nant-y-derry. A sense of unease swept over her as she approached the front door, of foreboding, sending a shiver down her spine. She wiggled instinctively, as if to shrug it off, dismissing the experience as imagination running riot.

It had been a long day. She lifted the besmeared brass daffodil knocker, recalling how polished it used to be when Mam was well, how dazzling in the sun. She knocked on the door, nothing. Did that curtain twitch? She couldn't be sure. She knocked again forcibly, and finally heard a stirring. "Come on Mam. It's me Carrie-Anne. Let me in. I could do with a brew and a Welsh cake."

Mam's Welsh cakes where legendary in the village. The only competition she faced was from Mrs Pritchard, the vicar's wife, who lived in the village rectory. A short woman of ruddy complexion, medium frame, and white hair tied back in a bun; she was generally clothed in a grey jacket and skirt suit with tawny stockings and brown flat shoes.

She would talk rapidly without taking a breath, often spitting through her ill-fitting false teeth. Her best friend was her oven and she baked unremittingly, as if her life and reputation depended on it.

The cottage door opened slowly. Then, Afon's face appeared, as if peering in disbelief. Carrie-Anne stiffened immediately and her voice changed. There was no love in this exchange.

"Is that you Carrie-Anne? Is that really you?"

"Where's Mam? I've come to see Mammy."

Afon fully opened the door. "You had better come in and sit down. Do you still want a brew? I'll fetch one anyway. Only got tea I'm afraid." He acted as if there was a time bomb waiting to explode. Indeed there was.

Carrie-Anne was completely on her guard. It took all her effort to sit on the lounge chair, perching on the edge as if ready to run. Her arms were defensively folded tightly across her chest.

Afon entered from out of the kitchen. "Is a mug OK Carrie-Anne?" Carrie-Anne never replied, she leant forward and gripped the mug with both hands continuing to quiver; she felt sick.

"Sugar?"

"No, No thank you. Where's Mam?" She glanced at the stairs leading to the bedroom.

"Carrie-Anne, I don't know how to tell you this. Believe me I tried to contact you." He stuttered, "God knows, I tried, but I had no idea where you were." He went on. "I'm afraid your mammy is no longer with us."

"I'm not surprised; Mam should have reported your bully boy tactics to the police ages ago. Now she's left you. It's about time. Where is she?"

"No, hold on Carrie-Anne. You don't understand." He began to ramble. "She became so distant after you left, locking herself away for weeks. Not talking or eating. Her eyes became almost lifeless, as if her very soul had gone. I tried to encourage her to see someone, a doctor, or psychiatrist, anyone, but she wouldn't listen. Then one day I came home from the farm…"

He placed one of his large hands to his forehead, shaking his head. "She had locked herself in the bathroom. There was no answer. When I called out, there was no reply. I finally broke the door down. There she was, lying in the bath, fully dressed. She was wearing that red party dress and white stilettos; you know, the ones she had kept for years. She had tied her hair back with a red band. Around her neck was this heart shaped pendant. The one she was always holding onto and dreaming. You'd better have this…"

He handed it to Carrie-Anne. Then took a brief pause; there was no easy way to say this. "There she was, all still, she looked peaceful. She had slit her wrists. There was

47

nothing I could do. I called the emergency services right away, but it was too late. They tried, but there was no hope." He could not get the words out fast enough now and began weeping.

"Your mother wrote on the bathroom mirror in lipstick, 'Waterloo Sunset'. I have no idea why. At times, it's true, I became so eaten up with jealousy, I would fly into a rage. Her constant reference to this Terry lad drove me insane. It so clouded my judgement. I became angry, bitter, hurt. I lashed out, I know it was wrong. I just couldn't help myself, she seemed obsessed, bewitched. It haunted our marriage daily. We definitely had our differences. But you need to know that I really loved Rhian, and I miss her greatly."

He tried to place his arms around Carrie-Anne. She was having none of it. She hurled the full mug across the room in a fit of temper, smashing it straight through the Victorian glass cabinet filled with stuffed wildlife, screaming and running out of the house as if something had possessed her.

CHAPTER 13

Griffin Autos, Uxbridge Road W12 –

Date: 28th March 1989.

The Pirelli calendar took pride of place on the garage wall, featuring a young, busty, semi-clad girl, with sponge and shampoo in hand, leaning suggestively over the car bonnet of a classic car. Terry could hardly take his eyes of Miss March, but forced himself to continue his erotic forage past Miss April, May and June and rested his eyes on Miss July, where underneath he duly booked his staff summer break.

Terry pencilled in the third week of July (15th-22nd). He looked at the leggy blonde girl (wearing little more than a pearly white smile), straddling a gleaming Harley Davidson, holding a rather large monkey-wrench suggestively to her bottom lip. His blood raced, and his penis stiffened, pushing hard against the flies of his bottle green overalls.

"It's no good looking at her Terry, you'll go blind. Blimey, she'd eat you all up and spit out the pieces son. Now, if it's possible for you to walk with a stalk on, could you kindly return to your bench and get some bloody work done, you horny little bastard?" Lenny deliberately yelled, catching the attention of everybody in the garage.

All the lads laughed and jeered. It was accompanied by the animated gesture for one off the wrist and raucous cries of "You tosser."

Terry tried and failed to hide his embarrassment as he returned to his work. Fortunately, due to the interrupting nature of the moment, his excited manhood gradually shrank back and normal service was resumed.

His propensity for astute money management allowed him to keep on the edge of fashion. He loved music. His recent and favourite acquisition was U2's *The Joshua Tree*, which he thought superb. For leisure, he enjoyed a couple of frames of snooker on Friday nights in the hall above Burton's Menswear and attending the local hot rod racing at White City. Downing a few pints with the lads on a Saturday night was a must, after which he'd religiously grab a meat loaded pizza with double cheese and French fries, getting home in time to watch *Match of the Day*.

Without extravagant spending, it enabled Terry to save for his holiday. Eventually, with the generous help of his boss Lenny, he was able to pass his driving test and obtain a 1978, silver Mark 2 Ford Escort, RS2000 with 7inch RS alloys. With some tender loving care and dedication he kitted it out with two front bright red bucket seats, small leather bound steering wheel, four enormous second -hand rally lights, new embossed gear knob and a radio cassette player from a Mondeo write-off. He didn't have the looks of George Michael and could not play guitar like Eric Clapton, but now his dream machine had arrived and so had he. He counted impatiently the days until his holiday.

CHAPTER 14

Golden Dragon – Fulham Palace Road –
Date: March 7th 1987

Harry and Jenny Mead agreed to celebrate their wedding anniversary at their old friend's restaurant the Golden Dragon. Jenny being progressively worn down by the debilitating effects of chemotherapy did not fancy a great fuss made of her. She much preferred an intimate, reflective time with Harry, rather than the surprise party that just about everyone knew about and was never any surprise at all.

Harry tried wholeheartedly to be everything that he could that evening, but inside he was eaten up with despair and sadness.

A pale looking Jenny took on the most loving and gentle demeanour. "We've had some good years together Harry. We have been very happy. You have always been the one for me. Now…" She stretched out her hand and embraced his taught knuckles. "Listen, you must be strong; Terry will need you. Life will go on." She hesitated. "Look Harry, please understand this, I've always loved you, and I always will, but I want you to find someone to take care of you in the future. You know you're hopeless without a good woman behind you. I don't want to think you'll be on your own, especially in your old age." She smiled trying to lighten the moment. "Just make sure, she doesn't bake cakes as good as me."

Harry replied trying to be encouraging. "Come on Jenny, we can fight this together, don't talk like this; we'll be here next year celebrating. In fact, look if we save up, we can even go to that place you're always on about. You know, Venice, that's it, Venice. What do you think? You'd like that." He so tried to be positive, it was a poor attempt. Immediately he wished he had said something more profound and helpful.

Jenny grinned. She loved him dearly. "OK, now when is this meal coming, I'm starving?" She picked up her chopsticks and started banging them on the table like a schoolgirl.

The food was good, in fact excellent. Harry was just about to ask for a pot of jasmine tea when Shanyuan and his wife arrived at the table.

"My friends, it is so good to see you again. I hope you enjoyed your meals? Now if you will allow us? This is just our way of celebrating with you; please accept our little gifts and a very happy anniversary to you both."

Just then, Lijuan approached with a beautiful tray of Chinese desserts. Lijuan was a demure lady, always smiling, of a sanguine nature and generous spirit; it truly reflected her Chinese name (beautiful and soft). She set before them a delightful array of coloured *ang ku kueh* (a type of *gaos*, steamed rice-baked snacks) and moon cakes. "This is for you," she said, with a broad radiant grin.

Jenny interjected, "Lijuan are you always smiling?"

She smiled even more. "My father taught me an old Chinese proverb. Do not open a shop unless you like to smile. My husband and I wish you the very best today and our sincere and prayerful hope for your future."

"Thank you so much Shanyuan, and many thanks to your beautiful wife Lijuan," said Harry, now standing up. Then again, looking at Lijuan, "You my love, are a real diamond, he's a very lucky man." He planted a big smacker of a kiss on her little cheek. Jenny nodded appreciably. Shanyuan put his arms around Lijuan and spoke gently.

"A bit of fragrance clings to the hand that gives flowers." He continued, "Something the two of you might find interesting. Have you heard of the Year of the Rabbit? Chinese Zodiac? This only happens once every twelve years. Harry, it is a remarkable coincidence that you were born May 1939, the Year of the Rabbit, you were married in March 1963, another Year of the Rabbit and today you celebrate your wedding anniversary in my restaurant. Would you believe, it again it falls in the Chinese Year of the Rabbit, 1987?"

Harry and Jenny looked on as if to say, "Yes, OK, go-on, what's it mean?"

Shanyuan placed his hand on his jaw and began. "The rabbit or hare is ranked fourth in the Chinese zodiac. Although the rabbit is associated with a fixed element, that of wood whose energy is *Yun*. It is also tempered by one of five Chinese elements throughout its twelve year cycles. They are metal, water, wood, fire and earth. Essentially, what does it tell us?" Now he had their full attention. "It reveals something about your nature, important, to be aware of. Harry you're amiable, kind and humorous. That goes without saying. But, you can also be reluctant to reveal your mind, with a tendency to escape reality. You must not be over cautious and miss good opportunities, but be careful, for you can be taken great advantage of. Bear this in mind Harry, remember, rabbits should never give up half way when striving for something."

"I'm always taken advantage of, aren't I Jenny?" he laughed.

Jenny replied, "Stop being silly Harry, this is interesting. So are you saying that these coincidences are in fact not coincidences at all, and in some fashion predict and shape our lives?"

Shanyuan continued, "It is for you to consider. You have to ask yourselves whether these events that we face are simply coincidental, or could there be some higher plan.

55

That there is a mystical relationship that ties lives to the laws of this zodiac." He lightened the mood from its intensity. "Anyway, to remind you of this, I would like to give you these small tokens." He held up a small fluffy patchwork rabbit, and a bouquet of snapdragons. "The snapdragons are your lucky flowers." He handed them to Jenny and kissed her cheek. "This is for you Harry." He passed over a fluffy rabbit. "Keep it secure now; it will remind you and Jenny of this day. Who knows, all that lucky rabbit stuff we hear about might amount to something after all?"

It went extremely quiet; Harry looked at Jenny who broke the silence. "Well that's got you taped, right on the button. Well done Shanyuan." She laughed out loud; hurriedly they all joined in the laughter, which eased the moment greatly.

"It's been a great evening, but we must go now. Lovely meal, lovely company, once again thanks for everything. We'll see you again soon."

"Your carriage awaits," said Shanyuan.

They all shook hands, kissed and were on their way.

Jenny snuggled up to Harry in the back seat of the taxi like young lovers. "Did you notice anything unusual about Shanyuan tonight? Anything different, you know, strange or odd about his behaviour or manner?" Harry yawned.

"Not really, maybe he was just a little tired; he's a busy man, lots on his mind." Jenny squeezed him tightly and shuffled in even closer.

"He just seemed edgy, uncomfortable, not himself. I hope he's OK."

"Not to worry Harry. Thank you for tonight darling, it was lovely, and don't forget we have the patter of tiny feet to look after now." She held up the toy rabbit and giggled. She kissed him tenderly. Harry held back the tears.

CHAPTER 15

Queens Head Pub, Brook Street, Hammersmith –

Date: Saturday 17th January 1987

Harry aligned the saturated beer mat, rested his pint, and dragged the ashtray to his side of the antique oak table. He sat down heavily; what was on his mind was replicated by his body language. He nestled below a capacious, Rococo, gold framed portrait of the nicotine stained Queen Victoria. This was his usual and favourite hideaway in the corner of this historic pub.

Withdrawing into the shelter of the low lighting worked just fine for him. A regular haunt since he began to comprehend fully the extent of Jenny's illness. He became a shadow of his former self. Often welling up in self-pity and then feeling guilty about his obvious selfishness.

"How are you doing Harry?"

Harry looked up, curiously glancing across the bar through the cloud of smoke he had just created, while puffing heavily on his cherry wood pipe.

"It's me Spider, Spider Harris."

Harris strolled across the room with a swagger, and stood at the edge of Harry's table. This was Harry's personal space and it was just about to get invaded. "Can I join you? Mind if I take a pew?"

Before Harry uttered a word, Spider was sitting down.

"You still in the taxi game? Haven't seen you for a while; been hiding? No wonder you can't get a sherbet dab when you need one."

Harry knew Harris, but he wasn't his favourite cup of tea. Harry always viewed him with a degree of suspicion, something he could never really put his finger on, just a gut feeling.

They played in the same darts team a few years ago; Harris was a mean dart player. Harry recalled the match night. Harris arrived cock-a-hoop sporting his new spider's web tattoo. It spread from his wrist to his knuckles on the back of his left hand. How exaggerated his dart throws were with his little finger, Bristow fashion, pointing upwards. Like a strutting peacock, he proudly displayed his indelible motif.

Harris's 164 finish. Treble twenty, treble eighteen, bull's-eye, gave them the District League Cup, regaining the trophy from their old adversary the Salutation in King's Street. From then on Freddie Harris became Spider Harris or simply Spider.

Spider was a stall holder in Shepherds Bush Market, selling second hand jewellery. He had already plummeted to the dizzy lows of visiting HMP, The Scrubs, serving a small stretch for grievous bodily harm and receiving stolen property. A wheeler and dealer, he didn't mind a dodgy deal, but watched his back very carefully these days. He was entertaining, gregarious and wily, edging on the devious.

"Yes, I'm doing a couple of earlies, a few graveyard shifts, but to be honest, since the missus has been so ill I've lost all interest. All my get up and go has got up and buggered off." He hesitated. "I need a sodding change, that's for sure Spider."

He downed his beer and studied the empty glass. "I'm getting a thirst on; another one pal?" Without waiting for an answer, Harry upped and returned quickly with two pints in his hands and resumed, "I've got to get it together, or I'll be no good to man or bloody beast."

Harris leant over the table in an exaggerated fashion and spoke quietly. "Listen pal, I might have just the job for you, right up your alley. A man with your driving experience would be just the ticket. After all, with your down the drains there's not a frog and toad in London you don't know; it'll be a doddle. I'll tell you what, no lies, it'll earn you more dough, and you'll be able to treat your missus to a few luxuries; make her comfortable, etc. After all, you know she deserves it, poor gal. What you got to lose?"

Harry nearly smiled; he sounded just like Mike Read, the cockney comedian. Harris being the product of three generations of market traders was determined to preserve the art of cockney rhyming slang. If it ever was to become extinct, it was not going to be while he was alive.

"It's a couple of business geezers doing well in the city, buying and selling etc.; import and export, that kinda thing; plenty of bunce. They need a personal courier, delivering packages around the city. No questions asked. Just button your gang and mob, low key, bees in your sky, no probs." Harris took a large gulp of beer, looked around from side to side and went on, "Well, what do you think, is it worth a butcher's?"

Harry banged his pipe heavily on the side of the ashtray, as if with every knock he was trying to forget something. "Doesn't sound above board to me Spider?" That was a huge understatement, but Harry didn't expand his reply.

"Look," Harris shrugged his shoulders, "I don't know all the ins and outs, but I think it's kosher, anyway a man's gotta make a living. Stuff the establishment, look after number one."

The thump of finger against microphone interjected their conversation. "Testing, testing. Good evening everybody; great to be here."

How bloody sincere was that? What a load of bull shit, thought Harry.

"This is Brett Vegas, I'm going to start the evening with a little number recorded by Tony Orlando and Dawn called *Tie a Yellow Ribbon Round the Old Oak Tree.*"

Harry shook his head and groaned, "It's that star spangled prat with the black wig and flared trousers. On his best day he sounds like a cat being pulled through a mangle. God, that's all I need right now."

"I'm coming home I've done my time…" warbled out of the speakers.

"Anyway, give it some thought." Harris finished his pint and slammed the glass on the table. "Gotta fly; gotta date with a nice little number from off of Wood Lane. Were having a ruby in the Taj Mahal then it's up to my drum for a little nightcap." An overstated wink followed, to emphasise the double entendre. "Here's their number Harry. Give 'em a bell on the old dog."

He quickly shook hands with Harry. Then fighting to be heard above the music yelled, "Chin chin," and he was away into the night

Harry took the slip of paper and gazed at it with mild interest. 'Fraser & Fraser, Antiques and Art Dealers, Pimlico Road. SW1.'

He stood up and glared at the second rate entertainer who was now in full flow with added vibrato. Then, whilst shaking his head again at the irritating vocalist, placed the note into his top jacket pocket and returned to fill up his empty glass.

CHAPTER 16

Carrie-Anne in Usk –

Date: Sunday 28th November 2010

Carrie-Anne, desperately short of money, emotionally drained, with no home or family to retreat to, gathered her muddled thoughts and attended to the traumatic dilemma she now faced. With no time to spare, she set her face as a flint and hitchhiked to Usk. She had a few friends there, people she knew from her old school days who lived and worked in the town. They may just be able to help, she mused.

Usk itself is an historic market town in Monmouthshire, located by the beautiful River Usk from which it bears its name. She remembered it with great fondness; her early days around the town were full of interesting memories. Carrie-Anne loved history, it was her favourite subject at school, and her home town was steeped in significant historical events and ancient sites. It once housed a large roman fortress (55AD), medieval market place, and hospital. It was home to the last Catholic martyr, Dafyyd Lewis, executed (1679). Then there was the impressive castle overlooking the town, dating back to humble beginnings (c.1066). It is also renowned for the valiant attack on the English by the Welsh prince, Owain Glyndwr (1403). This with its historic pubs made it an atmospheric place to live, particularly if you had a vivid imagination.

Today, making her own history, it was here Carrie-Anne ventured. After numerous enquiries, she managed to locate the whereabouts of one of her closest old class mates. Fortunately Helen Jones had not gone on to university, but had stayed local and was now running the family hairdressing business Scrunch 'n' Curl in Bridge Street.

Dwelling above the shop in Primrose Pad, Helen rented a modest two bedroom flat. It was her first step to independence and she loved it. Moving out of her family home was like a statement to the world that she was all grown up.

After the general hellos and great to see yous, Carrie-Anne unfolded her story, followed by a salient plea for a few nights stay and possible links to employment.

Helen had always liked Carrie-Anne, often wishing she possessed the same adventurous spirit. But she was far more down to earth, analytical in nature and sombre in dress. A procrastinator, it would take her a fortnight to decide what mascara to buy. So she welcomed Carrie-Anne as her desired alter-ego. Even at school she had always been attracted to her lively conversation, a little envious of her sense of humour and gregarious nature. Honestly, she wished her own character displayed some of these more forthright, outgoing qualities.

"Stay till you get yourself sorted Carrie-Anne, take the spare bedroom. Make yourself at home. By the way, the bathroom is through there. I'll make us both a coffee. Only instant, I'm afraid. Black or white?"

"Black, please Helen, no sugar; got to keep this muffin top at bay."

"Muffin top? What do you call this then?" Helen grabbed a large flab of her own stomach and squeezed it. "Trouble is, I love chocolate."

With that, Carrie-Anne took her backpack through to the warm bedroom, slumped on the single bed, tickled her fluffy travelling companion under the chin, and let out a huge sigh of utter relief.

CHAPTER 17

Pimlico - City of Westminster –

Date: Friday 21st July 1989

Harry's new employers were pacing the office floor. The atmosphere was tense, urgent, disconcerting. Eddie smashed his fist on the table, dislodging a sizeable globe paperweight, which dived headlong into the wastepaper basket like a synchronized swimmer.

Eddie Wood, the taller, older and wiser of the two brothers, took exaggerated deep breaths, causing his stomach to swell visibly. He was trying hard to hold back his overt aggression, that when lost, likened to an active volcano ejecting its molten lava, voraciously swallowing up all that stood in its path.

The younger sibling, Danny, was easily led and in awe of his brother. He would do anything to impress him, constantly seeking his approval. Danny would have been just as happy as a milkman doing the rounds like his late father. He enjoyed the high life and its rewards, but had no real stomach for violence. Unfortunately, caught up in the web of notoriety, he was now pigeonholed, like his brother, as a low-life crook.

"We have to put a stop to this right now. I don't care how we do it. If we don't get a handle on this, we'll be fucking yesterday's news," bleated Eddie.

"What do you suggest we do, raise a small army, go in there all guns blazing? It's not our style. Bloody hell, the last thing we want is a turf war!" replied Danny.

"Listen Danny, they are already muscling in on our drug distribution. Our transits are running scared. Our dealers are so far underground they'd give fucking moles a good run for the money. Our porno business is gonna look like a Sunday school picnic if they squeeze it any more. These fucking Chinese bastards are here to stay. They mean business, and I mean big time. Let's hope the stuff we've got on Mitchell will cause her to intervene, to save her own neck."

"They're not just Chinese opportunists, Eddie these are bloody gangsters, triads from out of Hong Kong, Chinese Mafioso. We mess with them, we better arrange our brass handles first. I'm telling you. Half the fucking Met are being paid off, and the other half turn a blind eye. The only way is to do a deal, to negotiate, or else we might as well sod off with what we have and relocate, preferably to Argentina."

Just then the phone rang. "Hello, who's there? This is Eddie Wood."

"Hi Boss. It's me, Harry, Harry Mead."

Eddie lowered his voice. "How many times have I've told you not to call me on this fucking number? It better be good, cos' I'm in no mood to be ponced about with. Now speak up for the love of Mary, and make it pronto."

"You've gotta get round here, and for Heaven's sake hurry. There's a deal going down tonight and the bleeding ducks and geese have got wind of it. You need to be here, it's vital, I can't say any more on the dog. Just get here! Otherwise we'll all be spending the rest of our days in Parkhurst."

"Stay focused Harry. Hide that package; you know the one, make sure it's out of reach. Somewhere safe; it could be our only chance of hanging on in there. For God's sake, don't let Mitchell get hold of it."

Eddie replaced the phone and grabbed his car keys. "Right, I don't know if this is for sodding real, but we gotta check this out. Tell you more in the car. Get tooled up, this could be messy."

They arrived at Harry's place about 7pm, jumped out of the car and legged it two stairs at a time onto the balcony. Harry's door was ajar. They stood tentatively outside; one pushed the door gently with the point of his gun.

"Harry," Eddie whispered. No reply. "Harry, are you there?" Then he let loose. "For God's sake, Harry, stop fucking messing around!"

They walked in cautiously and wide-eyed.

"I don't like this," whispered Danny, who seemed to be taking one step forward and two steps backward.

"Button it." Eddie gestured to his brother to move into the lounge, "Fuck me; it's like *Nightmare on Elm Street*, Freddie Krueger." Eddie placed his hand over his mouth, turning away and shaking his head from side to side.

"Who the hell could do something like this Eddie, and why?"

Harry's pale, lifeless body was lying on its back, his hands had been had tied together in front of him, bound by electric cable. His head contorted, leaning right cheek down to the floor. Blood had haemorrhaged from his nose and mouth. He had been violently stabbed, many times; the blood-soaked carpet bearing witness to the flagrant brutality.

There was a silence, then noises from outside the apartment. Eddie tried hard not to lose control. "We've been sucked in here, and blown out like a couple of kippers. The cunning bastards have set us up. We gotta get out of here and fast. Danny, don't touch anything whatever you do. On my mother's grave, someone's gonna get really fucked for this, and it's not gonna be us."

They bolted down the stairs faster than when they arrived, legged it to their Porsche, and sped out like their tails were on fire. Eddie was gripping the steering wheel so hard, as if he was already strangling the life out of somebody. He drove out of Busch court.

"What about the package, Eddie?"

"I don't fucking know Danny. Now they've really pissed me off."

CHAPTER 18

Busch Court, Charecroft Road, Shepherds Bush –
Date: Saturday 22nd July 1989

Terry turned the key of his VS2000, and as it throbbed with life, he turned on his cassette player to near deafening proportions, hitting the accelerator and beginning the arduous drive back to the city.

It passed uneventfully, apart from a minor traffic hold up from Junction 7-6 (M4 east) and the bizarre sight of an upturned touring caravan, with the strewn debris of its late insides stretching out for about 500 yards on the westbound stretch of the motorway.

He arrived at his home in Charecroft Road about 4.00pm, and parked the car erratically without paying due attention. He was sidetracked by the amount of police vehicles, the numerous uniformed personnel milling about like ants around sugar, and the posse of news reporters with flashing cameras and loud questions. Then he focused on the centre point of their operation, and walked faster, hastening even more as the realization dawned.

The axis of attention was his father's flat. The crowded balcony and the human resource personnel that were funnelling in and out of number 41 were proof enough. "What's happened? What's going on? Is my dad OK?" he pleaded with a uniformed officer at the base of the stairs.

"Just a minute sir, there's no one allowed up there right now. This is a crime scene, and forensics don't want any intrusion or any interference from anybody right now."

"But officer, you're not listening to me, it's my dad who lives in that flat!" He raised his voice with urgency. "He's got to be OK, do you hear?"

Terry went to grab the policeman, but refrained. The policeman beckoned to a smartly dressed, lithe, middle-aged woman leaning over the open car door of her white Volvo. She was engaged, talking intensely on her Mobira Cityman 1320.

"I want an APW (all ports warning) put out on suspects Edward and Daniel Wood. AKA the Wood brothers," she continued. "Last seen driving a silver Porsche 911 Turbo. At present we've no positive ID of the men or vehicle as to their whereabouts."

"Inspector Mitchell, I have a lad here, says he's the deceased victim's son. He would like a word, if you could spare a minute?"

Terry caught the word deceased and became extremely agitated, like an incensed dog trying to get off his leash. It was unfortunate, unprofessional and insensitive of Sergeant Wilkins, speaking in that manner. It was totally unacceptable, and irresponsible. Rest assured, he would be severely reprimanded for this later.

"OK, I'll be right over." She walked vigorously over to Terry, ignoring a cluster of inquisitive, rumbustious reporters.

"By the way, its *Detective Chief* Inspector, don't forget that in future Wilkins."

Just as they met, there was a cacophony of chaotic sound behind them. Terry looked around sharply. Two burly men from the LAS kitted out in green shirts and cargo trousers, were trying to stretcher a covered body into the ambulance through the pressing crowds.

"Hello I am DCI Mitchell from the Metropolitan Police." She displayed her ID card, which failed to register in Terry's fuddled mind.

He declined a hand shake. "I'm Terry, Terry Mead, Harry Mead's boy. What's going on here? Please tell me this isn't happening."

"There is no easy way to say this Terry; I'm afraid your father was found by a neighbour, a Mrs Whittaker from number 40 at around 2.00pm this afternoon. He'd been severely beaten, struck violently about the head and stabbed repeatedly in the chest and neck. He has since died from his injuries. This was a brutal, vicious and frenzied attack. Signs of false entry are evident and the whole place has been completely ransacked. Whoever did this was certainly searching for something. Obviously, we are treating this as a priority murder investigation, and forensics is currently checking, trying to determine the weapon or weapons used in this assault. Terry, I know this is a horrific shock for you, but if you know of anyone that would like to hurt your father, or who had a grudge against him, please get in touch, time is of the essence."

Terry was numb; part of his world had just collapsed. This was like some classic TV police drama being played out. The rhetoric and phraseology sounded like a script out of *The Sweeney*, but rest assured, this was no TV film, this was all too real. He looked to the heavens, held his arms upwards and screamed into the air, "Why, why, why?"

He frantically hustled his way through the masses, nudging and elbowing anyone in his path. Just as the paramedics were about to close the ambulance doors, he hollered, "Wait, hang on. That's my dad, wherever you are taking him, I want to be there too! Do you understand? Am I making myself clear?" The driver gave a swift glance at the DCI for approval. Mitchell nodded.

With tears now streaming down his cheeks, he leapt in the back of the ambulance, perching down by the side of the stretcher, laying his head on his father's chest. "I love you Dad. Whatever happened here?" he mumbled and closed his eyes.

This trauma was insufferable, completely and utterly blighting the early morning emotive interplay between Carrie-Anne and him. The van's flashing lights and siren were in full operation as it sped out of the Busch Court to the awaiting Path Lab.

DCI Mitchell began to saunter on to the crime scene when she was met on the balcony by Detective Inspector Brindle.

"What's it like in there Brindle? Give me the rundown. Any further news from forensics, any idea what they were searching for?"

He leant over to Mitchell with a bullish bearing, and spoke his mind. "Whatever trash did this, must have gone berserk; there's enough blood in there to keep Dracula happy for a fortnight. The bastards must be covered from head to foot in the poor sod's claret. There is no further news from the Body Invaders as yet?"

The first thing Mitchell thought was how to listen and hold your breath at the same time. Brindle had obviously been on a pub lunch attacking the garlic bread again. "Well done Brindle, explained in your usual eloquent and articulate manner." She took a breath.

"Harry's son has arrived back from a holiday in Pembrokeshire; we'll check his alibi later. We've put out an APW on the Wood brothers. They fit the frame. We have a possible lead, three lads skateboarding on the ramp leading out of the service entrance last night. They witnessed two men running hard and jumping into a silver Porsche, but unfortunately didn't get the plate number. The lads' statements will be taken later at the station. These men were looking for something, something worth killing for. We need to find out what that could possibly be. Check all Harry's friends, his work colleagues etc. Find out if he was involved in anything dodgy, if he looked worried or disturbed lately. We must find out what these men were after."

"I don't get it these days," quizzed Brindle. "Villains used to have some strange code of respect. But whoever did this, they were real animals. Forensics suggests that there's evidence of torture pre-death, they're some sick bastards."

"OK Brindle, cut the graphics, you've made your point. I did notice that. So let's get onto it!"

"I'll get on it right away, ma'am."

He made an exaggerated gesture of inhaling heavily through his nostrils as he passed Mitch the bitch, smiling unashamedly. Then he strolled off, laughing to himself, tossing his car keys up into the air and catching them on the way down as he approached his Ford Capri Laser.

CHAPTER 19

Detective Inspector Mike Brindle – The Met Police

Date: Sept 1974

Mike Brindle joined the police force in 1974. He was just eighteen. Trained in Droitwich, this keen, young, qualified constable, gifted with a considerable acumen, entered the service complete with whistle and truncheon. In those early days he had a real sense of duty and purpose, willing and wanting to make his mark in the war against crime. Unfortunately, time and experience revealed that the inevitable damp squib of towing the party line, adhering to police protocol, bogged one down in a sea of treacle. He likened it to a case of unwitting, chronic inertia, like riding a bike with no wheels, peddling like mad, exhausting, but getting nowhere fast.

He was locked into a world where ambition and status appeared to be all that mattered. Where too many of his colleagues, by hook or by crook would invest into this egotistical bun fight, to rise to the top, just to get there.

Mike was no boot licker, no sycophant. He had no propensity to scale the greasy pole of the Met. His lack of rank reflected that. He preferred the ways of the old school, avoiding playing always by the rules, but getting the job done. This did not encapsulate the current police philosophy or procedure. He became disenchanted, and disillusioned.

Mike had joined the force to be a crime fighter. To pit his wits against the villains and in his words, "Bang um up." His accountability to the hierarchy, for every action and conversation, drove him nuts. How could anyone scratch where it itched whilst wearing a straitjacket? The laborious hours of relentless paperwork were for office freaks, bureaucrats, not for him.

In the late 1980s, it became increasingly obvious that the new force had no place for dinosaur thinking. No place for lone crusaders. After all, they were all computer literate social workers now, spending their spare time down the fitness centres, or brown-nosing on the golf courses.

Frequenting the local pubs, slipping the readies to the local grass, for inside info, that was the real deal. Part and parcel of police life as far as Mike was concerned. His methods were instinctive, outdated, and dangerous, in spite of the positive results. He truly was a rebel without a cause. To him, DCI Mitchell was of the new breed, ambitious, arrogant and ruthless. She was fast tracked by the powers that be. If that was not enough for him to get all belligerent about, she was a woman.

These last few years he became increasingly abrasive, cold in emotion, indifferent to his colleagues. Now at thirty, his manner reflected his demeanour. He was six feet two inches with thinning, salt and pepper hair, dark brown eyes and a dimpled chin. He was slowly morphing into a beer bellied, chauvinist. He slumped around in a light tan leather jacket, polo shirt, grey trousers and brown suede Hush Puppies. He loved nothing more than getting out there on the streets, and pitting his wits against the villains, what he called being a real detective. To get results, solve crime, the victims deserved justice. That adrenaline rush, the chase, coupled with an intense sense of smug satisfaction after a conquest, was better than any designer drug. Every success was added to his imaginary trophy collection, like an obsessive big game hunter.

CHAPTER 20

Golden Dragon Restaurant – Fulham Palace Road –
Date: August 15th November 1986

It was 1986 when the triads entered the Golden Dragon. This was the perfect location for operations. After major threats to Shanyuan and his family, the triads had secured the upstairs, and their safe house was established in Fulham Palace Road.

Shanyuan had no options. If he wanted to remain in business and keep his family from serious harm, he would do as he was told. From here and other strategic safe houses around the city, the triads began to put their stamp on the criminal fraternity, dealing at first with the Asian and Chinese communities, and then turning their attention to other gangs and syndicates working in the area.

They feared no-one, and were completely driven by the need of an expanding criminal empire. The triad groups, such as the 14k, Wo On Lok, and Sun Yee On, fled from Hong Kong in the early eighties after the signing of the joint declaration between China and U.K.

These triads where constantly competing with each other for dominance of the Chinese underworld. That ruling power shifted frequently from one group to the next.

They controlled drug trafficking, importing from Germany and the Netherlands. Their seedy criminality included tax evasion, counterfeiting, illegal gambling, protection rackets and the extortion of legitimate businesses. These were all part of their avaricious mandate.

That is where the Golden Dragon restaurant fitted into the triad's machination. Shanyuan's dream became a nightmare. His beautiful eating house had become a nerve centre for organized crime. He became nothing more than a puppet in their dirty hands. Sure he would continue to manage the restaurant as if everything was OK, but nothing could be further from the truth. Such was the occasion when Harry and Jenny shared their last anniversary meal together. Shanyuan lived scared, frightened and defenceless. The product of years of hard work for him and Lijuan had been muscled in on, interloped, by a group of rapacious thugs.

CHAPTER 21

Hammersmith Cemetery – Margravine Gardens –
Date: 2nd August 1989

It was a hot, but breezy August Morning. Terry stood wistfully by the graveside of his father. He was uneasy, irritable, the high pollen count didn't help, his eyes itched like crazy and his nose blushed red from his constant hanky rubbing. He was accompanied by a few of Harry's cabby colleagues who presented an impressive blue and white taxi shaped wreath. The colours thoughtfully planned, in tribute of his dad's love of the Super-Hoops. Shanyuan and Lijuan where present from the Golden Dragon restaurant, along with Lenny the boss from Griffin Autos, three long-serving drinking pals, who readily admitted the cribbage nights at the Queen's Head would not be the same, and various neighbours from the Busch Court tower block.

As Terry turned away from the plot, he was surprised to notice Detective Inspector Brindle observing the service, leaning against a gnarled cedar tree about twenty yards away. He had met Brindle at The Yard during the interviews, and had warmed to his maverick manner. He was Terry's kind of copper, an uncut diamond, a results guy, but more importantly, underneath the steely persona, he believed he actually really cared.

Lenny Riley came dressed in his blue Teddy boy suit, trimmed with black crushed velvet on collar and cuffs. He nudged Terry, and gestured to him that it was time to place some earth on Harry's casket. The portly vicar continued, "…ashes to ashes, dust to dust…"

Lenny hugged Terry, then in true Elvis dialogue continued, "Antihistamine buddy, you need antihistamine. I'm really sorry man; your dad was one of the good guys. He was cool for an old dude. You need me anytime, I'm around pal."

He slapped Terry affectionately on both shoulders, spat his bubblegum out whilst trying to avoid the vicar's gaze, and walked hastily towards his imported 1973 Lincoln Coupe. Driving away to the sound of *Summertime Blues* and realising within seconds how inappropriate that was; he frantically reached out to turn the volume down.

Terry shook hands with the other attendees; they in turn extended their condolences. He looked to wave in acknowledgement of Brindle's presence, but he had taken leave. There was no bite-to-eat buffet, canned beer, or small awkward after talk to follow. In the cars and away, that suited Terry, forgetting to thank the vicar, who in turn raised his eyebrows, scraped the mud off his shoes, mumbled something disapprovingly, and walked away most disconsolate.

CHAPTER 22

The Old Barn, Hayward's Heath, Sussex –

Date: 27th July 1989

"You dealt with the car?" Eddie inquired

"Yeah, it's out of sight, backed it into that old store barn behind the cow shed. Guess what? I saw a scruffily dressed man with a long beard in there. He was asking for something to eat. Don't think it was Jesus?"

"What the bloody hell are you raving on about?"

"You know Eddie, *Whistle Down the Wind*, Hayley Mills and all that?"

Danny started chuckling and Eddie obliged almost in sympathy. "I swear you need a psychiatrist, you gormless twat. It's bloody freezing in here; see if you can start the fire in that old fireplace."

"That's rich Eddie. Where the bloody hell, do you think I'm going to start a fire, on the fucking sofa?"

You never know with you Danny. Now shut your rabbit and get on with it. I'm brass monkeys in here. There are a few old logs just outside the front door, hope they're not too damp or they'll just smoke us to death."

Danny moved to the door, tripping over a jutting floorboard.

"You clumsy bastard, Mum always said you had two left feet. Listen, we'll keep our heads down for a few days; plan some kind of way to get out of this poxy mess."

The boys were holed up in a derelict farm building in Sussex just off of the A23.

"Won't someone notice the smoke out of the chimney?" said Danny.

"What do you want us to do, sit here like a couple of frozen turds? If I find those bastards that set us up, I'll kill the fucking lot of them."

It was bravado talk mostly. Eddie and Danny weren't mindless killers. They liked others to believe so. It gave them more street credibility. They could carry the weapons, talk the talk, look the part, they could certainly put the frighteners on, but the reality was they were thugs, but not the mindless animal variety.

They woke up early next morning with the breath billowing from their mouths like two sweating race horses, clearly visible as it hit the damp, chilly air. Eddie went about putting the kettle on. Danny was tucking his shirt in, and trying to clean his teeth with his finger at the same time.

"Sod it, I've forgot my blood pressure pills. That's great, that is. How the…"

They were startled by the sudden noise that blitzed the air. "Edward and Daniel Wood, this is DCI Mitchell of the Metropolitan Police. You are surrounded. Now do yourselves a favour, and leave the building calmly, holding your hands up where we can see them."

"Christ, what the hell!" exclaimed Eddie, chucking the kettle across the room.

The message was repeated parrot fashion once again by Mitchell. Then she handed the megaphone over to Detective Inspector Mike Brindle, who was just itching to get involved. She walked back to her car. "Delegation is everything Brindle. Don't make a hash of it."

The boys inside shuffled and cursed like Casanova being caught with his pants down.

"What the fuck are we going to do now Eddie?"

"How the bloody hell do I know? How did they know where we are?"

There was no trap door in the floor, no secret panels, no underground tunnel leading through to the woodlands. That only happened in the movies. They were inside, surrounded and out gunned.

"This is D.I Mike Brindle. Come on the pair of you. There is no way out of this; we don't want any bloodshed. We don't want anybody getting hurt. You're hardly Butch Cassidy and the Sundance Kid. So get your arses out here now, and we can all go and discuss this down at the station."

DCI Mitchell withdrew the cigarillo from between her lips and visibly cringed.

Eddie poked his nose through the slightly opened door, and shouted, "We want a telephone and a lawyer. Do you hear me?"

"Sure you do, and I want Spurs to win the FA Cup," Brindle replied.

"Get yourselves out here, you got two minutes."

They vacated the farmhouse like a couple of scolded dogs who still knew how to growl but had forgotten how to bite.

"Don't say anything Danny, keep it shut."

Danny nodded.

Brindle was really hoping for more action. This was a little bit of an anti-climax. It had all the potential of a long, arduous, stake out. On the TV there would have been smoke bombs, hostages, helicopters. But this was Sussex. Now he'd be back in the Yard by lunchtime. "Well well, if it isn't Ronnie and Reggie. Oh sorry, I forgot, it's Fraser & Fraser, how's the antiques business, boys? Sergeant Blakely, get them in the car."

They were cautioned, handcuffed, and bundled into the back of the Rover SDI V8 to the tune of Eddie yelling, "You crazy bastards, you're making a big mistake; you won't get away with this Mitchell."

Brindle turned to DCI Mitchell, "You know ma'am, these boys, they haven't got the balls for a killing, at least not like Harry's. It's not their style. They might put a contract out, but not themselves. Extortion yes, drugs yes, fraud yes, but not this brutal murder. I can't believe that somehow they were responsible for Harry Mead's death."

"Well Brindle, at this moment they're prime suspects. Get someone to find the car; it's got to be around here somewhere. Check the outbuildings and the lanes. I want that Porsche found and thoroughly searched, even if they have to strip it down to the chassis."

"Yes ma'am, will do," replied Brindle.

"Oh and Brindle, Butch Cassidy and the Sundance Kid?" quizzed Mitchell.

CHAPTER 23

Terry – Armed Forces

Date: February 12th 1990.

Terry resumed work at the garage after his father's funeral. The current, traumatic events seemed to cling to him, judging him. Could he have done more? Should he have gone away? He knew his father's problems, his inability to cope after losing Jenny to cancer, it was well known. Did people apportion much of the blame squarely at his door? Then, there was the endless gossip and speculation about his dad's activities. He needed to get away for his own sanity and well being. It became too claustrophobic. He would wait until the New Year and check out.

One such employment opportunity grabbed Terry's attention. A field mechanic for the armed forces, this would certainly serve his purpose right now. After enquiring at the army recruiting office, he found that his skills could be essential to the maintaining of army vehicles. The pay wasn't bad, and the travel was interesting. He was up for it, and after the formality of the interviews and security checks, he was duly accepted. He packed light, taking just a few of his personal belongings, along with various items of sentimental value. He relinquished his tenancy of the council flat in Charecroft Road.

Terry dropped by the garage to say his farewells to the lads, especially to his boss Lenny. Immediately, Lenny wiped his hands on his oil stained rag, tossed his cigarette to the floor and crushed it with his size 10 winkle-pickers. He hugged Terry, as the workmates approached. He then went on, "Well Terry, all the best in your new adventure. Man, all of us grease monkeys are gonna miss you. You dig? All the lads have clubbed together. It was tough to get any money from these tight bastards, but in the end they came up trumps. Guess they must like you. So here, just a little going away gift; hope you like it man."

The gift echoed Lenny's own image. Terry tore off the packaging to reveal a heavy black leather belt, with a large embossed brass buckle featuring a Harley Davidson with the words, 'Ride to Hell and Back'.

"Remember Terry, if it doesn't work out man, there's always a job here for you. Your old locker will remain in the wash room, I promise. Hey, just a minute, I forgot, we all thought you might need this to take with you." Lenny handed him a 1990 Pirelli Calendar. "Look out for Miss August. What a pair of Bristols on that. She couldn't fall flat on her face, that's for sure."

"Thanks Lenny, and thanks guys; keep on trucking."

He was now ready for a new life, with new beginnings in the REME (Royal Electrical and Mechanical Engineers). Within as many months, after the initial technical training, he was posted abroad to a Light Aid Detachment in Germany. The British presence centred on the 1st Armoured Division. With Army vehicles stationed in many places around the world, opportunities for postings were extensive. Who knows, he thought, today Germany, tomorrow the world.

Rhian was now just a distant memory, like a dream of a foregone era. Salad days, before the raging tsunami of real life kicked in, sweeping his cosy existence into oblivion. He was not aware, back in Monmouthshire, a little girl, his little girl, Carrie-Anne, was growing up without her daddy.

The army became Terry's life for the next twenty years. Corporal Terry Mead went on to marry an attractive, vivacious, young girl called Natalie who resided in Paderborn. They married in Germany on the 10th June 1995. She was a real go-getter, a party animal, loving nothing more than to live life to the full. Natalie was a wily girl, selfish in nature and highly manipulative. She knew how to get her own way. It was never done by shouting and screaming, crying or pleading. Likened to the female black widow spider, she was enticing, promoting a promise of sheer Nirvana. Men would become like putty in her hands. You know the rest.

There was no question; half the men in the garrison would have loved the opportunity to *fick sie*. She was a real prick teaser and she knew it. Terry thought he'd died and gone to heaven, he was about to experience some of the most erotic times of his life; unfortunately it came at a very high price.

Lance Corporal Wiggins stood on the front of an armoured FV430 performing for his squaddies. He grabbed his genitals through his pants, followed by several suggestive thrusts and a raucous tacky laugh, directing his sarcastic jibe at Terry. "Steamy Nat, she's got legs right up to her armpits; I don't know whether to feel sorry for, or jealous of Nobby Mead. He's either got a tool like a donkey or a wallet like Rockefeller, or both!"

Terry was nicknamed Nobby, surprisingly not because of his ardent sex life. On manoeuvres, single-handedly, without sharing a crumb, he demolished a whole packet of rough oat Hob Nob biscuits (called The Nobby). Hence he became Nobby. He could live with that. It could have been worse; Hobnob Mead?

He endured and enjoyed three years of a highly charged relationship, encompassing tempestuous and soul sapping ordeals. When it was good, it was unbelievable. When it was bad, it was horrendous. She had an unquenchable lust for the good life. When she had exhausted Terry physically, mentally and financially, her lust moved on, so did she. Terry swore never to marry again.

CHAPTER 24

Police Interview – Brindle and Eddie Wood –

Date: Saturday 29th July 1989

"Right, let's run through this again Eddie," said Brindle, shuffling the papers on his desk. "You're telling me, you had a call from Harry Mead on the day of his murder. At what time was that?"

"Just after six in the evening. I and Danny were sorting out some delivery schedules, and we were running late at the office."

"We'll come to your deliveries later Eddie. So what time did the two of you arrive at Harry Mead's place in Busch Court? By the way, it's 'Danny and I'."

Eddie looked puzzled.

"Never mind Eddie, I can see it's lost on you; go on."

"Look I've already told you. It was about 7pm; the door was open; I shouted out, there was no reply. Danny followed me in. That's when we found Harry, he was lying on the lounge floor in a twisted position, there was blood everywhere and the room was taken apart. That's it. We heard noises and legged it. We were only in there for a few minutes. I swear we did not kill Harry. Why would we?"

"You forgot to mention the shooters; you were carrying guns. Hardly necessary for a social visit was it?"

"Look Mr Brindle, we didn't know what to expect. Harry sounded stressed, even frightened."

"So let's see," said Brindle, with both elbows firmly placed on the interview table, staring at Eddie like a falcon eyeing up its dinner, "you're telling me, that you responded to a cry for help out of the kindness of your hearts, arrived at Harry's door, walked in, and there's poor Harry's body covered in blood, sprawled across the floor, and his place wrecked. You realised he was dead, so instead of calling emergency services or the police, you simply strolled out, got in the car and drove home?"

"Well no. I mean, yes, Mr Brindle, we panicked. We just had to get out of there and fast. We knew this was a set up. We were being framed so to speak. We did not want to go down for poor Harry's death, so we thought we would disappear till it calmed down a bit. You understand?"

"Look, let's cut the bullshit, Eddie. We know what you and your brother have been up to for a long time. You have been unloading packages of cocaine and heroin all over London, using poor sods like Harry Mead as couriers to deliver large packages and brown envelopes. Paid in cash, no questions asked. We won't mention the porno distribution just yet. Oh, I just did. Is that right Eddie?"

"Yes Mr Brindle but…"

DCI Brindle interrupted. "I'm gonna tell you what I think happened that night. Yes, you received a call from Harry about 6.15pm. You were concerned about whether he was going to the police, because he inadvertently found out what he was delivering and wanted to quit. You see, Harry didn't mind being a courier for a little bit of *Emmanuelle goes to Hollywood*, a few blue movies. But drugs, no! You couldn't let that happen, could you Eddie? Even worse, he could blackmail the pair of you for a tidy sum."

Brindle continued, "So, you go up to Harry's to put the frighteners on. If that didn't work you'd have to shut him up. Harry wasn't playing ball was he? So one thing led to another, and it got out of hand. Didn't it Eddie? You couldn't use your shooters, too obvious. So you made it look like a frenzied attack. Some bungled burglary by a desperate druggie looking for a fix. You grabbed a kitchen knife and turned into Mad Frankie Fraser."

"No, No, No, I had nothing to do with Harry's death! Yes, he was working for us. Dropping a few things off here and there, but we had no problems. No reason to kill him. Harry was loyal, a good man. We got on. Ask Danny."

"Oh I intend to Eddie, make no mistake about that. Did you know you were seen scarpering? You and Danny were eyeballed running away from the scene. Your car was spotted and later identified as the getaway car."

"Yes, we were there, but you've got it all wrong!" Danny's voice increased in volume. "You've got it all wrong. I tell you, I don't know anything about the kitchen knife. Never saw or touched any kitchen knives."

Eddie stood away from the table, pushing his chair over in the process. The escort policeman guarding the door unfolded his arms, replaced the chair, watching Eddie at the same time.

"Then it's funny how we found the knife in the boot of your Porsche, wrapped in cloth covered with Harry's blood, concealed neatly under the spare wheel. How do you account for the first-aid box containing £500 that was found tucked under the front seat of your car? Furthermore my old son, that box had Harry Mead's fingerprints all over it. Explain that."

Eddie pleaded his innocence. "What first-aid box? I know nothing about any first-aid box or your bloody £500."

"The interview stops now, it is 4.35pm Saturday 29th July 1989." Brindle turned the tape machine off. "OK, officer, take him back to the cell."

Mike was not convinced that the crime analysis he presented to Eddie was what really happened that night at Harry's flat. He had to push all the buttons. Turn Eddie upside down, see what comes out. For one thing, it really wasn't their style; secondly, even they would not have been daft enough to leave a murder weapon and money in the

98

back of their car. No question the boys would go down for their illicit and illegal dealings, but murder? Brindle wasn't satisfied.

He supped up the dregs of the lukewarm coffee, aimed the paper cup at the wastepaper basket, lobbed, missed and then left the room. Work to be done. He would make a few enquiries of his own. The scent was in his nostrils. That's how Brindle operated.

CHAPTER 25

Golden Dragon Restaurant –

Date: Friday 6th March 1987

It was late evening. Shanyuan had just closed up the Golden Dragon Restaurant. It had been an accustomed Friday evening, good business, busy and demanding. Start of the weekend, pay-packets had arrived and been readily opened. Eager to spend customers flocked in for their favourite oriental food. Shanyuan yawned, he was ready for bed. As he began to enter his downstairs quarters, a disturbing dissonance of fierce arguing and loud sobbing spilled out of the upstairs tenebrous main room.

Mengyao (superior handsomeness), was a ruthless egomaniac with one thing on his mind, power; he assumed all the other benefits would follow like a faithful dog. A determined, dogged man, possessing no sense of compassion or compunction for his rivals, he was unflinching; nothing should stand in the way of his ignoble pursuits. A man to be feared and obeyed or you were simply expendable. He was the oldest son of a triad leader and knew only too well his time would come. He would prove himself here, at any cost.

Mengyao was five feet eleven inches, Shaven head, dark brown eyes, twisted features with pitted cheeks and crooked teeth. Broad shouldered, he always dressed immaculately with his expensive suits and shoes. Large gold rings featured on both hands, one of which was a vintage Good Fortune symbol ring. It was well known in the syndicate, that if he began to twist this ring on his left index finger with his right hand, it was a sentence of death. A man was about to die.

Two deep blood red rubies had disappeared out of the upstairs safe. These were very rare indeed, flawless, and weighed in at several carats. Somewhere, somehow there had been a switch. The green velvet bag that Mengyao withdrew from the safe contained nothing more than synthetic stones of little value.

"This rat who gnaws at a cat's tail invites destruction. We will find this traitor, and when I am finished with him, he will beg to die."

Pleading, begging, showing pictures of his wife and family meant nothing to Mengyao. This underling was given charge to safeguard these precious gemstones. He had failed and would pay the ultimate price. Mengyao would send out a clear message to any other would-be traitor that swift retribution would ensue.

He cried and screamed out in agony as some of his fingers were cut off at the knuckles. Then without further ceremony, Tingfui, one of Mengyao's henchmen, slid the blade of a sizeable meat cleaver swiftly across the throat. Mengyao looked on the execution, all that registered on his face was a slight sucking of his pockmarked cheeks, as if he had just swallowed a bitter pill to relieve a headache.

He left hurriedly with his henchmen, pulling on his leather gloves whilst descending the fire escape stairs at the back of the restaurant. His car door opened, he stepped into his chauffeur driven black Mercedes, leaving his lackeys to dispense with the body.

It was 5am. Shanyuan stirred from his bed and wandered quietly up to the restaurant kitchen. He switched on the stark tube lighting, poured a whisky and took a large gulp as he grabbed the biscuit barrel. He sat down at the battered stainless steel table, and took another swig to calm his nerves. Then he put his hand into the jar, retrieving several biscuits. He was digging like a boy looking for the last chocolate chip cookie. With a final grope, his shaking hand emerged with small, velvet, green bag. He listened, and looked in all directions before placing the cloth on the table and unravelling. There in front of him were two of the finest examples of Burmese rubies you will ever see.

In those early hours of the morning Shanyuan went about his wary plan. An old man, a mere pawn, whose life, premises, and finances had been insidiously and cruelly robbed. No one suspected him, or at least, not yet. Or so he thought. Unbeknown to him, lurking in the shadows was a young lad peeking through the half closed door that led to the stairs.

Shanyuan was unaware of the quiet onlooker. He would pay these bastards back and create a new life for his wife and family. After all, he thought, a man digs a well before he is thirsty.

CHAPTER 26

DCI Mitchell and DI Mike Brindle – New Scotland Yard

Date: August 8th 1989

DCI Mitchell was satisfied that with the amount of evidence set before her they could go ahead and charge the Wood brothers with the wilful murder of Harry Mead. Now it was up to the court to decide.

Mitchell confirmed her conclusion with Brindle. "They had several motives. Harry was under their employ. He could have stolen drugs, threatened to tell the police, tried to blackmail them, give many of their contacts to other gangs for pay-offs. Who knows? They were on the scene around the time of the murder; this was not a social gathering, a tea and biscuits shindig. They were looking for money, drugs, and answers. They were seen leaving the building in a hurry. They absconded to lie low in Haywood's Heath. Their car was identified, the same car that was found with the murder weapon, money and the blood of Harry Mead on the cloth. There was no alibi."

Brindle was about to speak, but before he uttered a word, she steamrollered in. "Let's wrap this up Brindle, those boys are guilty, I'm convinced. There are no questions to ask. Let the jury make its own mind up."

"Ma'am, do you know anything about some dodgy photographs?"

Mitchell's mind went on total alert. What was Brindle going to say next? She replied, "Nothing comes to mind, no, nothing comes to mind Brindle."

"Oh, it's just that Eddie Wood mumbled something about some photographs he acquired, but on following his lead, we couldn't find any evidence to substantiate his claim."

"There you go, desperate men, desperate measures."

Brindle said nothing more, but thought loads; he bit his tongue to prevent an outburst.

"That'll be all Brindle, no more enquiries now. Case closed, do you hear? Well, what are you waiting for? Work to be done. Don't just stand there like an accident waiting to happen. Go and brush up on your social skills or something, and close the door on your way out."

A more determined than ever Brindle left that room.

Mitchell now alone in the office, jabbed her fountain pen hard into the desk, scrambled to open the box of her cigarillos, lit up, and inhaled deeply, aggressively stubbing it out in the ashtray after beclouding with nicotine smoke the chair which Brindle had just vacated. If only she was a dragon and breathing fire, she would happily burn him to a crisp. She then went on to pick up the phone.

CHAPTER 27

Carrie-Anne at Crosskeys Inn, Usk –

Date: December 2010

Carrie-Anne needed to reconstruct her life fast. Fortuitously she had secured temporary accommodation, and was notably grateful to Helen for her generous help. She felt extremely uneasy about not visiting her mam's grave before she left. Her priority now was to get back on her feet, and then when composed and ready, she would return to share her intimate private goodbyes.

Helen was unable to accommodate Carrie-Anne with any full-time work in the hairdressers, just the occasional cash in hand, for a few hours, if and when. Within two or three weeks a lucky break ensued for Carrie-Anne.

'The Crosskeys Inn' Require Bar Staff – Evenings Only, Monday - Saturday. Enquire Within.'

Carrie-Anne had fitting credentials, competent in restaurant and bar experience from her brief Spanish adventure. She was a relative local, with an outgoing nature, countless energy and what's more (which aided her immensely), many of her contemporaries were away at university.

The Crosskeys Inn was in itself of significant local interest. Its frontage facing Bridge Street was constructed in circa 1368 and became established as a pub during the 1830s. Its centrepiece featured a grandiose fireplace in the lounge bar. The exposed timbers were originally ship timbers supplied from Newport Dock. True or not, it boasted a resident ghost and cellar gaol that once housed condemned prisoners, until facing the gallows on the town bridge.

It fitted her like a handmade glove, and she started work over the Christmas period. In at the deep end, she soon became a real asset to the bar. She could live with the daily innuendoes and double entendres that she encountered from the regulars, those, who sat around the circular table by the inviting log fire every late afternoon. The crude, repetitive, tedious comments induced whilst polishing the ale pumps, taught her how to fake looking amused.

She reached above the bar one afternoon to place her fluffy rabbit on a shelf above the optics. All eyes from the round table peered at her shapely backside as she stretched upward. Like any other woman she knew it, but no harm done and it pleased the old sods, she mused.

"What's that then Carrie-Anne?" asked a rather short, corpulent gent in a mustard coloured jacket, duly dressed as if he'd just arrived from a pheasant shoot, as he kicked a large log further into the welcoming fire.

"That's Dandy, my fluffy bunny, he's my little travelling companion."

A copious flow of hop, carrot, and bits of fluff jokes cascaded from the lounge bar. Inevitably, the final joke dribbled out like the last spot of air in a punctured tyre.

In fact, she quite liked the banter with these local characters, conducting herself admirably, when the odd suggestive comment went too far. After all, they were all old enough to be her father and many her grandfather.

What really floated Carrie-Anne's boat was the stream of well-built young men from the local rugby club that visited the pub every Saturday for their beer, pool and buffet. One such lad, a certain Sam Jenkins, caught Carrie-Anne's eye, and in her own feminine way she transmitted reciprocal feelings. The body language, the eye contact, the coy looks and the eager response when he ordered his beer, all announced her 'I'm available and I want you' signal. It was such a great pursuit; subtle as the proverbial sledgehammer. She was reeling him in like a tuna fisherman. Poor old Sam, he thought he was in the driving seat when he asked her out one Saturday night and she said, "I'll think about it."

Soon they were dating. It was one such night, shortly after closing time, Carrie-Anne and Sam left the Crosskeys to order an Indian take-away at the Spice Hut, planning to wash it down with a nice glass of merlot back at Helen's flat.

"You go ahead Sam, order yours. I'll just give Helen a call; see what she'd like to eat." Carrie-Anne lifted the mobile to her ear.

Sam entered the Spice Hut and stood in the alcohol fuelled Saturday night curry queue. He laughed while he waited; he pictured himself dancing to *Hot Stuff* as the guys did at the job centre, in the movie *The Full Monty*.

Carrie-Anne was unable to receive a clear signal. She crossed over, and stood close to the Three Salmons Hotel car park. It began to ring. "Helen, hi, it's me, we're just about to order an Indian. What…" She was taken back; a cold chill grasped her, as if someone had just stood on her grave.

"Carrie-Anne, are you still there? I'd like a chicken balti and mushroom fried rice, please. Carrie-Anne, Carrie-Anne, can you hear me? Are you OK?"

Carrie-Anne paid no attention to the mobile phone; she was transfixed, as she witnessed a tall man sitting at the driver's wheel of a black Audi A6. It was the Chinese man she had encountered at the airport in Malaga. He looked across at her briefly and she instantly recognised those dark piercing eyes. Those, she would never forget. In a moment of fear, mobilised by panic, she rushed at the car. "What the hell do you want?" she screamed. "Leave me alone!"

On pure impulse, she swung her handbag at the car door; it snagged on the wing mirror and ejected a trail of cosmetics all over the road. Sam and others rushed out of the Spice Hut to investigate. What was all the commotion about? Helen was racing towards them in her bath robe and slippers. The mystery Chinese man smiled, waved at Carrie-Anne and accelerated away. In seconds he was gone. She flung herself into Sam's arms and began to shake and cry.

"It's that man again; it's that bloody Chinaman. I'm sure it is. He's following me. Why? why? Help me, please help me."

"What man? Now calm down. How do you know? It's dark tonight, you may have been mistaken. He could just be visiting the family that work in the Pearl Garden down the street," said Helen unconvincingly. She felt it helped Carrie-Anne to think more reasonably, with perspective; it could just be a simple case of mistaken identity.

Carrie-Anne looked bewildered and confused. Surely she wasn't mistaken? How embarrassing if that were the case. Perhaps all that had come to pass with her mam's tragic death and her bitter resentment of Afon had slightly unhinged her mind. Maybe she wasn't thinking straight after all.

Sam responded, "Come on let's get you inside, in the warm."

CHAPER 28

Terry. Army Service and Resignation –

Date: February 2011

The years rumbled along for Terry. His involvement and commitment to the REME forces dominated his life, serving in strategic base camps both in Afghanistan and Iraq during the Iraq conflict in 2000.

He worked in harsh and often unforgiving environments. In truth, he functioned far better, with more dynamism and enthusiasm, when there was a prerequisite matter on the agenda. These troops needed reputable, reliable and intact mobility, their lives depended on such, and Terry rose to the challenge. He was not going to let anybody down. If England needed six runs off the last ball of the day to win The Ashes against Australia, Terry was your man. The need made him strong and determined to succeed.

This would play itself out in the coming years, for it moulded and shaped his character. One hundred and thirty-seven British service people lost their lives in that conflict and Terry knew some of those brave hearts personally. He thought he was a man when he joined up in 1990 and now realised he was just a Rookie then. He had grown up since;

every inch of him. His experiences, good and bad, crafted him into the mature, Teflon-coated, driven man he now was.

He remembered the years in Germany, when Lance Corporal Wiggins and his mates ribbed him ruthlessly about his failed marriage. They challenged his sexual stamina, his inert weakness in dealing with that man-eating, money grabbing bitch. He would know how to deal with her now, but it was over a long time ago. As for Lance Corporal Wiggins, it gave Terry no sense of redress to know that he was one of the fallen, as responding to a call for action his armoured truck struck a roadside bomb.

Now Warrant Officer (WO2), Sergeant Major Nobby Mead, he had a crucial decision to make. It was October 2009 and he had been selected for promotion of rank. The dilemma, he could either continue serving at the elevated rank in the British Army, or make the transition to civvy life while he still had the age and energy to pursue other goals. Warrant Officer Nobby Mead, with some misgivings it has to be said, eventually decided to resign from the army.

He proceeded to arrange through a London agency, a two-bed, ground floor rental in Tadmoor Street, just off the Bush Common. Terry was returning to his manor, his old stomping ground. He returned as a civilian in February 2011, after serving 21 exhilarating, and at times, onerous years in the R.E.M.E.

Now what would the future hold for him?

CHAPTER 29

Shepherds Bush Market –

Date: 25th July 1989

The famous Shepherd Bush Market straddled itself between the Uxbridge Road and the Goldhawk Road in Hammersmith. Located just behind the old railway viaduct, it presented a cornucopia of merchandise, a cauldron of sound, a composite of languages and a cocktail of aromas. It is a place where east meets west and marries comfortably. If you couldn't buy it or order it at the market, it simply wasn't available. It was a pickpocket's paradise and a shoplifter's dream. That is, until you got rumbled. Then if you were smart, you would disappear faster than a rat up a drainpipe.

Mike Brindle weaved his way through the market stalls like a snake through a thicket. He knew the jungle drums would beat out his arrival. It always gave him great satisfaction to know the wide boys and the duckers and divers were slamming their suitcases shut and scurrying to the exit on the Goldhawk Road. The ferret was in town, and the rabbits were scampering.

Mike bought himself some cockles from the seafood stall, saturated them in vinegar and piled on the pepper. Then, with his cocktail stick he began to pierce and feed, whilst stepping on the rolling grapes and kicking the satsumas that had spilled over from the greengrocer's stall. The legit traders' banter echoed around the market place with the same resonance as their grandfathers'. The voice may have been new but the script was old.

"'Ere are missus; gavver round. Tell you what, today's your lucky day. I'm in a good mood, so 'ere's what I'm gonna do. I'm gonna give you a free one, and it's a big un, but for gawd sake don't tell yer old man." He placed a marrow in the lady's carrier bag, and now the performing trader had enticed a giggling curious crowd.

Brindle arrived at the second hand jewellery stall. "Hello Harris, how's trade these days?"

"Swings and roundabouts, Inspector Brindle; bit here, bit there; you know how it is."

"Oh I know how it is son." Brindle paused to finish his cockles. "They were bloody lovely; now, tell me Spider, you heard anything useful about these Chinese thugs operating around the manor?"

"Not really, can't say that I have Inspector. I'm trying to keep my nose clean these days, earn an honest living. You know, be real kosher, above board, behave myself."

"Yeah Spider, sure you are, and I'm the Shah of Persia. Now stop fucking me about. Word is out that you were hiring for the Wood brothers. Correct?"

"Well I was asked if I knew of anyone that could do a bit of running around for them. You know, on the side so to speak, upset the old taxman, bees in your sky. But I didn't know what they were up to, honest Inspector Brindle."

"Please don't say you swear on your mother's life, Harris, I couldn't bear the insult. You not only placed poor Harry in the den of these vipers without any regard for his wellbeing, you knew exactly what they were up to, didn't you?" Brindle went on, "Do you know any reason why Harry Mead was murdered? Have you any idea? Did anybody ask about him? Enquire about him? Approach you in any way, for any information about him or the Wood brothers? Think Harris, because if I find you're lying, telling any Tom Peppers, you'll be an old man by the time they release you from the nick. You'll still fancy women but you'll have forgotten why."

Harris's nerves got the better of him. "They will kill me Mr Brindle; they really will kill me if I tell you anything. I'll be brown bread; there'll be pieces of me all over London. They're not like us, they're really mad bastards; they're fucking crazy. They do things to geezers that you can't imagine. They make Vlad the Impaler look like Florence fucking Nightingale."

Brindle wasn't moved; he reached out to the jewellery stall and picked up a silver pocket watch. "This is a nice piece of kit. Woodford Full-Hunter. Worth a few bob I shouldn't wonder. Have you got a receipt for this Harris?"

"Look, I can't Mr Brindle, they'll do me in."

"Right, say goodbye to life on the outside, you're nicked. I'm going to throw the book at you, and when I've finished you're going to wish you were dead son."

"OK, OK, but I want some protection; you promise me Mr Brindle?"

Brindle had no intention of offering any protection to Harris, but he nodded. He was working on his own agenda and off the record. This was his baby and he knew he was on to something. He'd show those pen-pushing, sycophantic, excuses for policemen how crap they really are, and stick it up Mitchell as far as he could.

"There were these two Chinese men, tough bastards, built like brick shithouses. They grabbed me on the way home from the market. Pushed me into the alley, grabbed hold of my right hand, spread my fingers out on a house brick and drew out this fucking great meat cleaver. They gave me thirty seconds to tell them of any contacts of Eddie Wood and where they lived. I was shit scared Mr Brindle, wouldn't you be? I gave them Harry Mead's name and address. That's all."

"Well, you could join them Spider. You know, become a triad. Then we could call you Chopper Harris," Brindle guffawed.

"Do you get it Spider, Chopper Harris, Chelsea... Oh, I'm wasting it all on you, aren't I son?" He continued, "Then you'd better run, scarper, as far away as possible, before they find you, or you might lose your darts hand, web and all."

"I panicked, Mr Brindle, contacted Eddie Wood and told him that the triads were going after Harry Mead. Don't you see they would have to do away with Harry fast, before he blabbed the contacts. These were all high class players, big names from the city. No question Mr Brindle, they were gonna have to shut Mead up, polish him off, he knew too much."

Brindle just stood there, eyeing up a silver boxing trophy. 'Royal Artillery Division, Light-Heavyweight Champion. 1947-48 – Harold Kemp'.

"Mr Brindle, you promised me, you promised me."

"No, not me son, I don't do deals with scum. You play with fire, you eventually get burnt, or in your case Spider, dare I say it, chopped." Brindle raised his eyebrows, slipped the silver watch into his pocket and turned and walked briskly out of the market. He'd got what he was hoping for.

CHAPTER 30

Tadmoor Street. London W12

Date: Saturday 2nd April 2011

Adjusting to the English weather was going to take some time. Iraq was mostly dust ridden, with a high heat intensity reaching temperatures of 70-80 degrees Fahrenheit. He wondered how long it would be before his suntanned body would return to its pale white colour again. Thank God for central heating. It was bitterly cold for an April day.

A few weeks passed and Terry settled in. There was no rush to return to work. He was a single guy. In Iraq there was only so much money one could spend. His savings were considerable, and serving twenty years in the forces, his military pension was available at the age of 43.

His love for cars had never diminished. His aim was to purchase a classic car and restore it to its pristine beauty. He took a deep breath as via Classic Ads, he considered the outlay for a pearl grey Aston Martin DB4, and was torn about what action to take. "Yes that may be a bridge too far old son." It needed a complete overhaul inside and out. To put it bluntly, it would take years and plenty of cash. But that was the project, and he was up for a venture. If he still felt in a couple of weeks' time that this was a worthwhile project, he would investigate more.

What he needed next was an accessible garage.

CHAPTER 31

Old Bailey, Central Criminal Court, London –
Date: Friday November 17th 1989

In truth, they would have needed Harry Houdini as a defending barrister to escape the overwhelming weight of evidence that pointed to Eddie and Danny Wood as the perpetrators of the murder of Harry Mead. The jury were not privy to all of their criminal activity or previous convictions over the years, but it didn't take a rocket scientist to realise these were professional crooks. Clearly they were better off the streets; any reasonable doubt? – Not much. If there was any doubt about them killing Harry Mead, it would only be a matter of time before someone would get killed directly or indirectly through their criminality.

"How do you find the defendant Edward Wood, guilty or not guilty?"

"Guilty, Your Honour," stated the presiding member of the jury.

"How do you find the defendant Daniel Wood?"

"Guilty, Your Honour."

"Will the defendants please rise, Edward Wood you have been found guilty of the wilful and premeditated murder of Harry Mead. It was a brutal and heinous crime of which you show no remorse at all. It is the sentence of this court that you shall be taken to a place of confinement where you will serve out the mandatory life sentence for your despicable crimes." The sentence was repeated ad verbatim for Danny Wood.

Brindle sat in the gallery and shook his head from side to side. There was a flawed argument by some to suggest the Wood brothers deserved all they got. After all, how many kids were laying in gutters or dead in squats because of their illegal distribution of class 'A' drugs? But he had a point to prove to Mitchell and her cronies. She was wrong about this, and he would love nothing more than to find the real villains of this crime, just to wipe that self-satisfied smugness off, in his words 'that hard-faced cow'.

Eddie Wood looked up to the gallery and stared straight at Brindle as if to plead for his life. Then he was shuffled out of court.

Too little, too late Eddie, too little, too late; like lambs to the slaughter, Brindle thought to himself. He hurried away to his parked car about a stone's throw away from the Central Criminal Court, Old Bailey. He entered the car, adjusted his jacket, looked into the cosmetic mirror on the sun visor and began to push back his thinning hair. Then he started the engine, revved and began to fasten his twisted seatbelt.

Suddenly he noticed a brown A5 envelope on his passenger seat. No sign of breaking and entering, he was sure the doors were locked when he arrived. He'd puzzle that out later. First things first, he grabbed hold of the envelope and with his right thumb ripped along the seal to open it. He withdrew the contents slowly. There was no letter attached. Brindle honed in and scrutinised the photographs. He felt like a baying hound that had just hooked onto the smell of the fox. This was dynamite. They were real, they did exist after all.

CHAPTER 32

Primrose Pad, Usk, Monmouthshire –

Date: February 2011

Sam Jenkins was 24, loved his rugby with a passion but was never going to climb to the dizzy heights of the major clubs. He treasured the camaraderie and the banter. He relished the sheer physical exertion and exchange of the game. Now, something else, or should I say someone else, had entered his life, and it was a whirlwind of a distraction. There had been girls before, quite a few in fact. He wasn't the stud of the rugby pack, but he certainly could put it about. He enjoyed every moment of his quest for carnal knowledge, or as his mates would say, 'a good shag'. This was somehow far more than that.

Carrie-Anne was not just fun, a bit of skirt, or just another conquest for Sam. She had an indescribable charisma, even as she carried the weight of circumstances that now pervaded her life, something shone out of her that attracted him like a moth to the light. She was no pushover and he recognised that. In fact, it was she that had him dangling on a piece of invisible string. He just wanted more of her. Carrie-Anne also began to awaken to the fact that although she fancied him, this was more.

Their first sexual encounter together was hardly the ideal. But somehow that made it all the more exciting, hoping Helen was unaware of the unrestrained copulation taking place in the small bedroom. It gave it the edge. Of course, Helen knew. She might not be the brightest bubble in the bubble patch, but she would have to be as thick as a whale omelette to be oblivious to their frisky cavorting.

Sam and Carrie-Anne exited the bedroom as if they had just been playing a game of Scrabble.

"Would you both like to join me with a glass of vino? It's Australian Merlot. Do you like it smooth and full-bodied?" asked Helen, whilst trying to keep her composure as the red-faced pair sat down. Then without any qualm she immediately blurted out, "By the way, how was the rumpy-pumpy?" Her brimming mouth erupted like a turned on garden sprinkler, spraying red wine all over the coffee table as she tried not to laugh.

Carrie-Anne echoed Helen's laughter, only with much more vigour. Pretty soon, all of them were in stitches. As the wine flowed, the more humorous it all became.

It was about 11pm, when all of a sudden there was a knock at the front door.

"Who can that be at this hour of the night?"

"That's a heretical question Carrie-Anne. How can we know?" Helen slurred. "Were not clairvoyant are we?"

"You mean rhetorical question, and you're as pissed as a fart," laughed Carrie-Anne.

They all giggled again, everything they said now seemed hilarious.

"How you said clairvoyant, beats me," Sam continued. "I'll go." He placed his wine glass on the table. "Fill that up girls."

Sam tackled the stairs carefully; he was pretty well soused himself.

"It's addressed to you Carrie-Anne, delivered by hand. There was nobody outside when I looked. The streets are dead tonight."

That all too familiar dread began to creep over Carrie-Anne; the wine would anaesthetise, take the edge of her stark emotion, but even so, she was real uneasy. She stood, opened the letter and asked Sam to read it out loud.

"Sometimes it is not who you fear that brings the danger. So be alert, sometimes you have to scale the mountain before you face a clear horizon."

Carrie-Anne's explosive outburst had no laughter or joviality attached. She grabbed instinctively at her mam's silver pendant that she now wore religiously. It was as if somehow her inner consciousness transmitted a heartfelt cry, beckoning her parents for protection and help. "Tell me,

126

what the fuck's going on Sam? I don't get it. What the hell does all this shit mean? For God's sake, am I going crazy or something?"

"Calm down, Carrie-Anne, it's only some prankster," Sam blurted whilst trying to sober up. "Maybe some mistake, delivered to the wrong flat which often happens; after all, does the note make any sense to you Carrie-Anne?"

The mysterious letter unnerved her, but in time the ample imbibing of red wine put her fast asleep. She felt better in the morning, more in control, after all, it was just a letter, some crank probably, who gets his thrills out of frightening people, or one of her old school pals playing a trick on her. She'd put it behind her.

CHAPTER 33

Griffin Autos, Uxbridge Road, London –

Date – April 8th 2011

Terry wondered if his old boss Lenny Riley was still operating out of Griffin Autos, whether the old workshop was still there. After all, it had been roughly twenty years since he left to pursue his army career. His motive was not purely self-serving, although without a doubt, acquiring a garage for his restoration work came pretty high on his agenda. He really would like to meet up with his buddy for old time's sake; to catch up on what's been happening around the manor through the years.

It was Wednesday afternoon, a brighter day with a lazy wind. He caught a taxi, asking the driver to take him to Griffin Autos on the Uxbridge Road. The cabbie never gave him that puzzled look, no shaking of the head. That was a good sign, thought Terry, It must still be there.

He then disappeared into a world of his own. His thoughts meandered back to his father Harry. Memories entered his head, one after the other, like a fast flowing stream, starting with the first day Harry took Terry around London in his brand new taxi cab. He subconsciously licked his lips, as he recalled the inviting smell and taste of that greasy, bacon laden, crusty roll, washed down with a large mug of milky tea with spoonfuls of sugar at the local transport café.

Then, there were the Saturdays at Loftus Road, when as a small boy he used to huddle next to Dad during the cold match days, wiping his runny nose on his woollen gloves, proudly wearing his bobble-hat and enthusiastically waving his blue and white scarf that Mum had lovingly knitted for him, cheering loudly for the Super Hoops. How his dad hoisted him above his head when Rangers scored a goal, and then his mum's ticking off when he returned home, for dropping ketchup and fried onions all down the front of his duffel coat.

"Here we are mate, Griffin Autos," announced the cabbie.

Terry still had that mischievous boyhood smile on his face as he returned to Planet Now. He paid the fare, and stood looking across the road. GRIFFIN AUTOS – CAR HIRE – FILLING STATION.

Nothing resembled the decaying asbestos roofed workshop that Terry remembered. Gone were the old metal shutter doors, the haphazardly placed piles of car tyres and rusty exhaust pipes that used to litter the entrance. Now standing before Terry was a large red- bricked workshop, with a white pebble-dashed frontage. The entrance featured

129

large glass folding doors. Adjoining was a modern office reception block and motor spares shop. The tarmac forecourt boasted a fleet of cars for hire and two rows of state of the art petrol pumps.

Terry entered the reception with grave doubts about finding Lenny Riley. The attractive young girl at the reception desk placed the phone down, picked up her pen, and with a big smile said, "Hello sir, can I help you?"

"Look, it's a bit of a long shot; I'm looking for a Mr Lenny Riley who used to own the old garage here many moons ago. Before the girl could answer the question, a door opened from behind the counter. "No, it can't be? Is that you Lenny?"

Lenny glanced up, shifted his glasses to the end of his nose and peered over the top. His brain suddenly began to register. "Terry, Terry Mead, well, I never thought I'd live to see the day." Lenny walked out from behind the counter, reached out and shook Terry's hand strenuously, talking in rhythm to his hand shake. "Come on, you got time for a coffee?"

"Absolutely Boss." That brought back some funny memories.

"Mandy, can you fetch us some coffee and bickies through to the back office. If anybody asks for me, I'm not in, got it? We've got a lot to catching up to do. This strapping man here is my buddy; used to work for me years ago, until he found a real job…" he chuckled, "…for queen and country," and then saluted.

"Mandy, I've been out in the Gulf for so long, swallowed so much sand, you could turn me upside down and use me as a bloody egg timer," quipped Terry.

Lenny no longer wore those greasy overalls. He had filled out as the years went by, and his Teddy boy hairstyle was just visible as he tried to make the most out of what little hair he had left. Now he was a shirt and tie man, looking swanky in his navy blue pinstriped suit and black brogues, every inch the guv'nor.

As they walked through to the back office, Terry couldn't resist. "Can't quite get into the drainpipes now then Boss?" He would always call him 'Boss'; it just kind of cemented the nature of the relationship in a mutually agreeable way. It rekindled the old days, remembered with fondness.

"Are you taking the piss young Terry?"

They spent a good couple of hours treating themselves to a catalogue of exchanges, some hilarious, some interesting, and some mindful, sombre reflections.

The rise of Griffin Autos was a small miracle to put it bluntly, but there it stood as a living testimony to hard work, ambition and a lot of luck.

Just as their time together was drawing to its natural ending, Terry popped the question of classic car restoration and possibilities of space in the workshop.

"Come with me Terry."

They began to walk through to the very back of the new workshop, passing by all of the modern equipment, a far cry from the dishevelled, cold garage Terry remembered.

"I've only got one car space available, its right in the back corner, but you will have to help me clear the area as there's a lot of old rubbish to be shifted."

They kept walking and approached a rather large tarpaulin covering what looked to be car shaped. "Go ahead Terry, pull off the canvas. You reckon you can get rid of this old junk?"

As Terry tugged away at the dust laden cover, choking as he did so, he was staggered. For there before his very eyes stood the first car he had ever owned, his old Dream Machine.

"Take your time Terry, have a look around the old girl. The keys are in the glove compartment, including your locker key." Lenny pointed at the rusted, green locker, parked against the back wall. "See, I promised you I'd keep it all just in case you came back. I'd better go check with Mandy that everything's OK, before she goes home tonight. No rush, I'll be back in about half an hour."

Terry was like a bee around a honey pot. He didn't know whether to laugh, cry, shout or sing. But in the space of about ten minutes he had achieved all of them. He sat in the front, and then sat in the back. He looked under the bonnet, then into the boot. Finally, it was time to check out the glove compartment. It creaked open and he placed his hand inside to pull out its contents, a couple of music cassettes, screwdriver, some snooker chalk, chamois leather, pack of cards, an old leather wallet, various road maps, loose change and an extremely old bar of Nestles chocolate. He grabbed his faded wallet and opened it up, searching out its insides. A book of postage stamps, snooker hall membership card, dry cleaning ticket and gift vouchers from the petrol station, then, just as he began to close the wallet, he noticed, that tucked down in the credit card sleeve was a passport type photo. He gently raised it to his eyes recognising Rhian and himself embracing one another. It all began to flood back. The joy of that week, the pain that followed, all the what could have beens and the should have beens, and he wondered what Rhian would look like now; whether she ever married, had children, moved from Wales.

"You ready Terry, were going to close up soon. Are you nearly done?" shouted Lenny from the front of the workshop.

"Give me five; just have a butcher's in the locker."

"OK."

He was met with an array of overalls, work boots, rubber gloves and cans of degreaser. On the top shelf was the prize of all prizes. It was the old battered radio, Lazarus. He went to slide it out, and as he did so, two envelopes of different dimensions and colours fell to the ground.

"Come on Tel, time to go."

"OK Lenny, I'm right with you. Can you drop me off at the Queens Head on the way home? I fancy a pint."

Lenny nodded. Terry placed the envelopes in his inside jacket pocket and hurriedly sat in the car. They drove off.

"Lenny, I've just found two envelopes in my locker by the side of the old jukebox, do you know anything about them?"

"Bloody hell Terry, they've been there years. I'd forgotten they were in there. They were delivered just after you went to Germany. Never thought they were important, but I put them aside for you. I'm sorry mate, they completely slipped my mind. Still, it's a bit late to pay your bleeding water bill." Both laughed it off. "Here we are buddy. It's a regular time-warp in there. I don't think they've changed the beer mats since the Coronation. See you soon."

CHAPTER 34

New Scotland Yard, Westminster, London SW1 –
Date: Monday 20th November 1989

Brindle arrived at the office mid morning, hung his overcoat on the singular coat hook, rubbed his hands together and felt for the radiator. Files, binders, dossiers, notes and photographs were piled several inches high, randomly strewn across his desk, featuring an indelicate topping of take-away menus. He had the kind of untidiness that any teenager would be proud of. "I must make a start on these soon; alternatively I could just file them under miscellaneous (synonymous with wastepaper basket), second thoughts, I don't reckon this stuck up paper brigade would appreciate that."

Anyway this was a day of days. The minute he'd been waiting for was about to arrive. He felt a deep glow inside, one of righteous indignation, justice, and smug satisfaction. "Let's nip to the canteen, I'm starving."

He left his office and strolled down the corridor swaying from side to side whilst singing, "You're just too good to be true, can't take my eyes off you…"

It was 3pm.

"Brindle, you wanted to see me; make it quick, I'm busy enough as it is without you trundling on about this and that. By the way, when are you going to do us all a favour, shift your arse and catch up, or simply just take a very early retirement?"

"Do you know Detective Chief Inspector Mitchell, I was going to consider the latter, but something's come up. By the way, if you don't mind me asking, as you're a very ambitious lady, have you ever considered a career change yourself?"

"What are you waffling on about Brindle?"

"Well I wondered ma'am, if you ever thought about modelling, not with clay or plasticine, nothing like that," Brindle was enjoying this, "but as a fashion model. You know, catwalk and all that stuff?"

"Brindle I don't have time for this," she raged. "Get to the point you irritating man."

"Well, it was only that I personally think you take a very good photo." He slammed the photos on Mitchell's desk and felt like he had just risen to the summit of Everest. He leant over the desk and whispered, "Tell me, what you think?" and winked with a 'cat that got the cream' demeanour.

The photos displayed a telling sequence of events, beginning with a lone Mitchell taking a sizeable package off of a vicious looking Chinese man who was seated in the rear of a black Mercedes with his window fully wound down; a shaking of hands; Mitchell opening the package revealing a wad of cash; counting the money; placing the stash in her bag; and finally, driving off.

"You have been a very naughty girl, haven't you Chief Inspector? Brings a whole new meaning to a Chinese take-away, don't you think?"

The last thing Mitchell was prepared for this afternoon was the one that presented itself in front of her right now. She was swift of thought, and intelligent enough not to go into free-flow, in case anything would prejudice her future statements.

"I am going to bring you down. It was you that contrived and connived in the plan to frame the Wood brothers. You knew that by taking the Woods out of the equation you would allow the triads to take full control of the manor, aiding the expansion to their seedy empire, and that in doing so, you could receive generous payoffs. I find it hard to come up with enough adjectives to describe you; you're a cold, calculating, menacing degenerate. You deliberately framed Eddie and Danny for murder."

Mitchell scowled, brazenly facing her accuser. "You can prove that can you? I don't think so."

"Poor old Harry Mead was just an expendable asset, so that you could line your greedy pockets. I knew I could smell a rat with you Mitchell. You just needed nabbing and sending back into the sewer where you belong, along with the entire flea infested vermin you colluded with. By the way, did I forget to mention? Chief Superintendent Lovell, you'll be pleased to hear, he has assigned me to the case. It is an indescribable pleasure for me to ask you to vacate your desk."

Brindle raised his voice to summon in DS Blakely who was poised attentively just outside in the office corridor. He leant forward invading Mitchell's personal space and continued, "You're being placed under suspension, pending further enquiries. Personally, I would have arrested you right now. Would you kindly escort this woman off the premises Sergeant Blakely? Oh Mitchell, don't disappear, I would hate to have to come and get you."

Brindle edged behind Mitchell's desk, seated himself on the black executive chair, and began to spin like a child on a merry-go-round.

CHAPTER 35

Primrose Pad, Bridge Street, Usk, Monmouthshire –
Date: Sunday 20th March 2011

There was no work available in the Scrunch & Curl today, so Carrie-Anne agreed with Helen to get on with some domestic duties. Helen was not going to be home tonight, she was travelling to Bristol to stay with some uni friends. There was a Champagne and Fancy Dress Party at the students' hall, and she had an eye on an archaeological geek called Simon. She was going to dress as Helen of Troy, hardly original, but she would look nice, and of course she had the entire wherewithal to arrange the hairdo before leaving.

It was Sunday; Sam had arranged to take Carrie-Anne to watch a movie at the Savoy Theatre in Monmouth. The theatre was about 20 minutes away by car. The root of this old cinema was part of its charm. Originally the site of the Bell Inn in 1794, launched as the Theatre Royal in 1850, later, by popular demand, it was converted to a roller skating venue called the Rinkeries. Then in 1910, it became Monmouth's first cinema, the Living Picture Palace. Now today, this atmospheric, historical venue stands as the

Savoy Theatre Royal. This was not just watching a film, but a whole evening experience.

Carrie-Anne started to shower early, for tonight she was going to pop her cork and dress up. Very rarely did she wear a dress, but this evening it was going to be the whole nine yards: a new hairstyle, elegant evening dress, sheer stockings, high-heeled shoes, alluring perfume, and accompanying accessories. She gave a twirl, pursed her lips, and checked herself out in the dressing room mirror. As she did so, her mind took her back to the tattered holiday snaps of her mam wearing that gorgeous prom dress, on her date with Tad. She so wished her parents could see her now. "I'm sure they would be proud of me."

She was going to knock Sam dead, blow his mind. He would have to be wearing a suit of asbestos to resist the heat of her erotic advances, which she had planned for him tonight. She was dressed to thrill this evening. Helen was away in Bristol for the night. Primrose Pad was exclusively theirs, and Carrie-Anne would be in like Flynn.

CHAPTER 36

Golden Dragon, Fulham Palace Road, London –
Date: February 26th 1987

Shanyuan was going about his usual business, checking that his customers were happy with their food and service. He ventured to a little booth that rested in the corner of the restaurant. "Hello Madam, I am Shanyuan, the owner of the Golden Dragon. I am just checking to see if your meal is OK tonight?"

The lady raised her head and shook his hand firmly. "The meal is fine; your reputation goes before you. I'm Vicky Mitchell, pleased to meet you. Do you think you can possibly spare me some time? It may be in your best interest Shanyuan."

Shanyuan indicated to his staff that he would be indisposed for a little while, and hand gestured for some drinks to be brought to the booth.

Mitchell spoke softly. "I know about the safe house upstairs. I also know that your life and the life of your family are in danger. Your business and your future, it's all being threatened by those slimy excuses for pond life."

The young waitress placed two liqueurs on the table, nodded her head gracefully and backed away like a ballerina.

"I have the power to get you and your family safely out of this. Not only that, if it all goes to plan, enough money to help you set up again, anywhere you like, away from all of this. What do you say?"

Shanyuan looked directly into Mitchell's hazel eyes and responded. "Vicky, if the first words fail, ten thousand will not avail, you can stare at the profit and step into the pitfall. We will talk further but not tonight, and not in here."

CHAPTER 37

The Queens Head Pub, Brook Street, Hammersmith –
Date: April 8th 2011 – 8.30pm

It had been an enjoyable, profitable afternoon for Terry at Griffin Autos. First, the welcomed renewal of friendship with Lenny, and second, by Lenny's marked generosity, he was able to restore his car in the very garage where he learnt his trade. That was fantastic.

Lenny was correct, for over two decades there had very been little change to the Queen's Head. Terry glanced around the bar, yes, everything is as it should be, and the familiarity was comforting. This was a veritable time capsule, which favoured, and invited the nostalgia of bygone days, good laughs, funny stories, and happier times.

Then hesitantly, he turned his head to view the table in the corner that his dad used to frequent. For just a few seconds, he visualised Harry sitting there raising his pint to his mouth, then puffing away on his cherry wood pipe, interjecting with thoughts out loud on the latest match at Loftus Road, or the unnecessary changes to the cabbie business. Terry laughed to himself, as he remembered the occasions when his mum accompanied dad to the pub, how she would hold his arm, sip her wine, listen to the same old jokes and stories that she had heard so many times before. As love is love does, and she never let on.

Terry ordered his beer, grabbed the pub's newspaper, strolled over to the table and sat down. Then impulsively, he spoke out loud as he raised his glass. "Here's to you Mum and Dad, you're the best. Missed but never forgotten."

Now he settled to enjoy his pint, gather his thoughts, and read the news. As he began to read he remembered the envelopes in his jacket pocket. Inquisitiveness got the better of him, and within seconds the first letter was on the table ready to open. Whatever experiences he'd faced in the armed forces, nothing was going to quite prepare him for this.

Miss Rhian Lewis
Arnant, Nant-y-derry
Monmouthshire

Date: May 22nd 1990

Dear Terry,

I have since heard of the tragic news about your father's death. I cannot begin to understand the pain that you have been going through. I will only trust that in time you will be able to rekindle your love for life. I know this is going to be

144

a shock, but I feel it is only right to let you know, that you are the father of a beautiful baby girl called Carrie-Anne, born on the 28th March. I hope this will bring some joy into your life.

Please understand this is not to lay any claim on you or your future. I know this was unexpected for both of us. I just felt it be wholly irresponsible for me not to let you know. To give you this chance to see, love, and hold your own little girl.

If you do not want to make any contact with me I will sadly understand. But, at least I have told you.

Love you loads – Rhian xxx

P.S. Enclosed picture of Carrie-Anne, and I still have Dandy the Bunny – Remember?

Terry sat trance-like, as his mind wrestled with the enormity of what he had just read.

CHAPTER 38

Police Interview Room – New Scotland Yard –
Date: Tuesday 28th November 1989

Brindle entered the barely functional Interview room, which looked about as inviting as a park toilet. The décor consisted of cream painted brickwork and bottle green gloss on the two huge radiators and skirting boards, four non-matching chairs and one highly distressed table with a wonky leg. The room housed stale air, and the metal framed, single-pane windows, had multiple coats of white gloss going back generations. You would need a crowbar to open those. If this was not enough, the fluorescent strip lighting would blink and flash intermittently with a life of its own.

"This room is in serious need of an interior designer or a demolition expert. What do you think Blakely?"

Blakely didn't reply, just shrugged her shoulders. DS Blakely was used to the cut and thrust temperament of Brindle. She was well above average intelligence, with a glowing career in front of her. Unfortunately Brindle's reputation for kicking against the pricks, and how he loved the obvious innuendo, worked against her. Still, she thought, someone's got to do it. Truth be known, she enjoyed working with Brindle. She never knew what was coming next. Average height, of Jamaican parentage, she was a feather in the cap of the Met, who were avidly encouraging more applicants from the black community to join the police force. She was humorous, generous, considerate, and above all, diligent. Brindle was lucky.

He was a man with a mission. He made a point of producing the falsest of smiles, scratched his nose vigorously, and apologised. "Sorry about that. I have this allergy; some irritating, adverse reaction to certain perfumes. Incidentally what kind of fragrance are you wearing today Miss Mitchell?"

Mitchell returned defiantly, "There would be little point in conversing with you over the finer things in life, Brindle. You're a complete plebeian. You couldn't tell the difference between a Cabernet and a Shiraz... if it didn't have a label on it."

He pushed the button on the tape machine. "Police interview with DCI Mitchell. Interview starts at 11.15am on Tuesday 28th November 1989."

"Now DCI Victoria Mitchell let's get on. You have a lot of explaining to do. Shall we start with how you appear to be on these photographs colluding with triad gangsters? Would you like to give some plausible explanation as to why you were there parleying with these criminals?

147

Undercover work perhaps? You know, police work of a discreet nature maybe?"

Mitchell's representative presses her arm and shakes his head, confiding, "You really don't have to say anything."

"Yes, well thank you Perry Mason. Tell me Victoria, may I call you Victoria? Because this is just about the end of the line for you, if you get my train of thought."

Brindle enjoyed that.

"Is this bright young solicitor hired on police expenses, or are you footing the bill? Either way, it seems a waste of time and money, after all I could tell you that for free." Mitchell stared with utter contempt at Brindle. You could almost detect 'murder' in her eyes. If she could turn the clock back, she would have found a way to eliminate him.

"So, I was thinking back to the day of Harry Mead's murder. You know, the one you arranged with your Chinese friends. Why for instance was the room ransacked? After all, in your sick scheme to have Harry eliminated, framing the Wood brothers, it did not require a ransacked room. That would complicate the issue, pointing to a random, frenzied attack from a desperate drug user or something. The Wood brothers already told me that Harry was as sound as a pound. They trusted him. They weren't looking for something that night were they? They responded to Harry's urgent call, which you or your accomplice forced Harry to make. So, if they didn't pull the place apart, and why would they, who did, and what for, I ask myself?"

Mitchell spoke up for the first time, the obvious pent up anger inside her gushing out. "Look you pathetic, dithering excuse for a policeman. What makes you think that the Wood brothers did not smash that place apart to make it look as you said, a frenzied random attack, to avoid detection? If you're so clever then answer me. Why would I need to get involved? The triads or the Woods could chop themselves into little pieces; they certainly didn't need me for that!"

"Protection, it's all about protection. Yes, they could have paraded the streets making dog meat out of each other. But, the game was spreading. Big shipments of drugs and precious stones were being smuggled in. The stakes were high, the rewards huge. That's where you came in, wasn't it Vicky Mitchell? You see, what you offered, they couldn't refuse. Protection at a very high level, someone right at the heart of New Scotland Yard batting for the triads, someone who very few people would dare cross. That's you DCI Mitchell, and you would be handsomely paid for it. I believe you and an accomplice ransacked Harry's room sometime after the murder. You were searching for something that neither the triads, nor the Wood brothers were looking for. I have no idea what that is or was, but you do, and I am going to do all in my power to find out."

"How do you know I even set foot in that room? How do you prove that one then?" Mitchell yelled as her solicitor tried to calm her down and shut her up.

"Let's go back to the day of the murder shall we Vicky? Remember our conversation in Busch Court. I left Harry Mead's flat, walked down the stairs and met you by your car. As I recall, I began to explain graphically the murder of Harry. By the way, I enjoyed breathing the garlic in your face, anyhow that's by the by. I mentioned Harry had been tortured pre-murder."

"So what?"

"Well, you told me that you had not yet visited the crime scene. I checked with forensics, they had not mentioned this in their initial report. They were just in the process of making out a detailed analysis at the murder scene, which you were not yet privy to. Yet, you told me you knew about the torture. How?"

Brindle continued in full flow now. "When I passed by you to go to my car, I took a couple of deep sniffs. It was a sarcastic thing to do, but I wanted you to know that I knew you hated my garlic breath. As I came away, I smelt a strange aroma. No it wasn't your expensive perfume Vicky. I wondered where it seemed familiar. Then as I sat down in the car, it hit me. I knew. It was at the flat. The flat was permeated with the odour of Harry's unusual piped tobacco.

150

You Vicky, would have had to been in that room for a long time to smell like that.

"That evidence would never stand up in court, Brindle, and you know it."

"Maybe it will. Maybe it won't. But I know the truth. I will find out what you were looking for, if it takes me a lifetime. Just to see you squirm. One thing is for sure, Mitchell, you won't be able to talk your way out of taking backhanders from murderous gangsters. God knows how many people you stitched up; how many people have conveniently disappeared; what nest eggs you've hidden away. There'll be a full investigation, no stone unturned, I assure you. Your police career is finished and a lengthy sentence is awaiting you. I couldn't be happier. Interview terminated at…"

"You bastard, Brindle; I should have had you dealt with a long time ago."

"That's as it maybe. Off the record Mitchell, you're a greedy, vicious, murdering miscreant, and I would like nothing more than to see you go down for life. Rest assured you won't need a solicitor; you'll need the Messiah himself to get you off of this lot. While I am alive, if you get out, watch your back, because if you so much as fart loudly, I will have you back inside. Incidentally, for the record, Victoria Mitchell, I prefer a quality Merlot myself."

CHAPTER 39

Tadmoor Street –

Date: Sunday April 10th 2011

The impact of the letter opened in the Queen's Head was truly mind blowing. Terry sat in his downstairs flat staring at the photos of Rhian and Carrie-Anne, wondering how to respond. His past was tapping him on the shoulder, causing him to look back and revisit. If only he hadn't read the letter. But then again, linked with the obvious disquietude of his situation, were the intriguing possibilities of a reunion with Rhian, and a chance of meeting his new-found daughter. He simply never questioned the alternative, whether the child was his or not. Perhaps, that was a revealing indicator of how much he wanted this to be true.

Somewhere out there, they had spent a life he was totally unaware of. He had learnt from his years in the forces not to react impetuously, but survey the ground, consider the consequences, think what action was appropriate, or indeed possible. Impulsiveness was for heroes. This had to be treated delicately.

Carrie-Anne would now be in her twenties and Rhian around her forties. No bull in the china shop advance for

Terry. He certainly didn't want to damage anything. His primary task was to cautiously enter this new dimension, another world, one of which he had never made claim to before, that of fatherhood. The questions he asked himself, he could not answer, but it put him on a sound footing. His ignorance of the letter until recently – would Rhian even believe him? Did she even care? Was he now too old, too far removed to enter their lives? Rejected or accepted? Hundreds of thoughts flooded through his mind; every one heaped another concern upon his broad shoulders; mentally, it was like carrying three military backpacks all at once. He would prefer driving an armoured car over the mine strewn roads of the Gulf, than tackling this one. But tackle it he must. He had the address, thanks to the letter. That would be a start.

He would borrow a car from Lenny at the garage, pack a few things, and travel to Monmouthshire, South Wales. First he would settle in the area, planning to stay in a nearby hotel. If there was any forthcoming information that would prove they were still living locally, he would bide his time, patiently waiting, till he felt it right to make contact.

CHAPTER 40

Triad H.Q, Soho, Wardour Street, Greater London –
Date: Friday 20th March 1987

Mengyao and his bodyguards entered the tacky strip joint with the moth-eaten chairs and shiny copper tables. Pictures of club acts yet to perform adorned the walls. Large dusty spotlights sat in rows just above the stage, shedding coloured glows upon one of the artists, who was practising her exotic act to the muffled tune of the heavy breathing *Je T'aime*, whilst complaining about how cold the venue was.

Sultry Sandy Gold, as she was called, moaned. "How can I possibly perform? Look, my body has goose bumps everywhere; I look like a plucked chicken." She grabbed her clothes from the floor and stomped off angrily, clattering in her high-heeled shoes.

At the back of the club there were stairs leading down to a converted basement. The room was elegantly decorated, almost regal. It seemed wildly out of place set here. There were no windows, but more than adequate lighting. A large room, it was perfectly set for a private club or organisation. After a stringent body search by the triad security guards,

Mengyao was allowed in. A triad inquiry was a fearful experience, for even the most tenacious.

Three elderly men sat behind a long, intricately carved rosewood table. This was business, triad business. Mengyao faced his accusers.

The wizened, shorter man in the middle leant forward. "As you know I am Longwei. No favours asked, none given."

Mengyao bowed his head in a frustrated submission.

"It is of great concern to all of us that you have continued to take lives without consultation. You have carelessly endangered the fraternity of brothers. Many things could now be uncovered, and that will be of great consternation to us. We could lose a major source of protection, and could well feel the wrath of Scotland Yard. You have been a great disappointment to us. We had such high expectations from you. It appears that you have lost something of ours that is very precious. Your pretentious ego and pernicious ambition have clouded your judgement. You have lost much respect amongst us. Do you know where the rubies are? Why should we trust you? You are as devious as a snake, cunning enough to blame others, when you could be holding these treasures for yourself. We cannot allow this. Even if not true, doubt is too dangerous a wound to heal. I can smell treachery; you fill my nostrils with its putrid aroma. You should remember the old saying, 'A bad word whispered echoes a hundred miles'."

Mengyao stood there amongst these old men and gritted his teeth. He hated their old ways, their long beards, and strict codes of practise. He would be much better, ruthless, powerful and single-minded; he would usher in a new regime. These old men had had their day; he held them in utter contempt. He began with his ritual of twisting his emblem ring as if in anticipation of their executions. In his own mind, he had transcended them all, and come the day, all would be his.

"We will have to consider what action to take in the light of your failure. When you become a threat to the nest, expulsion may be necessary; after all, a whitewashed crow soon becomes black again. You will exit the safe house at the Golden Dragon Restaurant and wipe it clean from our future intentions. Now go, you have disgraced us. You will hear from us shortly."

Mengyao left the building accompanied by two of his loyal triad members.

CHAPTER 41

Tadmoor Street –

Date: Monday April 11th 2011

It was early morning; Terry had not slept well. He spent most of the night writhing on the small leather sofa, creating an impressive array of farting noises as he pulled his sticky body away from the leather covering. He recalled how his first wife, a man-eating, gold-digging diva, would mutate into the female equivalent of Mussolini, an arm waving, foot stamping, finger pointing despot, who at the very sight of his used khaki socks tucked down the side of the sofa, would not cease until he capitulated, raising the white flag and dispatching the offending perpetrators into the laundry basket. He used to call it, her Italian moment. Natalie was more like the tyrannical fascist, than a tasty fettuccine, he pondered. No wonder they hung Mussolini, but what about her? he gleefully thought.

He had made his plans. On Friday he would be stepping through the wardrobe into the unknown. For the first time in ages he began to feel very unsure of himself. His confidence was at an all time low, and his stomach would not stop churning, lending its way to that horrible gut wrenching feeling, which he couldn't find release from since he heard the affecting news.

He was about to make himself some breakfast, porridge oats would do. None of that hot water and sachet rubbish, he loved porridge that you could stand your spoon in. Maybe the hot oats drenched in evaporated milk with heaps of sugar would comfort him.

Terry resumed his relationship with the beige leather sofa, placed his mug of tea on the side table, musing, tea on a coffee table, does anybody place coffee on a tea table?" His mood was not good, so the only sound to emerge from his pursed lips was a half-hearted chuckle; the quizzical thought was at least worthy of that.

He turned the radio on. Jazz. The first mouthful of porridge and the doorbell rang. Slapping the bowl back down on the table, he rose slowly and ambled to the front door. "Hello," he said, hardly raising a smile. Somehow his chuckle muscles were off duty this morning.

"Hello sir, recorded delivery for Mr. Terry Mead. Is that you sir? Sign here, thank you very much."

Terry yawned, "Ta Postie."

He shut the door and made his way back to the sofa. "Bloody cold porridge now, that's all I need. God, I am a miserable bastard this morning."

He slurped his tea. What on earth was in that neatly wrapped box parked next to his empty Super Hoops mug?

After all, he couldn't recall ordering anything. He lifted the package onto his knees, shook it, and began to tear at the gift paper. Discarded on the floor, he opened the box. He lifted out a medium sized, chocolate rabbit, wrapped in golden foil, complete with red collar with bell. There was a small label attached with the words,

Early Easter present, as I know you'll be going away soon. Enjoy.

There was no signature. As this distraction grew, so his stomach churning began to diminish. Who sent this gift and why? Who knew he was going away? Could it be an admirer? An army chum? What about Lenny from the garage? None of these were prime candidates. In actual fact, they were most unlikely. Perhaps Rhian, discovering that he was back from Iraq, but that can't be? She had no knowledge of him being stationed in Germany or Iraq in the first place, anyhow, but if so, why now? "Oh well, somebody loves me. I'm sure all will be revealed soon."

With that, he peeled the foil away, smashed into the rabbit and began to feast on the chocolate. "Just what the body needs right now, a good intake of tryptophan, this will generate my Serotonin levels, and I'll feel at one with the universe." He laughed heartily; it was like a dam bursting. He felt less stressed. "Nobby Mead, you amaze me, you're such a clever boy," he loudly proclaimed.

As he reached inside the golden foil for yet another bite of chocolate, he noticed a small paper scroll. "How did that get there?"

It looked very much like a Christmas cracker note, or a fortune cookie slip. He unrolled the piece of paper, and could just about read its contents without his reading glasses.

When two pieces become as one
The chase for its knowledge has only begun.
For others will follow with a mind on the prize
So keep your resolve bright eyes'.

Terry wondered whether to go back to bed and wake up again. He was bewildered. Perhaps it's a dream. Maybe, if he hit his head real hard in a Basil Fawlty kind of way, he would be back to realityville. As he focused onto the empty chocolate wrapper he confirmed, "Yep, this is real enough."

Life certainly wasn't dull since his return to London. He got up to face the mirror and before combing his hair, stared at himself and questioned the events set before him. He answered himself in a game's afoot kind of way, "Never mind about a two-pipe problem, I'll be smoking a pipe from now till kingdom come, before I'll unravel this bloody mind boggler."

Intrigue had arrived in person; curiosity had been aroused, little did Terry know, drama was close behind; a mystery was about to unfold. He tucked the riddle deep into his wallet, slipped his boots on, grabbed his jacket and left the apartment, continuing his preparation for his journey to Monmouth.

CHAPTER 42

Primrose Pad, Usk, Monmouthshire –

Date: Monday 11th April 2011

Lust and fun was one thing, but love, lust and fun, something else. It was a life changing moment for Carrie-Anne, something to build on. It had been a magical Sunday night she fully possessed him, body and soul. Sam responded with power and passion, intertwined with a real sensitivity of her sexual needs. This morning was a morning of new beginnings; the contented smile on her face said it all. She stirred from bed singing to herself. When she forgot the words, she simply made them up. She popped her slippers on, then clothed in her bathrobe, strutted her stuff through to the lounge as if she had just won the lottery.

Carrie-Anne would shower later; she switched on the TV, lay down on the couch with a mug of hot chocolate, placed her feet up on the arm rest, and grabbed her magazine. She began reading the juicy bits of gossip from the celebrity column. Robert Pattinson and Kristen Stewart (The *Twilight* movie couple) in break up rumours.

In half an hour she had read enough. She placed the mag down and glanced up at the clock. "OMG, its 11am! I must shift myself; enough of the high life."

She grinned, giving herself the mildest of a dressing down. "You're becoming a tardy old cow, Carrie-Anne. You know what your mam used to say. The Devil finds work… and all that stuff. Oh, wait a minute, what's this?"

Her eyes caught sight of a neatly wrapped gift box sitting by the side of the TV. She hadn't noticed it earlier; now it had her full attention. The label confirmed that this gift was for Carrie-Anne. She immediately thought of Sam, who else? Opening impatiently, she moved straight in on the prize. A chocolate rabbit wrapped in gold foil, with a red collar and bell appeared.

"Easter has come early. Thanks babe. Forever yours," she yelled, as if Sam was somehow listening.

She loved chocolate, but the new love of her life was going to share it with her. After all, she had read somewhere that it was an aphrodisiac. She peeled the wrapper, and broke the chocolate into sizeable eating chunks, noticing a small scroll of paper inside. She began to read its contents. Maybe another love exchange from Sam?

When two pieces become as one.
The chase for its knowledge has only begun
A shrewd tip now, the clues in a book
A nut leads the way to a weed – Take a look.

163

This letter in no way distressed or rankled Carrie-Anne, after all she had not yet descended from cloud nine. She was on a real high, residing in Nirvana City at the moment.

She accepted that this was a really weird note, with no apparent meaning, or use. She would check it out with Sam.

"Sam, hi babe, sorry to call you at work, but I just wanted to clarify something with you."

"What's the matter chick? I'm all ready for a clarification with you. I've heard it called some things, but that's a first." He belly laughed.

Carrie-Anne blushed slightly and pressed on. "Stop it Sam, I want to be serious for a moment. Did you leave me a gift box of chocolate this morning, before you left for work?"

"Hey, you are winding me up now. Don't tell me, you're two-timing me already?" he replied tongue in cheek.

"No, it's OK then, don't worry Sam, It must just be a friend sending an early Easter present. Daft dorks must have forgotten to sign it. Will I see you later babe?"

"Wild Horses couldn't... I love you chick, and I'll see you tonight."

Just hearing his voice gave her a strength and courage. She was no longer alone. That young man she enticed on that late Saturday night at the Crosskeys, was now her true love. They were now mutually cemented into a meaningful and exciting relationship. She stayed incredibly calm, placing the chocolate pieces into the fridge for later. "Great with a bottle of red wine," she thought.

Then walking back into her bedroom she tucked the mystifying note underneath her costume jewellery in her wooden box.

CHAPTER 43

George Pub, Wardour Street, London –

Date: Wednesday April 1st 1987

Brindle was sitting alone in his office reading the newspaper, comfortable, with his legs on the table, mug of tea in hand. He was well aware it was April Fool's Day, so he read with a degree of pessimism. *Yesterday at Christie's auction house, Vincent Van Gogh's iconic Sunflowers sells for £24,750,000.* "Well that's got to be legit," he mumbled. *Today, MP's will decide by voting For or Against the restoration of the death penalty.* Mike knew what he thought, but was not anticipating a 'Yes' vote. *Due to extreme changes in river temperatures, a great white shark has been seen swimming in the River Thames close to Putney Bridge. Her Royal Highness, the Queen, has announced a national day of mourning, as several swans have apparently disappeared…*

The door opened quickly, but not as quick as Brindle's legs flew off the table, and back onto the floor.

"Oh God, it's only you Blakely, I wish you'd knock! Look I've spilt tea all over my dicky dirt." He tried wiping it off with a handful of tissues. Now he was flustered. "What is it?"

"There's been an explosion outside the George Pub in Wardour Street. It's a car bomb, bit of a mess I'm afraid, sir; happened about half hour ago."

"OK, let's go Blakely, but you owe me a mug of tea, so don't forget."

*

"Is this Wardour Street, or bloody Piccadilly Circus?" shouted Brindle, slamming his car door and rushing to the scene of the explosion.

There were people milling about everywhere.

"Keep the paparazzi back beyond the barriers, and find me someone who can tell me what's going on. You do know this is a crime scene?" he said sarcastically to the youthful police officer.

Blakely introduced Brindle to the new kid on the block. "Sir, this is Dr. Emily Saunders, Forensics, and Fire Chief Craig Whitton."

"Perfect, then let's get a handle on this shall we? What do you know Craig?"

Craig was an old friend, a seasoned fireman, now in his fifties. He had a deep voice and a physique of a thirty-year-old. He was a strong, focused character, with legitimate commitment to his profession, but certainly not blessed with a sense of humour. "Explosive device of some description, placed in the engine compartment, triggered by turning the ignition on. No survivors. There were possibly three in the car, hard to say right now. Car is a black Mercedes; we are trying to piece together what's left of the number plates for traceability. Fortunately, apart from the unlucky street busker who sustained damage to his left arm, there were no other injuries to the general public, Mike."

"You mean he will never be able to play the guitar again? Thank God for that. Have you heard him? I'd pay him to shut up. Hope he wasn't playing, *Boom Bang-a-Bang*. Thanks Craig, keep me informed."

Brindle turned to Dr. Saunders. "Well, Dr. Saunders, I don't suppose you'll have a problem with the cause of death or the time?" He widened his eyes, checked her out, and continued. There wasn't much help to aid his invasive appraisal – a tallish woman, head to foot in a white all-in-one overall, plastic covers on her shoes, mouth mask and rubber gloves. Brindle thought, Blimey, it could be Lord Lucan in there. He investigated the debris. "Is there any way of finding out the identification of these poor sods? Obviously a key and kaboom job. Body parts everywhere, I would imagine. I don't envy you with this case; it'll be like putting together a thousand piece 3D jigsaw puzzle." He laughed and shook hands. "In at the deep end it seems." He walked back towards Blakely.

"DI Brindle, if you could spare a minute?" Dr. Saunders was beckoning him back. She removed her mask.

Brindle cracked a self-indulgent gibe, if ever there was one. "Well, at least you're not wearing a moustache, that's a relief."

Saunders looked at Brindle, with a confused look on her face. "Was that meant to be funny?"

Obviously he thought so.

She invaded his personal zone, stared into his eyes and let go with both barrels in a broad Scottish accent, which, unquestionably conveyed her comments in a more rapacious manner. "Listen, you may not like me for whatever reason, but I will not stand here and be patronised by a prehistoric Neanderthal like you. It may be April Fool's Day, but I am no-one's fool; have you got that? You may think in some strange way that your sarcasm is endearing, but let me assure you, it's not. Times have changed Brindle, moved on; women are out of the kitchen. Let me tell you something else too, we are here to stay, so you'd better get used to it."

She took a breath, stepped back, adjusted her demeanour, pulled off her rubber gloves and continued, "Now, on a professional note, witnesses say that they saw three Chinese men entering the car before the explosion.

169

The collateral damage will obviously create major problems with identification. We will have to refer to dental records, fingerprints etc. I suggest that we look into the possibility of using the new DNA opportunities introduced last year into police investigations. Although I have to mention, it is only in the early stages of its development. That's if we have anything on file. It's my guess, that they were illegal immigrants. Probably, as suspected, a turf war, triad style. No trace at present on the car. I can't see them being reported as missing persons, so it's going to be a tall order. Nevertheless, I will see if I can piece together any vital strings of evidence that can lead us to the ID's of these men."

They both looked at each other, just refraining from bursting out loud with laughter at the unintended turn of phrase, 'See if I can piece together'.

"Oh, there is one thing that might be of interest." Saunders held up a small transparent plastic bag.

"Go on," said Brindle.

"Well, we found this rather unusual ring, gold I'm sure. It's large, with an emblem of some kind. Found it on the charred finger of a detached part of a left hand, definitely male."

"Well, thank you Dr. Saunders for that enlightening talk. I'll think about what you've said over my Brontosaurus burger." He liked her, smiled, and so did she. "Upwards and onwards, we need to be thorough."

He called to Blakely. "Blakely, see if you can find any shreds that may be useful – paperwork, documents, that kind of thing; anything unusual that might give us a lead. Meanwhile, I'm going off to see a certain Chinese gentleman who might just be able to shed some light on all of this carnage."

CHAPTER 44

Three Salmons Hotel, Bridge Street, Usk, Monmouthshire
–

Date: Sat.15th April 2011.

It was a marvel Terry kept safe on the motorway. His mind kept drifting backwards and forwards, trying to make sense of everything. He lowered his speed after crossing the Severn Bridge entering into Wales to pay the toll. Preoccupied with events, he couldn't remember passing the Swindon or Bristol exits on the M4, which caused some concern.

In another half-hour, all being well, he should be arriving at the Three Salmons Hotel. His agenda, park the car, visit reception, find his room, unpack, shower, visit the bar, do lunch, read the paper and chill out. After all, he would relish any calm before the expected storm of events that would surely follow.

The Three Salmons was a well established country hotel, centred in the heart of Usk. For about three hundred years it had been a pivotal part of community life, an important thread in the tapestry, woven into the life of this historic market town. It was an ideal location for Terry, Nant-y-

172

derry, and the village where he was hoping to find good news of Rhian and Carrie-Anne was just a few minutes away by car.

It went pretty much to plan; Terry relaxed in the hotel bar. Mid-afternoon it was relatively quiet, just a few elderly couples sipping their after lunch coffees and nibbling their complimentary ginger biscuits. There were more cafetieres on the lounge tables than gin and tonics. Terry visualized the famous Agatha Christie sleuth, Jane Marple, seated in the oak panelled lounge, slowly knitting, whilst eyeing-up the array of scrumptious cakes, enticingly placed on the Royal Doulton plate stand. She certainly would not have been out of place.

This flight of fancy was embellished and legitimised, heralding its credence, when the barman asked the oncoming customer in the tweed jacket and deerstalker hat. "Good afternoon, Colonel, would it be your usual sir?"

The River Usk rises from the northern slopes of the Black Mountains of mid Wales, eventually taking a southerly course where it meets the Severn Estuary. The river derives from a Brythonic root word meaning abounding in fish or water. The hotel name certainly echoed the former. Dedicated anglers pitted their wits against the fighting salmon, wading knee deep in the flowing currents and skilfully casting their lines. The hotel bar had several wall-mounted glass cabinets, of a, times gone by era,

173

displaying all kinds of antique fly-fishing equipment. On the walls were the ineluctable sepia photographs, exhibiting triumphant anglers, holding their whopping salmon in outstretched arms, paying tribute to their own 'look what I've caught' consummation.

He began to daydream, back to the one and only time his dad took him fishing at Ruislip Lido in Middlesex. It was a beautiful lake surrounded by wood, secluded swimming and allocated fishing areas. It boasted of long-based rowing boats, water skiing and a great cafeteria full of sodas and ice-creams. It was here that a young Cliff Richard recorded the single *The Young Ones.*

Terry was 11 years old, standing on a small jetty, yards from the bank, waiting for his dad to give the signal. He promptly placed his wriggling worm on the hook, adjusted the float, looked at Dad for the go ahead nod, and cast his line into the lake. Not five minutes later, the frustrated lad turned to his dad and groaned restlessly the immortal words which would sum up his life and character admirably. "We're not having much luck, Dad."

"Impatience and fishing don't go together son, it's like fire and water. The worm hasn't even got wet yet."

He was jolted back into the here and now by a loud and rowdy wedding group who entered the bar pursuing celebratory drinks before going upstairs to the awaiting reception. He couldn't help but ogle one or two of the ladies dressed in their finery, everything co-ordinated, including rather delicate and elegant fascinators. It began to arouse his carnal appetites. Since his early marriage break up Terry and sex was a rather spasmodic occurrence. He had the occasional steamy nights of playful sex, with eager girlfriends who wanted just that, no strings attached. He craved for more than these irregular and calculated mutual gratifications. Certainly sex was high on the agenda, but love, laughter, loyalty, and a future together became important now.

Two men dressed in full wedding suit regalia strutted like peacocks in their grey top hats and silk cravats, sidling up to the ladies, placing their arms around their partner's demure waists, hugging tightly. The message rang out loud and clear. These ladies are spoken for.

"Lucky bastards," Terry said under his breath. He was jealous of course.

Then a tumultuous hoard entered the hotel bar like a mini tsunami. Giggling bridesmaids, embarrassed page boys, exasperated grandparents, hyperactive, petulant toddlers, and a wailing, tired and hungry baby swelled the fractious noise in unison. This alloyed with juiced up cousins, uncles and aunts, made up life's sweet symphony, or if you read it like Terry, a bloody nuisance.

It was time to leave. Terry wondered whatever happened to the quiet country hotel he had spent the early afternoon

175

in. Unfortunately, many of the wedding party would be staying overnight of course. On that note, he left the building, took a deep breath of the cold evening air, and wandered along Bridge Street, a small but quaint high street, well furnished with local amenities. Usk was certainly not short of pubs or clubs. He stopped fifty yards short of the time-honoured bridge that arched over the River Usk. "What's it to be Terry?" he challenged himself loudly. "The Crosskeys or the In Between?"

CHAPTER 45

Crosskeys Inn, Usk –

Date Saturday 16th April 2011

Terry peered in through the small diamond paned windows of the Crosskeys Inn. Once he feasted his eyes on the large log fire in the lounge bar, he was hooked. The lounge was all dark wood and low lights, upholstered bench seats under the windows, and a variety of small tables spread around. In the middle of the room facing the glaring heat from the log fire was the round table. It soon became obvious that this was the focal point for the dyed in the wool locals, who enjoyed their social interaction, swigging the ales, and munching pork scratchings. These regulars took their turn in loading logs onto the hungry fire. It was attended to without any goads or demands from each other. Terry mused; this highly synchronized operation could not have happened overnight, it must have evolved over many wintry months, possibly years. They all played their part without any altercation. Very Darwinesque. He smiled. This may be a brand new word, he wasn't sure, but it described his observation perfectly, and made him laugh.

"Yes sir, what can I get you today?"

Terry's humorous pondering had sidetracked him temporarily. "I'm sorry, I was miles away. Can I have a pint of cider please?" He pointed to the pump of his favourite brand.

The young barmaid poured, serving the cider with a trained smile. "There we are, sir," and holding out her hand for the payment.

Something indefinable and inexplicable sent shivers down Terry's spine, seeming to drag at the very core of his soul. He looked again into her eyes and felt he was looking into a mirror image of his own. A sense of familiarity grabbed him, but how?

"I'm sorry sir, are you OK? That will be £2.80 please."

He fumbled awkwardly with his cash, as he pulled it out of his trouser pocket; this chilling encounter had unnerved him. Eventually he paid and sat down at the window seat.

"Carrie-Anne, can I have two more pints of the usual, please?"

"Yes Howey; fresh glasses?"

"No, I don't give a shit about health and safety, the bureaucratic, overpaid prats with their rules and regulations, the countries gone mad. God knows how we survived over all these years. They don't know their arse from their elbow. Sometimes, I think I've bloody lived too long. Do you know the other day…?" This was going to be a long story.

Carrie-Anne wished she'd never asked, chose her selective hearing mode, which basically meant she'd stopped listening, just nodding occasionally, hoping it was in the correct place. There was a collective resounding, "Yeah," from all his mates seated at the round table.

"I am glad I asked you, Howey; off your soapbox now?" she smiled. Howey laughed.

Terry was on full alert. Could this be? There was no way. It isn't possible, after all, there are many girls called Carrie-Anne. He took deep breaths. His mind was telling him one thing and his heart another. Then, as Carrie-Anne bent down to place the glasses in the glass-washer, he noticed a glistening silver necklace swinging away from her body, as she leant over. Terry recognised it immediately, even after all these years. Surely, this was the gift he gave to Rhian; the silver heart shaped pendant. It featured a lone diamond on one side, and a small engraved flower on the other. This was daunting and exciting, fearful and compelling. Could this really be his daughter, or just a hopeful cry in the wilderness?

He finished his cider and walked back to the bar. Carrie-Anne was beginning to feel uncomfortable, this man had hardly taken his eyes off of her since he entered. Her body language expressed her growing discomfort.

"Can I have a Jack Daniels, please? Please excuse me, do you mind if I ask you a couple of questions, you might just be able to help me out?"

Carrie-Anne always placed her arms across her chest when she felt awkward or vulnerable and this was a little creepy.

"Most people call me Nobby these days. Many years ago, I was a close friend to a girl called Rhian, Rhian Lewis. Have you ever heard of her? I believe she lived in Nant-y-derry, not far from here? I'm trying to locate her. I'm led to believe that she had a daughter, would be about your age now. She was called Carrie-Anne."

Terry hadn't noticed how quiet the lounge bar had become. No one was speaking; you could actually hear the pub's German shepherd snoring under the corner table.

"No, I'm sorry, I can't help you; I don't know of any Rhian Lewis."

Carrie-Anne tried with all her might to stay composed. She glanced across at the locals; they began to converse again, as if conducted by her modest nod and wilful eyes. He swallowed his Jack Daniels with one visit of the glass to his mouth, placed the glass back on the bar and apologized. "I can see I bothered you, I'm sorry. Please if I may, one more question. That pretty necklace you're wearing, where did you get that? Only it reminds me so much of a necklace

I gave to my girlfriend, many moons ago. We were on our holiday together at Pendine Sands".

Carrie-Anne held the necklace defensively, shielding it from him. "This is mine; it's been mine a long time now. I don't know what you're talking about."

Terry held his hands up, palms facing towards Carrie-Anne in a, I surrender; don't shoot me kind of way. "OK, well I am staying at the Three Salmons for a week or two, so if you hear of anything, or something jogs your memory, you know where to come. Bye for now."

Terry left the bar and headed back to the hotel.

CHAPTER 46

Brindle and Saunders – Forensics –

Date Thursday 5th April 1987

Mike had a love hate relationship with the forensic lab. Viewing the remains of victims with their various organs adrift and the hideous injuries sustained quite intrigued him. On the other hand, the arrant sterility and clinical smell, which pervaded every part of the room, always made him feel like vomiting in the nearest waste bin.

"Any news, Dr. Saunders, on the Wardour Street bombings?"

Emily was a pretty woman, mid-thirties, tallish in stature, blond hair, blue eyes, fair-skinned with a good dress sense. When out and about she always looked smart, tidy and well groomed. She was a rare mixture. At work, articulate, precise, serious, cool and calculating. At leisure, playful, funny, trivial, erratic and down to earth. It was like the difference between Radio One to Radio Four. Maybe that's how she kept her sanity dealing day by day with the dead.

Saunders lifted her eyes from the lab microscope and walked towards the nearest set of charred bones that had been meticulously placed on the stainless steel table.

"Looks like you've got three John Does," Inspector Brindle. I can confirm all men, ages mid-twenties to mid-thirties, of Asian origin, possibly Chinese. Nothing else has come to light. We have no matching records, zilch on file, nothing much to go on. Approximate age, sex, and race we can determine. Cause of death, place of death, time of death, obvious. We discovered some jewellery, medallions, keys etc., nothing of particular help or significance; mainstream stuff, you can pick up in any high street store. You remember this gold ring, it's quite distinct."

She lifts up a sealed plastic bag with the exhibit inside. Saunders continues, "Other than this, there's some high quality clothing, and looking into that, the Versace looks like it belonged to the big fellow. But unless anybody, somebody comes forward with more information, they're anonymous, all of them. Two of the men were roughly the same height, about 5' 7" – 5" 8" tall, weights, both around 170lbs-190lbs. The other, a much taller man, 6 feet or more, wearing size 11 shoes; quality footwear, that is, what's left of them."

"I didn't think they grew Chinese men that big?" He grinned. He was met with silence. "Well, Emily," he quickly glanced up, observing whether calling her Emily was acceptable. Nothing registered in her eyes at all. He nervously cleared his throat and went on, "That large gold ring you found at the scene, it surely must be recognisable, traceable. It looks very old and probably quite rare. Got to be triad reprisal executions, looks like the triads are killing their own vermin. Bloody good job. While they're squabbling, bitching, and murdering one another, it saves us the problem. Let's hope they all kill each other, wipe each other out. Our streets will be a lot safer."

By this time Brindle was feeling a little queasy, and turning pale. Saunders looked at him and spoke quietly whilst shutting down her computer. "Come on; let's get you out of here. You look a little ashen. Fancy a nice cup of coffee, Mike?"

Brindle nodded and his interest was aroused. After all she called him, Mike.

CHAPTER 47

Mitchell in Prison, Pentonville –

Date: May 1990

Praying Mantis, she could see herself as such, devouring those who stood in her way. Her warped mind becoming increasingly twisted every day, her heart filled with contempt, greed and vengeance. It not only sustained her, it made her stronger. This was a massive injustice as far as she was concerned; after all, she was Vicky Mitchell.

Mitchell had exited the communal slate grey shower room and sat down on one of the rows of benches placed back to back in the centre of the drying area. She began to wipe her feet with the rough towel. She heard a cough, and as she looked up, the formidable presence of a stockily built woman faced her. Short, gelled hair, podgy face, with arms looking capable enough to carry a stag up a mountain, she was no pushover. Her abundant thighs, set as stanchions, upheld a considerable weight, supporting an extremely large posterior and plenteous stomach fat. "Hello Mitchell, I'm Frankie, settled in well? I thought it about time my friends and I paid you a little visit."

Mitchell knew this was coming; it was only a matter of time before the scum showed up. Before she could completely reveal her contempt for this moron, a wet twisted towel was thrown over her head and pulled tight across her mouth by one of two accomplices. Mitchell's head was pulled backwards. She wriggled, and as she did so, the towel that had been wrapped around her body slipped to the floor. She was naked and gagged, but somehow Mitchell still felt in charge of the situation.

Frankie moved forward, forcing her captive's legs apart and moving her fat hands up and down on the inside of Mitchell's thighs. "Bet it's been a long time since you've had a good fuck, Mitchell?" She grabbed hold of her pussy, twisted and squeezed hard. "I could do with another bitch, keep things fresh, you know what I mean?"

Mitchell was feeding off this; she thought, That's it you fat turd, keep feeding in the pennies, and you'll receive the jackpot.

"Anyhow, first I think I had better mark my territory," said Frankie." She moved her cheek to the side of Vicky's face and began to nibble her ear, whispering, "Your mine now…" Grabbing the edge of Mitchell's right ear with her teeth, she was about to bite hard into the lobe.

"What you up to Frankie? You're at your antics again? My god, you're a horny cow. Now leave her alone. Come on, get dressed, and let's get back to a degree of sanity shall we?" The prison warden had no sympathy for Mitchell, she deserved everything she got. She arrived a little late to the altercations, hiding out of sight while prison church served itself.

Mitchell stood up, and slowly began to move out of the washroom.

"I'll be seeing you later bitch." Frankie waved, poking her tongue out provocatively.

With that Mitchell erupted, turned and attacked. It happened so fast that the warden was taken by complete surprise. She grabbed Frankie's hair, and in one quick movement, Mitchell raised her leg, slamming Frankie's head down hard on her knee bone, cracking her nose immediately. The warden began to shout for help whilst, trying to grab Mitchell. Mitchell again slammed her knee into Frankie's bloodied face. The obese inmate tried to grasp Mitchell's neck, digging her fingernails deeply into the flesh and drawing blood as she dragged her nails downwards, causing a slash wound on Mitchell. Other guards arrived, and began to infiltrate the commotion, Mitchell's one last act of defiance, she head-butted a dazed Frankie, which caused her to reel backwards, tripping over the benches and smashing her head on the corner of the radiator. There was no movement, complete silence. The wardens ascertained the immensity of the moment, and then almost panicked as they endeavoured to deal with the scenario. They restrained Mitchell, checking Frankie's pulse and calling for a doctor. Frankie was dead.

"Looks like she won the payout after all," Mitchell sneered.

"Get Mitchell back to her cell now, and quick. You'd better make yourself at home, Mitchell. You're going to be in here a long time now. Murder or manslaughter, just add on the years."

There was no response from Mitchell. Her pecking order had gone to the top of the prison food chain. She remembered the praying Mantis.

CHAPTER 48

Primrose Pad –

Date: Sunday 17th April 2011

Carrie-Anne found it impossible to relax or sleep, wave after wave of countless possibilities, unanswered questions, powerful emotions, racked through her brain like a swirling storm as she tried to make sense of this last torrid year. Last night's conversation regurgitated all of the painful, confusing, and mind boggling events of the last few months, leaving her weary, angry and determined to get to the bottom of it all.

This she had to do alone. She had not confided in Sam. There would be a time for that later. Right now, the nemesis she had to confront could be life changing or earth shattering. But, confront it she must, no matter what the outcome.

She dressed, being extra careful of her appearance this morning, Sat down by the coffee table in the lounge and penned the note, nothing elaborate or revealing, just matter of fact. Later would be the time for explanations, confessions, information and conclusions. Dad or intruder? Acceptance or rejection? Truth or lies?

The coming few hours, if he showed up, was going to be frightening, pulsating and revealing. Love and hate could pour out in equal measure, and right now no one could determine the outcome.

She placed the note in the envelope and hurriedly dropped it off at the reception desk of the Three Salmons Hotel. This was about 7.30am. The next few hours, waiting for the liaison would seem like an eternity.

CHAPTER 49

Three Salmons Hotel, Usk. –

Date: Sunday 17th April 2011

Terry took his time before descending the stairs and entering the hotel lobby. He was hungry, but knew that the residing remnants of the wedding party would be down early, nursing headaches, and tucking into a Full English before heading off home.

"Morning Mr. Mead. A letter arrived for you this morning at about 8am."

The assistant manager tailored from a bygone era, complete with black patent shoes, brilliant white starched collar, chequered waistcoat, and stylised cufflinks, looked undeniably dapper. He asked Terry if his stay was to his liking, and then handed over the note.

"Everything's hunky dory my friend. Is it this way through for brekky? My stomach feels like my throat's been cut. I'm real hungry now. Nothing like a Full Monty; bugger the cholesterol."

Without registering any flicker of emotion, like a sentinel horseguard at the Royal Hyde Park Barracks, the aspiring hotel manager gently gestured with his right hand,

"Straight ahead sir, through the double-panelled doors, just on the right before the front entrance. Daily papers are on the desk inside the foyer, opposite the restaurant."

Terry sauntered on clutching the note and laughing to himself. That gentleman was inoffensive, smart, and almost word perfect. He was obviously an avid devotee of the inimitable Reggie Jeeves, the impeccable, stylish butler to Bertie Wooster. All he lacked was the slick backed hair style.

Terry chuckled. "I'll bet he didn't like me saying, bugger the cholesterol!"

The restaurant was everything one would expect of a five star country hotel. Faultlessly and tastefully laid out, and immaculately clean. Terry remembered desperately trying to eat breakfast on army manoeuvres, endeavouring to keep the blood sucking, potentially lethal sand flies (often referred to by the troops as 'no see ums') from biting him, while simultaneously, attempting the impossible task of keeping the swirling sand out of his tea mug. But that was another story.

He opened the note as the young waitress arranged the voguish china teapot. The cup and saucer, milk jug, and sugar bowl were placed onto the table with a military type precision. No question, I see shades of Jeeves there, He thought.

"There's extra hot water if you want it, sir?"

"That's OK; I've already had a shave this morning, just bring on the breakfast please. I'm past peckish and into ravenous." Well, Terry thought that was funny, but it was obvious that the quick fire joke went right over the young girl's head.

He began to read.

Mr Mead.

I have been thinking over our conversation in the Crosskeys Inn. I need to see you A.S.A.P.

Please meet me today at 11am in Sprokwobbles. It's a small coffee house on Bridge Street.

Carrie-Anne.

P.S. It's important.

CHAPTER 50

Carrie-Anne and Terry at Sprokwobbles Coffee House –
Date: Sunday 17th April 2011

There was never going to be an easy way to approach this union. Carrie-Anne already felt the pangs of nausea sweeping over her as she walked to the coffee house. One thing was for certain; she had made up her mind and would not enter the establishment until her contact was inside. That way, any last minute nerves or anxieties, could leave her with a swift departure, hopefully unseen.

Terry was inside pretending to read the daily paper. It gave him something to do with his shaking hands, which seemed important right now. He hadn't ordered. He would wait for Carrie-Anne.

She entered, having seen her intended liaison. Terry spoke rapidly as he stood up to shake Carrie-Anne's hand. "Hello Carrie, call me Nobby. First things first, what can I get you to drink?"

"A tall café latte, please." She felt uncomfortable calling him 'Nobby'. Nonetheless, she attempted it. It came out rather muffled, awkwardly, and instantly she dropped her head and pretended to read the menu of which she had no interest.

As he stood at the deli counter he could sense Carrie-Anne scrutinising his every move, and he shuffled uneasily. Coffees in hand, he returned to their table.

"Here we are. Tall café latte and an Americano with two shots for me. I can't stand weak coffee. What a strange name for a coffee-house, Sprokwobbles. What's that all about?" Terry asked.

"Apparently, it's named after a series of children's books. By all accounts they're very funny, the main character being Willit the Sprokwobble. So there you have it."

They both went to speak at the same time. A timid laugh followed. "Sorry, after you."

"No, after you Carrie."

"You mentioned at the Crosskeys about this necklace. I wasn't honest with you. It was my mother's, and it was extremely precious to her. It was only upon her death that my stepfather handed it over to me. You see, it was given to her by her first and only true love. A man called Terry. He's my real father, but I have never seen or heard from him. He caused much pain to my mam, and she never got over it. Although she married again, the marriage was a disaster, and she just gave up. Tragically, she committed suicide, and I was not there when I was needed." Carrie-Anne started to cry, and Terry handed her a serviette. He recoiled in a state of horror and shock.

"Rhian, Rhian Lewis, dead?" Whatever he expected today from this conversation, this was not on the agenda. There was no provision or planning that could have remotely prepared him for this. He wanted to hug Carrie-Anne, but felt he would be rejected, so sadly refrained. He mumbled to himself, "I didn't know, God help me, I didn't know." He smashed his fist on the table causing other customers to stare at him. "Let's go somewhere private, away from here, talk things over."

CHAPTER 51

Usk River Bank –

Date: Sunday 17th April 2011

It was a five minute walk From the Crosskeys Inn to the riverbank. The river was unusually high for this time of the year, due to the excessive rainfall over the winter months. In spring the River Usk was generally a beautiful sight, but today it looked uninviting, wild and cold. Soon, everything would take on a different hue. The river banks would be enhanced by the enriched flora. The swans would glide majestically in pairs, keeping a parental eye on their large mottled signets. The restive mallards resounded with boisterous rivalry, as they splashed and squabbled, breaching the tranquillity, vying over the scattered crumbs cast by eager pensioners. Fat wood pigeons bent the boughs of the overhanging trees. Songbirds hopped about, composing their own mellifluous symphony. The salmon fisherman in their waders would stand knee deep in the water, casting their lines up and downstream, as the on looking dog walkers strolled along its banks with their faithful tail wagging canines.

It was a very overcast day for April, vacillant, and the River Usk looked decidedly bleak. Terry and Carrie-Anne nestled together on the riverbank bench with a degree of discomfort. He began to confide in her, beginning with the course of events that had led him to this spot. He told of the letter he received, some twenty years after dispatch. The revealing photograph enclosed in that letter, verifying the young child Carrie-Anne. He told of the exciting and enlivening experience he had with Rhian at Pendine Sands, Holiday Park. The horrific circumstances that changed his life, returning home to find his Dad brutally murdered. How this precipitated into his escaping from it all. Explaining how he eventually joined the Army, where he would spend his life for the next twenty years.

Terry unfolded the letter, handing it to Carrie-Anne along with the photo. "Take your time Carrie-Anne; it's a lot to take in."

The wind picked up, blowing strongly along the riverbank. They both shivered a little and readjusted their clothes to shield them from the prevailing cold breeze. There was a long hesitant silence as she scrutinized the letter. First, a brief read to survey the facts, second, with more intensity. Finally, going over every word, as wave after wave of realization and emotion swept over her. It was as if she could feel the heartbeat of her mother in every word.

"I have so many questions; I'm confused. Does this mean that you are my dad? That you are Terry? That this necklace is the same necklace that you gave to my mam?"

She endeavoured to make sense of it all, gather her thoughts, as she began to unveil the tragic life of her mother, recalling the torrid, despairing marriage to Afon. Then, there was Rhian's continual yearning to be reunited with the man of her first and only legitimate romantic encounter. It became a regrettable obsession, wondering, if she had played it better, been more persuasive, assertive, maybe things would worked out better. But she was young, inexperienced, having no idea that Terry had never received the important letter of his child's birth.

Then out of the blue, Carrie-Anne asked Terry if he had any recollection of the song, *Waterloo Sunset*. "If you are my real dad, then you are the only man that my mother truly loved. My mam, unfortunately, became extremely ill in her last few years, depressed, isolated, and withdrawn. She lost her will to live; she stopped fighting her demons…" she hesitated and then went on, "So my mam took her own life."

Terry face turned ashen, he felt sick in the pit of his stomach. He was not ready for the crushing news he had heard in the last hour. He had learned in the army how to cope when news of a fellow comrade was killed in action, but not this. This was too much right now.

"In those last few years, Mam often sang that song. Do you know why she would write the title upon her dressing room mirror in lipstick? Why she would choose to put her red prom dress on just before she committed suicide?"

Silence was followed by a heavy cloak of guilt and remorse which encapsulated both of them, planting the seeds of, 'if only'. This by far outweighed the bitter wind that was now ripping along the riverbank. It seemed apparent, and without consultation both conceded they deserved any punishment that could be dished out. If that started with them becoming extremely cold, then bring it on.

Eventually they stood up. This was a telling point. Terry cautiously placed his arms around Carrie-Anne. She responded. The gentle hugs became strong and meaningful. It seemed they held each other for ages, nothing spoken, but much conveyed. Both lost souls in their own ways. Now suddenly, this uniting was the start of strength and belonging, like a soothing balm, healing and comforting the pain of years.

Meanwhile across the bridge on the other side of the Usk River stood a tall sinister figure, heavily clothed, with the upturned collar of a black woollen overcoat shielding his identity. He stood judicially coursing the departing couple.

CHAPTER 52

Golden Dragon Restaurant – Fulham Palace Road –
Date: Wednesday April 1st 1987

Brindle hurried from the scene of the carnage on Wardour Street, making his way to the Golden Dragon Restaurant. He needed to make a few enquiries; it was time to question Shanyuan.

Shanyuan patrolled the restaurant with a watchful eye, like a mother hen with her needy chicks, rather than the arrogant, strutting, look-at-me peacock. After years in the business, he became adept at reading the body language of his clientele. He mastered the art of predicting their desire for service and attention. He would gain useful knowledge concerning their appreciation or lack-of his cuisine. From their first mouthful of food, the following facial expressions were an epistle to be read. Too hot, too cold, unusual, favourable, or simply not keen. He keenly assessed his customers, whether they were patient, impatient, pedantic or simply drunk and out for trouble. He would warmly welcome his patrons, always trying to stay one step ahead, surmise the events as they would unfold, and compensate accordingly. That was the art to good business.

"Good afternoon, sir; can I show you to a table?"

"I am looking for a Mr Shanyuan; if he's in the establishment today. I would like a word with him?" There was no, please.

"I am the owner, Shanyuan. Come, follow me. He led Brindle to the very same booth that DCI Mitchell had warmed some time back. "Coat?"

"No, I'm OK, Mr Shanyuan."

Brindle sat down and Shanyuan joined him. He produced his ID card and slid it along the table towards Shanyuan. "DI. Mike Brindle, I'll get right to the point; I know you're a busy man. What do you know about the triad operation in these parts? Do you have any information as to their chief players, and their whereabouts? I need some identity as to a current situation; thought you might be able to help with identities.

"I have no idea, Mr Brindle." Shanyuan's body language gave away his discomfort. "Now I am a busy man as you have noticed."

Brindle had known about the safe house for a long time but kept silent. "I won't keep you much longer. Did you ever have any connection or meeting with a DCI Mitchell?"

"Not to my knowledge, Inspector, I think I would have remembered. Now if you don't mind, I would like to get back to my customers." Shanyuan stood, shook hands with Brindle avoiding eye contact and turned to walk away.

"Sure Shanyuan, don't let me stop you earning a crust. Just one thing I thought you might be interested in before you go. I don't know if you have seen the news. There's been a car explosion in Wardour Street. Bomb by all accounts. Seems to display all the hallmarks of triad retaliation; three men, sharing their body parts all over London. One of them was wearing a large distinct gold ring. Do you know of him, or anything pertaining to this sorry mess?"

Shanyuan just moved his head from side to side. "Well if you do hear, or have anything you want to share with me, here's my number, you can reach me any-time. By the way, I hear the food is good in here, I must give it a try."

"You will always be welcome, Inspector Brindle; I recommend the Szechuan King Prawns."

Shanyuan returned to his work. Brindle left knowing he had stirred up a nest, it would only be a matter of time before he would be back to see Shanyuan.

CHAPTER 53

Longwei in Soho Warehouse –

Date: Monday March 16th 1987

The pungent aroma of eastern spices permeated the heart of the Soho warehouse, veiling the unmistakable stench of rat urine. A modest, uninspiring staircase led to an upper office located in an outmoded shell of a mobile cabin, seated upon the steel gantry. Two hulking men stood either side of the entrance like a couple of granite gargoyles. Inside the racketeers were discussing vital shipments from Hong Kong, including further development and communication with useful allies, this would proliferate their criminal network and activity.

There was an air of pretentiousness, an egotistical invulnerability about them; a smug satisfaction of security and power. Longwei was a formidable presence for a small elderly man. His diminishing stature and looks had not dulled his intellect or cunning. He continued to earn the respect of his subordinates, who constantly bowed their heads in open obeisance to his presence and position.

The phone rang, echoing loud in the building. Nianzu, a younger associate who had scaled their ignominious ranks and carried some influence in this warped dynasty, picked up the receiver. "Hello, this is the Xiamen Oriental Food Manufacturers. Can I help you?"

"Never mind all that soy sauce and prawn cracker bullshit, put me through to Longwei. I have information of paramount significance. Let's just say, if nipped in the bud, it will be of mutual benefit. It's always profitable to dispense with lurking scorpions, don't you think? Let's crush the bastards before they sting us."

Longwei spoke slowly, with a gruff measured tone; nothing seemed to faze him. "This is Longwei. I understand you have information for me of a salutary nature. How much is this going to cost me for the privilege? We are talking money? Even over the phone, I can smell the seedy aroma of avarice. Be careful my friend, it can be all consuming, devouring the very soul, till man becomes lower than the beast of the field."

A sarcastic raucous laugh bellowed down the phone line. "That's rich coming from you, Longwei. The last thing I need is a pompous, Chinese, would-be sage like you spieling advice on piety. Come on, saints alive, you've spent most of your life wallowing so deep in your own excrement you'll need a snorkel to breath clean air. That's of course if you can recognise it these days? Lecture me about greed, I don't think so. Now, can we do business or not?"

"You have teeth and claws young lady, be careful they are not pulled out. Survival in the wild without both is almost impossible for predators. We have a saying, eggs don't fight with rocks; sadly there is only one outcome."

"Do you have a bloody proverb for everything? Well here you are, you'll be familiar with this saying; beware the ides of March. We're talking Caesar here. Now, forget the middle and forget the bloody month, just get the gist Longwei. Your imminent demise is already in the planning."

Longwei's facial expression never altered. He was familiar with death threats; they were part of the territory of this pernicious organisation. Like an old scarred lion, he was still king of the pride, resorting to Machiavellian tactics to stay ahead if necessary. His rise to power had meant inflicting severe retribution to countless would-be usurpers. "If this is true, you will be amply rewarded my little tiger."

"Look to the man with the prominent gold fortune ring, for he has the rubies you seek. Trust him at your peril. He has no respect or regard for you. He lurks, waiting his time in the shadows to pounce. My name is Mitchell, not little tiger, DCI Mitchell. You'll be hearing from me shortly, Longwei; after all, a favour deserves a favour, don't you think?"

CHAPTER 54

Natural History Museum, South Kensington –
Date: Wednesday 29th November 1989

It was a cold, grey, but dry Tuesday morning as Shanyuan made his way to the Natural History Museum. He had wisely missed the mad rush hour stampedes where it was every man and woman for themselves. To the fittest the spoils, in this case the prize being an available seat on a bus or train.

It was 10.30am. He entered the impressive main entrance of the museum. The Waterhouse Building, Alfred Waterhouse, a relatively unknown young architect completed the project after the sudden death of Captain Francis Fowke. Once described as a true temple of nature, this iconic London landmark boasted basalt columns and Romanesque architecture. It opened to the public in 1881.

A few steps inside the museum, immediately he was confronted by a huge replica skeleton of a Diplodocus (Sauropod), with a raised head at the end of an extremely long neck. Shanyuan began to read:

The Diplodocus (Double Beam), 90' long, 145 Million Years old, Jurassic age. Replica courtesy of Mr Andrew

Carnegie at the request of the King. This was the longest dinosaur that ever lived.

No matter how many times you saw this colossal skeletal specimen, it never failed to impress, immediately you were relieved by the fact that this immense creature was a herbivore and gladly of a past era.

His mind wandered and rested on his favourite dinosaur of all, the infamous, Tyrannosaurus Rex. How it truly reflected its description (terrible lizard). This was no herbivore. Rex was a true carnivore, a real predator. Of a time when primeval men were hardly top of the food chain and learning quick was essential to their survival. How this magnificent predator inspired thought. Shanyuan began to consider how history at all times, presents and confronts us with its own set of predators, those feeding off others. Of course, these days, as far as the non-veggies amongst us are concerned, your average rib-eye is taken for granted. Our senses dulled to the reality of devouring our fellow companions upon planet Earth. Unfortunately, some choose to satisfy other avaricious or lecherous needs, no matter how cruel or evil. The offenders could be countries, governments, regimes, businesses, gangs or unscrupulous individuals. The predators were here to stay, like a cancerous tumour, and for many people who fall prey to these forces, it really is, still a matter of survival.

"Better lean and good, than fat and evil." Shanyuan remembered his father's counsel. Just then, he was startled by a heavy nudge on his shoulder. He turned around.

"Blimey, he's got some neck on him," Brindle joked, pointing at Dippy and awaiting some humorous exchange. None came.

"Oh, hello, Mr Brindle, It is good that you came today." Shanyuan nodded and they shook hands.

They both scanned the area for a quiet, out of the way spot to continue their conversation. Not far from the main hall, by the side of the central stairway, they entered a small corridor featuring fossils and bones, exhibited in waist high glass cabinets. That led them into a seating area provided for the visiting enthusiasts to munch on their packed lunches. Apart from three Japanese teenagers who were checking their cameras, chatting enthusiastically and giggling in equal measures, it was reasonably quiet.

"I came to meet you as agreed. It's been a long time. I guess you're not here to discuss the ingredients of your chop suey?" Brindle smiled.

"No, Inspector Brindle, although the ingredients used to make our house chop suey are second to none." Shanyuan reciprocated the smile, and cautiously surveyed the eating area. He continued, "Before telling secrets on the road, look in the bushes." He pointed at Brindle. "I am afraid, I have not been entirely honest with you, and I deeply regret that.

Honesty, and dignity, should flow together; I am deeply ashamed of my actions. Now I must, how you would say, put the record straight."

He went on, "It was February '87; DCI. Mitchell, Vicky Mitchell, did visit me at the restaurant, to convey a mutual business proposition. For obvious reasons, I made arrangements to meet her away from my home and business. We met a couple of weeks later. She had known for some time that my establishment had been illegitimately secured as a safe house for the triads. She began to promote a deal, a deal that would promise protection, a future for me and my family.

"Go on," said Brindle, "What happened next?"

Mengyao, one of the triad bosses, had taken charge of a very special shipment worth a small fortune, blood rubies, weighing in at about four carats each. Now, at one carat alone, they would be worth thousands. But for this size, quality and rarity, they would fetch as much as twenty-five times their intrinsic value. These were fine specimens, remarkably unblemished, flawless to the naked eye, medium, dark saturation. Their value was unbelievable. They had come from Burma (Myanmar) via Hong Kong, falling eventually into the hands of the triads, who smuggled them into the UK.

Mitchell had done her homework well. She had learnt that formerly in China, I laboured as a professional locksmith. Did you know inspector Brindle, that the earliest known lock and key discovery was found in the capital of ancient Assyria, the ruins of Nineveh? Oh dear, I seemed to have digressed."

"Don't tell me, you were there at the time, even you're not that old Shanyuan," Brindle interrupted.

"Assuring me, that as a humble restaurant owner I would be above suspicion, her proposition was this; employing my latent skills, I would steal the rubies from the upstairs safe, placing them somewhere secure until a later date. Then, when the dust had settled, she would attain these rubies. I listened with astonishment and intrigue, as I watched one dog trying to devour another. There really was no honour among thieves. It reminded me of the *Heron and the Frog*, whilst the heron was trying to devour the frog, the frog had his hands tightly around the heron's neck."

"How did Mitchell get to hear about the rubies in the first place?"

"They were colleagues in crime. Mitchell offered police protection for triad pay-offs. Together they continued to plot and scheme their sordid plans. The rubies were always going to disappear. Mengyao also intended to steal the rubies and blame other sources for the disappearance. Mitchell thought she would get in first and clean up. Quietly, with stealth, biding her time, she would eventually inherit the rubies. By then, if all went to plan, Mengyao would hopefully be out of the way. Mitchell would make sure of that; she treacherously contacted the triad hierarchy, revealing his intention."

"Why didn't they plan to steal the rubies together, and share the fortune?" Brindle asked.

"A man's greed is like a snake that wants to swallow an elephant, it is all consuming."

At that moment, a plague of young school children descended upon them, fighting for the empty seats. The front runners were already opening their rucksacks and prising open their lunch boxes. The noise level increased sharply.

"OK you lot, stand up and quietly, if that's entirely possible? Pack your food away. It is not lunch time yet. I repeat, it is not lunchtime yet, you ravenous munchkins. Come on now, walk in order. We have to see the smilodon before lunch. That's a sabre-tooth cat to you lot, then you can scoff your grub to your heart's content."

"Sir, can we see the blue whale. My dad says it's huge," shouted a scruffy boy with a big grin, shirt hanging out and tie around the side of his neck.

"Evans lad, it's a pity your name isn't Jonah. You might be staying longer. Come on, let's go and hurry."

That was a relief. Brindle was noticeably agitated; they were interrupted in the middle of their conversation. "Bloody kids, don't you just love them?"

"If you hurry through long days, you will hurry through short years, my friend. Be patient."

Ignoring, Brindle hurriedly beckoned Shanyuan, to continue.

"I had no intention of handing over any rubies to Mitchell." Said Shanyuan

"But you did steal the rubies, didn't you?"

Shanyuan smiled. Was that enough to confirm his actions?

"You don't happen to know anything about a package of photographs, which magically appeared on my front car seat? Funny really, my car was still locked and you a locksmith. They contained clear evidence of DCI Mitchell taking a large bung from a rather ugly looking Chinese thug, no offence intended Mr Shanyuan."

"None taken, Mr Brindle."

"Wait a minute," Brindle in questioning the source of the deposited photographs, caused something to marry, it clicked into place. The ring, I knew I'd seen that ring somewhere before. How slow am I? The Chinese man who handed over that package, he was wearing a large gold ring on his left hand. It is hardly a coincidence that the remains of a left hand, bearing a similar, if not identical ring, was found at the scene of the car bombing in Soho."

Brindle began to get increasingly animated, like a hunter suddenly picking up the scent again. When he finished here, he would rush back to forensics to confirm his suspicions. Enlarge the photographs, examine the ring. "What happened to the rubies Shanyuan?"

"Do you believe in destiny Inspector?"

"Shanyuan, some things we cannot change, they are above our control and others, we can make the difference. We choose. Are you telling me that's destiny? That it cannot be altered? That it's predetermined?"

"Often one finds destiny, just where one hides to avoid it," replied Shanyuan, "It will all come to light in the Year of the Rabbit. For that, we will all need patience; only one every twelve years. There will be tests and trials, for the worthy will be rewarded, and the fools exposed. The chase will be on. No-one will gain its reward unless the riddles are solved. There is a watchman, even while we speak, who is out there, with the sole purpose of guarding this secret until the time revealed. I cannot tell you any more, Inspector, except, this man with the gold ring whose name you seek, it is Mengyao. It seems Mitchell's treachery succeeded. Brindle raised his eyebrows trying to cajole Shanyuan into revealing more.

"Any more beans to spill?" he queried, "Anything that I ought to know about?"

The only reply was a brief smile. Brindle turned to walk away.

"Oh, and Mr Brindle, Inspector, your destiny in this saga, believe me, is not finished. You could say it's only just begun."

CHAPTER 55

Mitchell's Release – Pentonville Prison –

Date: Tuesday 12th April 2011

Vicky Mitchell was out. She served her time. Years of grubby, claustrophobic, mind numbing, soul destroying days amongst the sweaty prison bitches, had not ceased to dull her bitterness and anger. In fact, it had fuelled her quest for revenge and remuneration. The years that had been taken away, stolen from her, would be repaid in full. One thing the slammer had given her was time to think. She was much older now, harder, wiser and full of hate.

The older Mitchell still maintained herself well. Her tall, lean figure was almost her trademark. Workouts in the prison gym had nicely honed her once softer and fuller body into a hard and muscular physic. Now, shorter hair highlighted her distinct flint like appearance, with high cheekbones sculpturing her alluring facial features, marred only by a two inch scar on the right side of her neck, which she obtained in an altercation with, described in her own words as, "A copper hating, hairy lesbian, built like Tugboat Annie." Unfortunately she never survived, after failing in the attempt of intimidating and abusing the new inmate.

Still, without question, an attractive, powerful woman, but hell hath no fury like this one. She had been scorned, and payback time left no place for romance in her wilful itinerary.

A cashmere-beige Lexus, with dark shaded windows, pulled up outside the prison gates.

"Hell's bells, you've come up in the world! Whatever happened to the white van man with the dodgy tyres and no road tax?"

"I thought you deserved some Plymouth Argyle (style) after your regrettable incarceration; after all, let's start as we mean to carry on. As for the posh jam jar, it's all about contacts ma'am."

Mitchell opened the rear door and sat in. She tossed her canvas holdall along the rear seat. The driver turned, smiled and acknowledged her.

"Good to have you back in the frame. It's been a long stretch of porridge. I'm sure you're raring to catch up ma'am?"

Mitchell eagerly responded, "Oh yes, but remember the hare and the tortoise, strategy, the waiting game, and then catch up, overtake, and finally full throttle to the finishing line. It has always been about hands on the prize, nothing for coming second, and now it's but a stone's throw away from becoming all mine."

Mitchell changed the subject and calmed down a little. "Right, let's get out of these stinking clothes, shower, have a good meal and a glass or two of Beaujolais. In fact, tonight my friend, might be a night to sink a bottle or two. The driver turned, placed both hands firmly on the steering wheel. No driving gloves revealed the faded spider's web tattoo on his left hand. The Lexus smoothly pulled away and proceeded towards inner London.

CHAPTER 56

St Peter's Church, Nant-y-Derry –

Date: Easter Sunday 24th April 2011

Carrie-Anne's world had been shaken to the roots; she had been catapulted from a degree of normality, into the bizarre, dark, incomprehensible future. She could anticipate or understand nothing, at least nothing that was making any sense. Events since Spain had been almost too hard to swallow. Following the tragic suicide of her mother, she'd been beset by the most inconceivable catalogue of circumstances. A mystery stalker, house intrusions, a weird unexplained note, and an Easter gift containing a strange riddle. If that were not enough, out of the blue, a man turns up after twenty-four years, claiming to be her estranged father. He shares a brief tale of a romantic holiday encounter, supposedly with her mam, after which he returns back to London to discover the devastating news that his dad had been brutally murdered. How to make sense of all of this? What next? So many questions still to be answered.

Carrie-Anne and Terry had agreed to meet regularly, deciding to press ahead, but in a sensitive and cautious manner. This was a fragile time for both of them. They acquiesced that it was crucial for the pair of them to visit the grave of Rhian. Together they would celebrate her life. For Terry, she was his lover, and mother of his only child. For Carrie-Anne, simply Mam, her best friend, loving, caring, unselfish and supporting, until that sickening disease of alcoholism took its toll, and like a ruinous thief robbed her of latter years.

They agreed to attend the grave on Easter weekend. Neither was of a particular religious persuasion, but somehow it brought a poignant significance, a sense of appropriateness of which they were both at ease with.

They parked in the deserted car park just inside the rusty iron gates, which led to the back of St Peter's Church. To the left, rooted against the old stone wall, was an age old yew tree and just a few yards from its shade stood the grave of Rhian Lewis, nothing grandiose, nonetheless congruous.

Terry wiggled his toes, staring at his tan suede shoes which seemed thirsty enough to soak up every available drop of water from the dew drenched grass. It had always been one of his pet hates. Funny for a tough squaddie like me, he mused.

He stood at the tended graveside with his arm around Carrie-Anne, as both their eyes alighted on the marble headstone.

In memory of Rhian Megan Llewellyn
Loving wife to Afon Llewellyn.

'Finally my Love – Rest, be at Peace'.

Carrie-Anne whispered her sorries to her mam, and brushed away the marks of her running mascara. Terry became restless, as he tried to come to terms with it all. Regrets and sadness clouded the pair of them, but somehow, that seemed to induce a sense of healing, fulfilling some deep need and longing for release. Both humbled and sincere about their shortcomings, a strange, unintelligible stimulus registered in both of them. For both, a heartening awareness, like a warm embrace, reassured them that Rhian harboured no feelings of bitterness, anger or hurt, but smiled upon them with love. Now she could truly rest in peace. Her family had found one another, united at last.

Carrie-Anne held Terry's hand, and spoke softly, "Goodnight Mam."

Terry squeezed her hand tightly. "Yes," he said, "I promise you Rhian, I will do everything I can to love and look after Carrie-Anne, to be there for her. Thank you for my beautiful daughter. God rest, my love."

A plump wood pigeon cut across the silence, as it brushed out of an adjacent tree with about as much grace as a startled warthog. Terry tried to lighten things up a little. "Clumsy birds aren't they? But I've heard they can taste delicious, couple of breasts, pan fried, with red wine gravy, roast leeks, wild mushrooms, and garlicky mashed potato." He over emphasised the licking of his lips.

221

Just then a school minibus pulled into the car park, and within seconds, children were pouring out of the van as if freedom was just around the corner. "Now listen, pay attention," bellowed a seasoned, middle-aged teacher, who had obviously done this a million times before and was now operating on automatic pilot. "When we get inside, I expect you all…" She clapped. "Are you listening?" She raised her voice even louder. "That includes you Scott," she said pointing her finger and continuing, "…to behave, try not to spread most of the chocolate from your Easter eggs on the outside of your mouths. You need to be clean and tidy for the Easter presentation. Right, Annabel and Ruth lead on… and quietly."

Terry and Carrie-Anne smiled at each other, enjoying the sideshow. Then they started to amble back to the car.

"That reminds me Dad…" (This was the first time he was affectionately called Dad. Terry would never forget how significant and embracing that was) "…I haven't had time to buy you an Easter card, let alone an egg."

"Well, believe it or not, before I came away to Usk, I had a chocolate Easter bunny given to me by a secret admirer. Strange note inside, I don't know what the hell that was all about. Still the chocolate was great, didn't last long."

Carrie-Anne stopped in her tracks and looked at Terry in utter astonishment. "Was it an Easter bunny wrapped in gold foil, red ribbon and bell around the neck?"

He laughed. "Aren't they all. You don't have to be a bloody psychic to guess that."

"No Dad, this is serious shit. Listen to me. I received one too, with a note just like you; some stupid kind of riddle or puzzle. Got no idea what it's all about, but I kept it at the flat in my jewellery box... Do you still have yours?"

"Yes, it's in the back of my wallet somewhere." He reached into his rear trouser pocket.

"Wait, let's get back to the flat and check them out. Something weird is happening here and I really want to get to the bottom of this."

"Rear trouser pocket, bottom of this, did you really mean that, 'cos that's bloody funny?"

"Shut up, Dad, I'm being serious, this is no laughing matter." Then she laughed.

It seemed instinctive for Carrie-Anne to scan the area, checking to see if anybody was watching. They quickened their steps to the car, and drove back to Usk.

CHAPTER 57

Bella Italia Restaurant – Chiswick Road – Brindle and Saunders –

Date: 30th November 1989

When he was with Emily he felt good. It felt good. Such was the time when they dined together at the Bella Italia Restaurant in Chiswick. It was uncomplicated and easy for both of them, no awkward movements or moments, no delicate nibbles and sips. They tucked in like a couple who had known each other for years. The evidence, Sicilian sauce around Mike's lips, playing into Emily's hands. She smiled, carefully wiping his mouth with her serviette. "Yes, I definitely think we can extract significant evidence from this sauce, looks like the man in question was enjoying a Bolognese, with a touch of parmesan. I must fetch it to the lab. What do you think Detective Inspector Brindle?"

"I think you should get out more."

They both laughed. It was at that consolidating juncture that their eyes met revealing so much more than any spoken words could match. For the first time in a long time, he had someone to impress.

Emily summoned up all her investigative skills, thus discovering that underneath that untidy, belligerent, exterior, was in fact, an intelligent, humorous, and caring man, not exactly bursting to get out though. One who had endured a volatile, acrimonious relationship, and after escaping, was in no hurry to retrace his steps. Scathed, bitter, and vowing he would never put himself through all that heartache again, he became dismissive and wary of women. He became increasingly disillusioned with society and his work within it; jaundiced against the legal system, who pussyfooted around in wigs and gowns, handing out pathetically lenient sentences to serial offenders. In fact, this flawed procedure, this keep net culture, as he called it, was truly demoralising. You'd spend countless hours, craft and experience to land a big fish, place it in the keep net, and in no time at all it was released back into the same river.

When Mike was with Emily, his second-nature disposition and dishevelled appearance transformed itself. His stance, unkempt appearance, bad breath and grumpy nature disappeared. Clean shaven, and wearing a pocket wrenching cologne, he scrubbed up well. Hardly the morphing proportions of the humble caterpillar to the resplendent butterfly. But nevertheless, underneath the years of hurt and disenchantment, now emerged a good looking male. Those deep furrows and inner sadness his face portrayed, stood as an open testament of tough life's experiences. Happily, those hard drawn features were dissipating as he began to learn, trust again, even love?

Emily found it engaging, focusing her considerable deductive talents on the living for a change. Her crusade was to pursue, and unearth the real Mike. She had dented his introspective shield, and Brindle began to live a little. His defence mechanism that had faithfully guarded him from any future hurt had also repelled possibilities. Now, it was slowly lowering like a castle drawbridge, as trust began to rekindle and stir old feelings.

"Well Emily, I think we can fully determine that after examining the ring in the photograph against the exhibit in our possession, that they are one and the same, that of Mengyao's."

Emily leant forward resting her chin on her hands. She didn't speak.

"Mitchell and Mengyao were obviously in cahoots. Mengyao made substantial payments to Mitchell for information and freedom from investigation. Mitchell raked in the dough. Then according to Shanyuan, the rubies come along, and both greedy sods wanted more than a piece of the action. They wanted it all. Mengyao's purpose was to fabricate the apparent stealing of the rubies, and pocket the goodies? Mitchell's to double-cross, arranging with Shanyuan to nick the rubies out of the safe some time earlier, then replace with fakes. She collects from Shanyuan when the coast is clear. Mitchell promises Shanyuan and his family money and protection from the triads. Then, that crafty bitch as cool as you like, phones the triad hierarchy and grasses up Mengyao. That would explain his execution in the car bombing wouldn't it?"

"Well, what can I say? But that would pose the question, if as you say Shanyuan never had any intention of handing over any rubies, if Mitchell or Mengyao never actually got their hands on the rubies, where are they?" asked Emily.

"What if Shanyuan, took the rubies out of the safe as planned, replaced them with the fakes? He smuggles them out of the restaurant. He followed Mitchell, the cunning little devil, waited till she met Mengyao, and then photographed the money exchange. Then bang, as easy as you like, when necessary, he drops the evidence straight into a copper's lap, or in this case, my car, and she's well and truly shafted him, big time."

"But that would mean Shanyuan actually knows where the rubies are?"

"Where they were or where they are. Yes it does, doesn't it? Unfortunately, we have no proof, and he is never going to tell us, even if it's true. It doesn't sit right. There is no way the Wood brothers killed Harry, they were set up. Mitchell arranged for it to look like a reprisal killing by the Woods, thus leaving the door open for Mengyao and his entourage to lord the manor."

"But why would Mitchell have such an interest in killing Harry and framing the Woods? OK, she may get more of the action, less competition, and more wonga, but it was such a risk; why would she take that, sheer greed?"

Wait, of course, it's beginning to make sense. I knew Mitchell was the first to arrive, probably with an accomplice, at Harry's flat. I cannot prove that, insufficient evidence, but make no mistake, she was there. The place was completely ransacked. Like you say Emily, why the risk?"

Brindle was almost falling over his words, it was all making sense. He let out an excited giggle and then a wry smile, pointing at Emily. "She was looking for something, something worth taking the risk for; something big enough to make the difference."

They both looked at each other, and there followed a brief silence. Then Mike, like a seasoned fisherman casting his alluring bait, waited for Emily to bite. Then, both with broad grins, they spoke in unison.

"The rubies!" Both lifted up their wine glasses, clinked them together.

"Well, done Sherlock."

"Well done Watson. Waiter, another bottle of you fine Italian wine, thank you."

Brindle cupped his hands, leapt to his feet. This was what he lived for, what made him tick. He was a damn good copper and he knew it. "Emily, you're a little darling, I love you." He blurted it out spontaneously, leaning over, holding and turning Emily's face towards him with his manful hands; he aggressively kissed her full on the lips. He now had the attention of all the restaurant diners; he hastily sat down. The diners returned to their meals and conversation with amusing smiles. Then, as the realisation set in, his eyes widened, and he looked apologetically at Emily, nervously rubbing his hands down his jacket. He wasn't really sure what to say. He mumbled, "Look, I'm sorry Emily, got a bit excited, it must be the wine, please forgive me." He lowered his head like a naughty schoolboy, hoping not to get the cane.

"Well, that's nice, are you saying you only kissed me because you've had too much to drink, Mike Brindle?"

"No, I didn't mean that, Emily. I just..."

Before he could say any more, Emily cut in. "Then, you'd better kiss me again, just to be sure." Her eyes radiated that seductive warm glow that any real man would instantly recognise, and Mike was no exception. The night was only just beginning.

CHAPTER 58

Mitchell Based in Hotel, London –

Date: 13th April 2011

"You still got it Mitchell," she smiled at her reflection in the bathroom mirror above the small circular wash basin in room 34.

Years ago she would never have entertained something so ignoble and mundane. She puckered her lips, rubbing Oil of Ulay on her slender hands. She glanced back at the large double bed, her discarded panties, stockings, and the disarray of the bed sheets paid silent witness to her frenzied night of passion. That smug, self-satisfied look was clearly visible. Not so much the cat that got the cream, more, the conquering, dominating, take it while it's out there feeling. Her conquest was a young, energetic executive, almost half her age, who when enticed, right on cue, was equally determined to improve his sexual status by satisfying this seductive foxy lady.

He had long gone. She failed to release any genuine warmth or concern for the young stud. But if needs must, she might call him up again. "Remember the Mantis. Well at least you didn't eat him all up Vicky, well not this time anyway." She licked her lips and a twisted smirk appeared on her face, like a sorceress that had successfully cast an evil spell.

A touch precocious and undoubtedly egotistical, nevertheless, she rated the sex as an eight out of ten, besides, she had been out of the sexual arena for a long time, and if truth be known, it wasn't quite like, once you've learnt to ride a bike etc., more like, practise makes perfect, and she was out of practise. "What was his name?" She let out a real gut laugh, trying at the same time to cover her mouth with her hand. "God, it was Ralph! Well, young Ralph, I hope I put a smile on your face, and a pain in your groin, you lucky bastard."

She gently placed her hand on her forehead, cautioning, "Too much of the good stuff Vicky. You're not used to it you know? What the hell, it's been a long time."

Just then, the internal phone rang.

"Hello, this is reception, am I speaking to Ms. Victoria Mitchell?"

"Go ahead, this is yours truly." She still spoke with that air of snobbish superiority which was extremely irritating, but she revelled in it.

"There is a gentleman in the lobby waiting for you. Apparently he's providing transport for you today. Shall I confirm that you will be down?"

"Sure, tell him to relax, rest his butt. I'll be along shortly."

Mitchell didn't hurry, she applied her make-up in the most calm and calculated manor. There was no rush. That was the telling precursor; her analytical mind dictated a place and time for everything. The pitfalls of haste, she had learned to her detriment in her youth. Now slow, deliberate and determined, she became a much wiser and dangerous adversary.

Eventually she appeared in reception wearing a black pencil skirt and jacket, ivory blouse, unbuttoned just enough to err on the provocative and high heels. Already tall in stature, high-heeled shoes matched her lofty attitude. She may not be in the force anymore, but her stylish, business-like code of dress would not alter.

"Well, Harris, you have the agenda for the day, take my luggage to the car, and we will press on."

She waited for Harris to open the car door and sat in the back with a steely look in her eyes. There were other needs she desired to attend to now. Spider made no attempt to verbally reply, he nodded, and then indicated as he turned the car onto the Uxbridge Road.

CHAPTER 59

Solomon Joseph, Jewellers, Mile End Road, Whitechapel – Date: 14th April 2011.

Pentonville had done nothing to reform this bent copper, on the contrary, she left its confines with a dogged and uncompromising determination to retrieve the blood rubies and then deal with, 'That interfering bastard' DI. Mike Brindle.

It was time to capitalize on her illicit gaining of the blood rubies. She had previously secured the merchandise, biding her time. As the months past, and the furore died down amongst the criminal fraternity, she had planned to sell the rubies to the highest bidder, and live the life she had craved and worked for. Regrettably, before she was able to retrieve the gems, her abrupt arrest and eventual conviction sentenced her to several years in prison. What kept her going from this huge setback was the venom for revenge, and the irresistible secret – she knew the rubies whereabouts. However many years it took, they were hers. Now the long awaited time was here, she opened the safe deposit box in complete solitude and gently lifted out the fortune that was now in her hands. The silken handkerchief slipped away easily revealing the gems in all their glory. Even Mitchell could not stop her large smile as she came to terms with her gained treasure. It almost took her breath away.

"I've done it, I've done it, and I've fooled the lot of you." She kissed the rubies."My little babies, you beauties, you're all mine."

She would seek out her accomplice from years ago, one who authenticated the blood rubies handed over by Shanyuan, and to whom she paid admirably for his expertise, and to keep his mouth shut. Hopefully he was still alive. First a genuine street valuation, then a drive for hard cash.

Mr. Joseph's business was his life; there was nothing that gratified him more than weaselling good money for inferior stock that added substantially to his profit margins. He reclined on his grand dark green leather chair in the back office of his high street jewellers on the Mile End Road in Whitechapel. He would do his own bookkeeping in the old fashioned way; he didn't trust computers, bankers or hired accountants.

The bell rang as she opened the front door of the jewellers alerting Soly. He shuffled into the shop. These days his body affirmed a profound stoop, his shoulders and upper back arched forward, causing his neck and head to rest in an almost horizontal position, there was no eye contact as he mumbled, "Yes, can I be of any assistance?" He scribbled something onto a notepad, and then raised his eyes almost chameleon-like to view his customer.

"Still alive then you old goat; you don't know how pleased I am to see you."

"No it can't be? Surely not? Is that really you, Mitchell? The years have been kind to you." Soly shuffled to the front door, turned the sign to 'Closed', pulled the shutter down, and returned to his position behind the counter. "It's been a long time, the old days; it's not the same anymore, the odd fence here and there, nothing like those times; a license to print money."

"It's about those times that I have come to see you Soly. I want you to assess the street price of…"

"My God, you haven't, you can't, you have the rubies? Come into the office; this way, mind the step."

His hands trembled as he raised one of the rubies to inspect it. He passed his magnifying glass backwards and forwards over the ruby, then again, and again. Then he picked up the other ruby, holding it up closer to the table top lamp. He looked disturbed, concerned, frightened. He whispered, "They're not real… the rubies are not real, they're fake."

"You must be mistaken, you authenticated them yourself, you were there. Shanyuan handed them to you."

She yelled, "You where bloody well there at the time, don't be such a fool!"

"I am telling you, that these are not the rubies I examined with you and Shanyuan. I don't understand, they were genuine, and these are just paste. Somewhere, somehow, those have been replaced."

Her face went ashen, the anger had contorted her looks, and she was some adversary when she was angry, and right now, deadlier then the male. "You mean I've bloody well waited twenty years for two pieces of fucking red glass?" She screamed as tears of aggression seeped from her now squinted eyes. "You bastard! You Heim, you had something to do with this, didn't you? You piece of shit!"

She pulled a gun out of her handbag allowing no time for Soly to move. Two bullets smacked into his forehead, forcing him to slump back heavily into his chair, the blood slowly emptying from his head wounds. "You cheating, lying bastard. I'll teach you to fuck about with Vicky Mitchell." She emptied the rest of the chamber into his body, as if with every shot she was gaining some recompense for the gross deception. Her final act as she left was to place her leather gloves on, grab the fake stones and empty the cigar ash from his alabaster ashtray all over his lifeless body. "There, you piece of worthless trash."

She exited the jeweller's taking care not to be seen, jumped into the Lexus and away.

"Does Solomon have any CCTV in the building?" asked Mitchell.

"You must be joking; that tight-fisted old git, you'll be lucky if he's got an inside shithouse. You OK?"

"Don't ask Spider, just don't fucking well ask!"

CHAPTER 60

Carrie-Anne and Terry at Primrose Pad –
Date: Easter Sunday 24th April 2011

The time was just approaching midday when Carrie-Anne and Terry arrived back at Primrose Pad from the cemetery. Thoughts of Easter lunch had dissipated since the enlightenment of the two mysterious notes. Helen had closed Scrunch & Curl for the Easter Holidays, attending some mud-laden pop festival on the Isle of Wight with her new boyfriend.

"Sorry Dad, I forget to mention that Sam won't be around for this week. He's gallivanting around with his rugby chums, they're touring in France (aka the bash and binge weekend). True to form and utterly predictable, he'll be nursing some niggling injury and a peach of a hangover. Still, he loves this calendar event and wouldn't miss it, even if his house was on fire."

Carrie-Anne rushed into her bedroom, lifted the jewellery box and secured the note that was sent in the Easter rabbit. Hurrying back into the lounge, she cleared the coffee table of an assortment of local rags and magazines, placing the note on the table, smoothing it out with her right palm. She turned towards Terry. "Come on Dad, where is your note?"

"Hey, slow down, Penelope Pit-stop, let me read yours first, see if it makes any sense."

Terry pushed himself along the sofa and nestled next to Carrie-Anne. He placed his reading glasses resting on the tip of his nose and began to read each line out loud.

"When the two pieces become as one.
The chase for its knowledge has only begun
A shrewd tip now, the clues in a book
A nut leads the way to a weed – take a look."

"This looks familiar and the writing…" He stopped, stood up, and delved his hand into his back trouser pocket. "Damn it, I always wrestle with this bloody wallet, it's like trying to prise a winkle out of its shell." Eventually and not before time, the offending article appeared from the dark recesses of his restraining pocket.

"Bloody hell, Dad, I'm sure I can hear it gasping for air; you're the only man I know that can suffocate a wallet. What on earth do you keep in there?"

After evicting several business, credit and loyalty cards, he began to ease the various notes out. First, phone numbers for car spares. Second, a crumpled letter including details of rent arrangements. It went on and then, just after the scrawled renewal dates for his MOT, the elusive note in question was found. "Thank God for that; I thought I'd lost it for a moment."

"What does it say, Dad? Come on hurry up, you're slower than a Skoda full of elephants."

Terry wasn't listening; he just glanced at the note. "It's definitely the same writing, look, and the same verse. No wait a minute, hang on, the last two lines on mine, their different.

"When two pieces become as one.
The chase for its knowledge has only begun.
For others will follow with a mind on the prize.
So keep your resolve bright eyes."

The atmosphere in the lounge was interfused with a degree of excitement and bewilderment. What had they got themselves into? What prize? Who will follow, and what will they do? The knowledge of what? Clue in a book? Was this just a hoax? If so, why?

They had only known each other for a short period of time, both leading totally separate lives until now. Who would know Terry well enough to send him a note, more to the point, why? After all, he had been in the army for some twenty years. What connection with his newly found daughter had sparked this off? Obviously, the notes they received on the same day, could only enforce the fact that someone was hoping both of them would meet. Or to be more specific, they knew that dad and daughter would meet, and this would culminate in their collective clues hopefully precipitating an answer.

It was beyond question that both sets of clues where needed if there was going to be any solution to this conundrum. They would not be aware of the enormity of these notes at present. It was enough though, to grasp that something well above the normal in their lives was taking place.

Their enthusiasm and tenacity for the unravelling of the riddles could only be described as watching two people engrossed in a game of Scrabble, both reluctant to concede until they exhausted every available letter in their bid to win. Two hours swept by as they discussed and picked each other's brains, trying to deliver any sense from the notes.

"When two pieces become as one?" Terry read aloud, "Two what?"

"Can that mean you and me Dad, you know, we have come together, haven't we? Now we are kinda one!"

"Could be Carrie-Anne, but wouldn't the verse state, two persons, rather than two pieces? The only two pieces that we know of, that have come together, are these notes, same writing, same paper, possibly from the same page; here look at the torn paper."

"Terry continued, "Quick Carrie-Anne, check if your note's torn edge jigsaws with mine."

You could not measure the adrenaline rush as the notes fitted like a glove.

"I need a drink Carrie-Anne, and I mean a drink."

"Yeah, come on, you hungry? 'Cos I'm starving. Let's pop across to Crosskeys, we'll grab something to eat, nothing fancy, regular pub grub, and a couple of drinks."

"Sounds diamond to me, by the way, it's on me and we'll continue this later," responded Terry.

"Cheers, Dad; with any luck they'll have the log fire blazing away in the hearth. It's a sight warmer than this bloody flat. Seriously, it gets that cold in here, penguins would feel at home.

"Carrie-Anne, you're nuttier than your dad."

They clothed up, raced down the stairs, slammed the door, and in three minutes where sitting in the Keys ready to order, eyeing up the huge plate of lasagne and chips served on the table opposite.

CHAPTER 61

Mitchell and Harris visit the Golden Dragon Restaurant

Date: Monday 18th April 2011

"You had better believe it, I'll teach those meddling bastards not to fuck about with me. They'll reap the whirlwind. As for Brindle, he's a dead man walking. Have you done all I asked you to do?" Mitchell ordered.

"To the letter, ma'am," was Spider's quick reply.

"Good, very good; if we upturn all the rocks, something will crawl out, and rest assured we'll be there."

"But you gave old Shanyuan the verbal, promising protection and dosh if he half- inched the rubies, giving them to you when things had quieted down."

"Yes, the rubies examined by Solomon, according to him, were kosher. Shanyuan was with me at the time. So, what games we play. Shanyuan and Soly in it together, fleecing me?" She paused. "What if Shanyuan somehow switched the rubies after authentication? The crafty old fox. We know Harry Mead was operating for the Wood brothers; Shanyuan and Mead were friends, they could have colluded together, passing on the rubies to his bosses for a sizeable cut. After all, the Woods had the ability and the contacts to dispense the merchandise safely. But why do that? Why not keep the merchandise for themselves? Why involve the Woods? Shanyuan and Mead, fifty-fifty split. That's the best percentage deal."

"So what are we saying here? You reckon its Shanyuan in league with Harry Mead? Well, Mead is brown bread. That means that Shanyuan's fifty-fifty split has become a nice, round, hundred percent."

Harris, for God's sake, leave the thinking to me, you'll wear out the only bloody grey cell you have left, and put that bloody cigar out, it smells like a Cuban bordello in here. Let's visit that devious old bugger, we'll toss his sweet and sour balls in a flaming wok till his eyes water. Then tomorrow, Riley, boss at Griffin Autos, we'll quiz him, see if we can locate the whereabouts of a certain Terry Mead. After all, you never know, Terry may have something to tell us about Harry's last days that will render a clue or two. We'll pay Brindle a visit when he's least expecting it. I want to shaft him big time. Somewhere in this mess of pottage, this hotchpotch, someone has stashed these rubies. I believe they're still out there. Years have only increased their value. These babies are my prized pension plan. I deserve it, God help me, and I've paid for it. No bastard is gonna stand in my way, do you hear?"

With total disregard for pedestrians and antipathy for traffic restrictions, Harris parked the car. His driver's side mounted the pavement; stopping abruptly, he yanked the hand break up and flicked on the hazard lights.

"Nothing changes," Mitchell ebbed, as she glanced at the Golden Dragon Restaurant. "Let's get this sorted. I've got a sneaky suspicion that Shanyuan is pivotal to all this. A pound to a penny he was involved, right up to his scrawny yellow neck. He knows something, and we need to squeeze it out of him. Those rubies didn't disappear into thin air.

Just then Harris noticed a traffic warden sizing up the car, checking her watch and writing on her PCN (Penalty Charge Notice). He opened the window. "Look out, it's the Gestapo; you got nothing better to do, like beheading or torturing peasants? I'd bet you'd like that, especially in that uniform? Turn you on would it, you sad cow? If you keep writing, I will take that pen and shove it…"

"That's enough Harris. Let the lady go about her work. Cut the abuse, and stop snorting like a frustrated warthog."

She continued her surmising, running over the possibilities time and time again. Mitchell's investigative experience only enhanced her wilful ability to succeed. "Shanyuan opened that safe, we made a deal, and he was the only one clued up and capable of cracking that code. What if that cunning little bastard duped me, passing on fake stones? How did he do that? So what have we got here? The rubies, possibly still with Shanyuan? Passed on to an accomplice? Now if Harry was the partner in crime, he must

245

have dispensed with the merchandise double quick. So suppose it was Harry, to whom would he pass on the jewels, if not the Woods?"

There was the sound of a scrape as the Yellow Peril lifted up the windscreen wiper, meticulously placing her ticket underneath. Harris growled.

"The week before Harry's demise, Terry left the flat, taking a holiday in West Wales. There's no indication to suggest Terry has come into money, no record of excessive spending or investments. He's certainly not high on the hog, but you can never be too sure. He could just be a dark horse. I don't want to under estimate him. You'd be amazed how devious people can be when there's a lot of money at stake, Harris."

"Tell me about it. Anyhow, what is he, a bleedin' hog or a horse? We won't know whether to roast him or whip him," quipped Harris.

"Hilarious, Spider, very funny; now, if you can forget about the mixed metaphors and concentrate, you might learn something, you daft bugger. Let's continue, follow up this Terry Mead hunch."

They entered the restaurant with purpose and went straight for the jugular.

"Where's Shanyuan?" Mitchell asked.

"May I ask who it is…?"

Before the attractive Chinese lady greeting them could finish her smile or sentence, Mitchell interrupted, "Look lady, I don't have time for all this protocol bullshit, I'll ask you once more, where is Shanyuan?"

"I'm afraid he is not here."

"Maybe I'm not quite making myself crystal. That's clear to you. Where the hell is he?"

"When I say, he is not here, I really mean, he is not here. In fact, he and his family have returned to China sometime ago. I have taken management of the restaurant for the foreseeable future."

Meanwhile, Harris's nostrils had been invaded by the pungent aroma that inhabits all Chinese restaurants, tickling your taste buds and causing a mild salivation. His envious glaring at the young couple tucking into the special fried rice began to make them uncomfortable. They adjusted their chairs and turned away from the intrusive onlooker. Instinctively, the young lady adjusted her top, to cover-up any over exposure of cleavage, and whispered to her partner," Who's that letch?"

Harris was only interested in feeding his face, but his lustful expression was misconstrued. Finally he backed off, as their uneasy response registered.

He regrouped catching the end of Mitchell's interrogation. "Would you fucking credit it?" he yelled. "All this poxy Harry Lime we've been waiting, and when it comes to the crunch, Fu Manchu has scampered, done a runner, back to bloody China."

Mitchell stared hard for several seconds at the new manageress, trying to ascertain whether she was telling the truth. Her body language gave no sign of deceit or cover-up. "Don't tell me, no forwarding address?" Mitchell didn't wait for a response; she knew the answer to that already. "If I find you're lying to me, any cock and bull, loosely translated, crap, I'll be back, and I promise you, I won't be quite as accommodating."

"Where to now?" asked Harris, as he simultaneously yanked the parking ticket from under the windscreen wiper and threw it to the ground. "I fancy something to eat."

"Button it for a minute, Harris. Stop thinking about feeding your face, I'm trying to think. If Shanyuan has absconded back to China with the rubies, we could be well and truly shafted. I am hoping he didn't try to smuggle them through customs. That's a calculated risk I don't think he would be willing to take. I'm guessing he's too smart to lessen his odds. I reckon that they remain here somewhere in the UK."

"Were talking about donkey's years ago, the trail's gone cold. It would be easier to find the Irish bleedin' Crown Jewels."

"The more reason why we don't waste any more time; let's visit Griffin Autos. How do you know about the Irish Crown Jewels?"

CHAPTER 62

Mitchell and Harris Visit Griffin Autos –

Date: 18th April 2011

"Looks like, you haven't been under a car for a long time Lenny?"

Lenny had no recollection of the woman that confronted him. Maybe he knew her, there was something vaguely familiar about her stance and forthrightness, and she obviously knew him. He answered, still racking his brain. Who was this woman? "Not any more, I'm a whistle and flute man now; look, no grease under my fingernails."

Mitchell wasn't interested in the small talk; she overtook the conversation, swerving in front like a Formula One racing driver. "We are trying to locate Terry Mead. We understand he was not only an employee of yours, but you were also good friends. He has recently retired from the army. Has he by any chance contacted you since his return? Do you have any idea of where he lives? Or a phone number where he can be reached?"

"Young Terry, good lad, calls himself Nobby Mead now. Yeah, he came in to see me recently. Always had a lot of time for Terry, shame about his father's death. Think he would have stayed with me, if it wasn't for that tragedy. Yeah, Terry asked if he could take some space in the garage. He rents a place in Tadmoor Street, but you won't find him there. He recently discovered to his utter surprise, that he had a daughter. He had no idea, stems from a holiday romance back in '89. So he's gone on a hunt to find both mother and the daughter."

"Do you know whereabouts?" Harris joined in.

"I understand they live in a small village in Monmouthshire, South Wales. Can't think of the name right now, but it's close to a market town. Usk, I think? Yes Usk. He'll be back, I'm sure, but he could be some time. Shall I tell him who called?"

"No, that's OK, you've been most helpful. Oh, just one more question?"

"Sure, go ahead, if I can help I will."

"Did Terry mention that he had come into a lot of money recently, or was about to?"

"What are you the police or something, why do you want to know?"

Harris answered, "Were just friends, we have some important private news to share with him, but we have to locate him quickly or he could miss out on it. There is a time limit. It seems from your understanding that Terry doesn't know about the inheritance yet."

"No, no, as far as I understand it, Terry was comfortable with his army pension, but nothing more or he kept that very quiet."

"Thanks, Lenny." Mitchell shook his hand.

"No problem, and if you meet Terry before I do, give him a hi from me, he's a buddy."

"Oh, we'll give him a hi, don't you worry," smiled Mitchell.

Mitchell's mind was in overdrive as she left the garage. Soon they were back at the London hotel.

"Pack your bags, Spider. Pick me up around 7pm tomorrow. We are going to take a small vacation in Taffy Land. Be sharp. We need to locate the mother of Terry's newly found love child. She may be a key. It's a long shot, but Terry might be in the frame, if so, he may have confided in her during that holiday. You never know, something relating to his father's actions or movements that previous week. That might just be the lead we're looking for."

Spider Harris nodded, released the hand break, found first gear, revved up, and began to lift his foot off the clutch.

"Oh, and Spider, while you're at it, find out if Brindle is still about. I'd hate to think anything has happened to him, yet."

Harris pulled away, merging into the late night London traffic.

CHAPTER 63

Terry at Three Salmons – Carrie-Anne at Primrose Pad –
Date: Sunday 24th April 2011

Terry had enjoyed the late bite to eat at the Crosskeys. He arrived back at the Three Salmons about 11pm, having swiftly hugged and kissed Carrie-Anne goodnight outside Primrose Pad. It was the most unusual and complex Easter time he had ever experienced.

Tonight, he felt drained, physically and emotionally. He tossed his keys and Cabot watch onto the bedside table, slung his jacket over the small armchair, kicked off his shoes, and plonked himself on the bed; still partly clothed, he pulled the duvet over him in one movement and he was fast asleep within minutes. Tomorrow, his first real duty was to search for a rental property within the area, somewhere less expensive, more reclusive, giving him time, space, and quiet, to develop these whirring thoughts within his head.

Carrie-Anne upped the stairs and purveyed the untidy flat, which somehow, had the uncanny annoyance of passing sentence without uttering a word.

"If Helen could see this, she'd throw a wobbly. What a mess. She'll be back soon, and you my girl will be in the doghouse. She wouldn't want to see me in this state. A Hoover wouldn't go amiss, before you start on the bathroom and bedroom."

Carrie-Anne responded as if this was a real conversation, curling up her top lip and replying out loud, "Do I look bothered?"

Paradoxically she began tidying up, smartly picking up her trainers from the middle of the room. She regrettably inhaled their pungent tang, then held them away from her body as if they were infectious. With a look of sheer disgust, she threw the offenders in the washing machine, slamming the door like she'd just placed them in quarantine before an outbreak. She then placed the stained coffee mugs in the sink with a drop of bleach and began seeking out the spray polish and yellow duster.

She showered at some length, hoping that the warm, cleansing water, like a comfort blanket, would ease her mind and body, unburdening her of the day's events. Could she feel uncluttered, free?

It was around midnight; she donned her fleecy pyjamas and fluffy slippers, deciding to phone Sam. She had missed him badly, but the intrigue and challenge of these crowning hours consumed the day quickly.

There was no reply, and no missed calls registering on her phone. That was unusual. She felt lonely, edgy and a little sad. Tonight she could do with a loving hug. She yearned to feel the warmth and strength of Sam with his broad shoulders and strong arms holding her tight. His sensible approach, humour and ability to put things into legitimate perspective, gifted her that confidence, security and reassurance that she craved.

Carrie-Anne struggled, trying to reject the intrusion of susceptibility that desired to take lodge in her mind tonight. As she finally lay snuggled within the sheets, concurring that her nose was extremely cold as she held it, she spoke her thoughts. "A shrewd tip now." What was the tip, the clue that would unlock this riddle? Time passed. Then without unravelling the puzzle she fell into a well needed sleep.

CHAPTER 64

Mike and Emily at Breakfast –

Date: Wednesday 20th April 2011

"Cholesterol on the table, Mike; hurry up, or you'll have a cold breakfast."

"OK love, be right there."

"Now, Mike," asserted Emily.

He rushed into the kitchen stumbling over his treasured red Chow-Chow, who yelped loudly, busily wagging his tail like a signalman's flag. "Come on Leo, out the way, you're my top dog, you're a beauty."

He kissed Leo on the top of his head. Then he pecked Emily on the cheek whilst trying to put his tie on, yet to do up his shoe laces.

"Second again. You're a real charmer, Mike Brindle."

Mike studied his breakfast." What no black pudding? Never mind Em, this is pukka, you're a diamond. I've always said it."

Mike sat and swigged his tea. "Ah, that's better. My mouth was as dry as a rattlesnake's bum. You can't beat a nice mug of Rosie Lee in the morning. He shook the bottle furiously, and then drowned the breakfast beneath a swamp of brown sauce.

"Breakfast with your sauce?"

Mike fed Leo the rind of the bacon. It was downed in no time. "OK, clever clogs, you can talk, at least I didn't finish off all the chocolates last night, but I see they've all mysteriously disappeared this morning. Or was that down to my poor old dog again, having a late night feed? He's amazing at opening fridges, aren't you Leo?"

Emily chuckled, "No, in all fairness, Leo did eat most of them; he loves choccies."

"He is not supposed to eat chocolates, they're not good for him. Anyhow, your nose is growing again, Pinocchio." Mike smiled, inserted his first forkful of bacon and egg in his mouth, starting to speak as the phone rang. "Bloody Hell!"

"Leave it Mike; eat your breakfast for goodness sake."

"Won't be a moment, erm, it's probably the office, calling for a rundown on the Fairclough case."

Emily sighed; she loved him, knowingly smiling in tolerance of his inability to let things rest. Will things ever change?

Mike picked up the phone, spoke the necessary, and awaited the caller's enquiry or request. He was correct.

"DI. Brindle, this is Detective Sergeant Blakely. We've had a call from Griffins Autos, the garage on the Uxbridge Road."

"Yes, yes, I know where it is."

"The owner, a Mr. Lenny Riley, says he only wants to speak to you. Seems one of the guys who used to work for him spoke very highly of you, said you were the real McCoy."

"A good morning wouldn't go amiss Blakely, and don't sound so surprised, it has been known you know! Now, be a good girl, bring round the jam jar, it'll save me going back to the office. Give me some time to eat my breakfast, or I think Emily might insert the sausage in a very intimate region of yours truly's anatomy."

"Yes, guv. Oh and by the way, you do know that fatty sausages are no good for you?" She could not contain the giggle that followed.

"Thank you, Blakely, very droll, very droll, but don't give up your day job."

He placed the receiver down, looked at Emily apologetically, and continued to eat his cold fry up.

Leo looked up with those big brown doggy eyes, waiting hopefully for the master's attention. Mike could never eat a meal at home without a morsel being torpedoed into Leo's jaws before Emily caught him.

As if she didn't know?

CHAPTER 65

Afallon Cottage, Llancayo-

Date: Tuesday 26th April 2011

The grey clouds and heavy rain did nothing to promote the property rental. Terry met the breathless estate agent at a small isolated dove grey cottage on the outskirts of Llancayo. It was only a few miles from Usk, hidden away in the country lanes. It was old, very old, and somehow the inside conveyed a much older look than the weathered outside. Everything was dated, but essentially, everything you needed, not wanted, was in the place.

"Welcome to Afallon Cottage, Mr. Mead. Sorry I'm a bit late, couldn't find the keys to hand. Anyhow, without further delay, now we are here, shall we enter?"

She unlocked the door with some difficulty, pushing the door open vigorously, disturbing several cobwebs and arousing the dozy woodlice. As she scraped her Wellington boots on the bristled door mat, a scrawny ginger cat startled both of them. It shot out of the opening door, hissing loudly and making its exit over the garden wall. The agent with hand on chest took a deep breath. "Must be feral, got in through the back window shouldn't wonder. I hate cats, creepy things, always staring."

Terry assessed. She looked a formidable lady, the no-nonsense type. Deep voice, country tweed, mid-fifties, large breasted and thick hipped. His mind turned to a worthy comparison, Margaret Rutherford playing that old sleuth Miss Marple. "I've heard of rural life, but this is a tribute to the Victorian heyday, a real museum piece," stated Terry.

He leant on the edge of a deep, square white sink, which sat below the distressed windowsill, and began to wipe the dust off the drainer, noticing the bare copper pipes and mildewed dish mop. That aside, you had the basics in place. That's all that mattered at present.

"I'll take it." They shook hands. "By the way," Terry quizzed, "What's Afallon mean?" He crumbled underfoot what he deduced to be mouse droppings.

Ms. Thomas seemed quite taken back at the question, as if he should automatically know. "It conveys blissful, Shangri-La, Paradise." She coughed awkwardly and continued. There was not a smidgeon of a smile, or an inkling of outward embarrassment, even in the light of the obvious paradox. "OK move in when you like, I'll go back to the office and set it all in motion. We'll deal with the paperwork later."

She disappeared quickly before Terry could change his mind, leaving the doubtless scent of lily of the valley hovering in the air, manoeuvring herself skilfully into the driving seat of a small Ford Corsa. It presented a real challenge, but one she had encountered many times before.

"Economy over comfort I guess?" He quipped.

As the car sped away Terry laughed out loud, as he read the name on the oak lintel above the door.

"Afallon."

CHAPTER 66

Carrie-Anne at Primrose Pad –

Date: Wednesday 27th April 2011

"Hello babe. Hi, it's me, Sam. Sorry I didn't give you a call earlier. Look, I'm not sure how to tell you this. Looks like I'm going to have to stay in the land of Camembert and Bordeaux for a little while. It's unfortunate, but things beyond my control babe."

Carrie-Anne lingered with that sinking gut feeling that always occurs before downer news arrives on your doorstep. He's dumping me over the phone. I can't believe it.

Tears started to well up in her eyes; she hesitated to prompt the next sentence that was to leave Sam's mouth. It would be painful. As if she didn't have enough to deal with. This took the biscuit. Why? What? Even worse, who? How could he do this to me, the rotten creep?

"Yeah, it shall be at least three or four weeks before they allow me to leave the hospital. I've broken my leg in two places, fib and tib apparently. For reasons best known to them, they do not advise flying at present. Still the food is good, and my French is getting better. Carrie-Anne, *je t'aime, ma cherie*."

Carrie-Anne started to back pedal. Her words fell over themselves as she responded with relief and care. "What and how did you do that? Trust you, never by halves. If you've got to break a leg you might as well break both bones. Can I help? What do you want me to do Sam? Shall I fly over? Contact anybody? Send anything? Wait a minute, I'll get a pen, I want the name and address of the hospital. Are you OK?"

"Wow, slow down Carrie-Anne, take it easy, everything is fine. I'm comfortable, and being looked after well. Chill out, I'll keep in touch, and if there is anything I need I'll call you. You got enough on your plate, what with your new found dad arriving and everything. I'll be OK. Now, here's the name and phone number of Saint Claire's Hospital."

Carrie-Anne scrawled the address as if Sam's life depended upon it.

"Now sexy, you look after yourself, because when I come home I'm gonna need plenty of loving care, and I mean loving? *A tout a l'heure ma cherie*. I'll see you soon babe. Love you."

"Love you too, Sam. Need you. I'll be waiting for all that *Cwtching. Dw i'n. Cariad*."

Carrie-Anne placed her mobile on charge, as her mind sauntered through all the recent events, like the ball on a casino wheel, whirring until it slowly dropped and nestled on the riddle. What could it disclose? What was the purpose?

"A nut leads the way to a weed?"

What's it trying to reveal? She became miffed at her ineptness. Her inability to lay bare the puzzlement frustrated her. She needed help to uncover the secret within the mind boggling notes. She wondered how her dad was progressing with the riddle.

Her phone rang again. It startled her, and its sudden, sonorous tone retrieved Carrie-Anne back from her intense thoughts. "Hurry, Carrie-Anne," She motivated, "It might be Sam."

"Hello Carrie-Anne, I am speaking to Carrie-Anne?"

"Yes, who's speaking?"

"Let's just say an interested party for now." The deep man's voice spoke calmly, with an articulate and concise acumen.

"What do you want?"

"You may have something that belongs to me; I intend to get it back. Unfortunately, your poor stepfather could not shed any light on the subject. We did try awfully hard to eject any possible assistance. Sadly, he had nothing to reveal, except a wayward stepdaughter, and a tragic wife who is no longer with us. That leaves us with you Carrie-Anne, and your new found daddy. Oh, and by the way, I know you and your stepfather didn't see eye to eye, so you'll be pleased to know that he has met with a very unfortunate accident. Surprising how farmers of great experience can become so familiar with things that they forget to take the necessary precautions. Still, they do say that familiarity breeds contempt. A date with a silage pit can be a nasty way to spend your last few moments. We don't want any more of those, do we Carrie-Anne? Otherwise someone might think it was done on purpose. By the way, don't even consider contacting the police, after all, it would be a shame to find, and to lose your new daddy so quickly. Don't you agree?"

Before Carrie-Anne could assimilate all the information and respond, the caller hung up. For a few moments she stood there like a rabbit caught in the headlights, unable to move. If ever she was in any doubt as to the substance and intensity of events touching base with reality, it was now. She suddenly felt a morbid chill, difficulty in breathing; she tried desperately to determine her next move.

Edging towards panic, she must call Terry. Scrambling for his phone number, the harder she looked the more abstruse it became. Her mind went blank. "Why don't I keep it on my phone?" She started to rummage in her handbag, dipping her hand in like a blade of a cement mixer, stirring the contents, hoping that something would rise to the top, chiding herself for being so disorganized. Angrily, she tipped her bag upside down, shaking it like a rag doll, screaming as the contents poured over the table. "Come on; come on, where is it? It must be here somewhere!"

What seemed like an eternity later, the illusive salon business card with the scribbled number revealed itself, much to the relief of the disturbed Carrie-Anne.

Just then the doorbell rang.

"That could be Dad; Oh God, please let that be Dad." She clamoured down the stairs.

"OK just coming." She opened the door and her anticipation was duly stolen. Looking up and down the high street there was no-one to be seen. As Carrie-Anne turned to go back inside she noticed a small brown package on the doorstep. She checked the street again, still no-one. She grabbed the mystery delivery, slammed the door, and returned up the stairs to the front room.

Like a nervous contestant in a game show, racing against the clock, she wasn't sure what to do first; the parcel or the phone call. She selected the parcel, and began tearing frantically at the wrapping. She discovered a country cloth cap, herring-bone pattern, distinctive and memory inducing. She'd seen that before, many times. It was Afon's, her stepdad.

"Oh my God," she groaned. "This is like a bloody horror story. I've gotta get out of here and fast."

CHAPTER 67

Brindle and Blakely at Griffin Autos –

Date: Wednesday 20th April 2011

Mid-morning, Brindle and Blakely arrived at Griffin Autos. Brindle belched loudly. "Pardon me, Blakely, I shall have to stop these fried breakfasts in the mornings, gives me terrible indigestion." He repeated it again, literally. "That's better. Right, come on then; let's find out what this is all about."

It began to rain, first those large drops that fall so slowly that you can count them as they splatter and darken the grey paving, then the downpour, merging the polka-dots into a stream of water, cascading off the gutter and away to the drain.

"Come on Blakely; let's run, we're going to get soaked."

Before they could enter reception Lenny approached them. "Inspector Brindle, is that you?"

"Never mind Inspector Brindle, let's get under cover first, I've already showered this morning."

They rushed for the cover of the garage. Mike brushed the water off his forehead with his palm, and then shook the water from hand to ground. "April showers, it's chucking it down. Why do they say raining cats and dogs, Blakely? You're bound to know, you're a clever clogs. Yes, DI Brindle, this is he, and this is Detective Sergeant Blakely. What seems to be the trouble Mr Riley?"

"Please, call me Lenny, everybody does. I wanted to contact you. A couple of days ago, two people visited the garage asking about Terry Mead. Tough looking tall woman, well kitted out, with a fairly shady looking sidekick, tattoos etc, mid forties. You remember Terry Mead? His father Harry was brutally murdered in his flat about twenty years ago. Hell of a mess. The Wood brothers went down for the murder, think it was something to do with drugs, a reprisal killing or something like that."

"Just hold your horses a minute." Brindle's spirit started to rise; it had been quite a while since that old hunter instinct kicked in. This was undoubtedly rekindling his interest. "Did this woman give a name at all?"

"Oh yes, she had no problem, very confident, very direct. To be honest, she's a real looker, not a young 'un, but I would, if you know what I mean?"

"I don't think you'd like to go delving into that honey pot Lenny. That woman is a real man-eater; she'd have her teeth sharpened if she could."

Donna Blakely lifted her head from taking notes. She focused on Lenny, then on Brindle, at which point she donned that womanly smile which always conveys 'typical' without uttering a word.

"All right, all right, ground control to Major Tom, come in Lenny, let's have it. What was her name?" Brindle's eyes lit up in anticipation.

"Let me think now, Mitchum, no, no, I know it began with M, it was…"

If Brindle could have raced down his throat and returned with the answer any quicker he would have done.

"…Mitchell, that's it, yes Mitchell; my brain these days."

Brindle had just won the jackpot. Mitchell was out. He knew that this would open up that old account. Something was going to surface soon, and he would be there. The rest of the conversation between Lenny and Mitchell was conveyed to Blakely.

She finished the notes, closed her notepad, popping it into her top pocket. "Thank you Mr Riley, or should I say, Lenny. If you can remember anything else, or if they contact you again, please call us straight away. It might be as well if you keep this to yourself for now." Blakely smiled again, and returned to Brindle who was sitting in the car fidgeting, like his brain had just had a shower, washing the mundane away, touching his spirit with a refreshing intensity.

"This is it, Blakely." He rubbed his hands together excitedly. "The fox has returned to its den. I've waited years for this. Mitchell never really copped all that was coming to her, but I'm going to make sure that conniving bitch does. Just wait for her to step out of line, and in the words of Michael Jackson, 'I'll be there', but it won't be 'to protect her'. Let's get cracking Blakely, keep this hush-hush for now, just you and me."

"Jonathan Swift, sir"

"Make sense Blakely, what are you on about? Did Riley mention Jonathan Swift? What's he got to do with this enquiry? We're not looking for Gulliver are we? Or shall we travel to Lilliput just in case?"

Blakely laughed, "No sir, but you've got the correct Swift. The most plausible explanation, Jonathan Swift's poem, describing a city shower in the 1700s. You know, cats and dogs."

"Blakely you never fail to amaze me. Come on, mastermind."

CHAPTER 68

Terry Arriving at Primrose Pad –

Date: Wednesday 27th April 2011

Terry sped towards Usk as fast as he could, negotiating the wet s-bends with impressive skill. Carrie-Anne was standing on the doorstep of Primrose Pad as if it were a bed of hot coals. Terry lowered the window of the ageing Range Rover to convey his, "I came as soon as I got your call, bloody tractors…"

Before he finished his sentence, she was sitting in the passenger seat. "Let's get out of here, Dad. Did anybody follow you? I'm really shit scared; this isn't a game anymore. They say they have killed my stepdad. Look, its Afon's cap. It ended up on my doorstep. It's a nightmare. If I speak up Dad, they've threatened to kill you and they're not bloody well joking. We have to hide somewhere and sort this out. Oh my God, I can't believe this; what do they want? What is happening? Can you think of anything, Dad? We need help; do you know anybody we can trust?"

Terry was struggling to take all this in. "Look Carrie-Anne, I've just rented this cottage near Llancayo. Nobody knows about it, and its miles from anywhere, off the beaten track. I've not even paid the deposit yet; we'll stay there and consider our options. You my girl, must try to chill, this could all be puff and wind. I think I know someone who can help us, maybe able to shed some light on this, because I haven't got a clue right now. This bloody puzzle has become no clearer, but the answer must be in there somewhere."

They arrived at Afallon, and parked the car yards from the front door.

"It's not the Hilton Hotel, but it'll do us for now. If we're lucky the rain might not pour through the roof tonight."

"It stinks of damp, Dad, like a smelly mausoleum, its bitterly cold. Look, this hasn't been dusted for years."

"Since when have you been a household deity?"

"What Dad?"

"You know, a domestic goddess? I've only just agreed to move in. This is the first time I've actually put the key in the door to let myself in. Obviously, it needs a woman's touch. So don't hold yourself back, feel free to smarten things up. You should have joined the army, you wouldn't complain about this then. This is luxury compared to some of our military exercises in Iraq. You'd think this was the pearl in the oyster."

Carrie-Anne responded, "More like the bottom of the barrel, Dad."

"There's supposed to be central heating. I'll try to sort the heat out, you find the kettle and a couple of mugs. Let the water run for a little while, or we'll be drinking rust soup. We'll feel better when we've warmed up. Be quite cosy really, and safe."

"Cosy, it's about as cosy as Bates Hotel."

Terry laughed.

Carrie-Anne snuggled under the rough patchwork blanket as she sat in the armchair supping her tea. "Prefer Hot Chocolate."

"Tomorrow I'll go get some supplies."

Carrie-Anne corrected, "You mean you're going to go shopping Dad. Supplies? We're not in Afghanistan now."

She shared her ordeal in a clearer, slower, and pensive manner, trying to add reason and logic into the unsavoury course of events that occurred earlier that day. Terry listened, holding back a protective anger that stirred inside him, that paternal instinct, to confront anybody that would dare threaten his daughter.

"Now listen up Carrie-Anne, I got a bad feeling about this. I think time is definitely of the essence. Will you be OK tonight? I need to shoot down to London. There's something I must do, and there's somebody I have to meet. I'll do all I can to be back ASAP. Nobody knows you here, so there's nothing to worry about. Phone me if you feel you need to, but don't phone any local friends, in case information falls into the wrong hands, and don't answer your phone unless you know who's calling. In fact, let them leave a message instead, that's safer."

"I don't believe this; you're not going to leave me in this spooky place all night all on my own Dad? What about the groceries?"

"Oh come on Carrie-Anne, you'll be just fine on your todd, you've been watching too many of those horror movies. What do you think, a mob of flesh-eating Zombies from *Night of the Living Dead* will be bashing down the front door?"

"Oh you're really helping, Dad. Why don't you mention werewolves and vampires, and don't forget the Boston strangler."

Terry couldn't help laughing, she was so dramatic. "I'll nip down to the local garage and pick up some groceries tonight, drop them off, and then head down to London. Anything you particularly would like princess?"

It was the first time Terry called Carrie-Anne, princess. She never responded negatively to his term of endearment, on the contrary, she quite liked it. She felt loved, wanted and special.

"Yeah, after your encouraging conversation, a bucket of tranquillisers, sprig of garlic, silver bullets, wooden stake, large cross, a twelve bore shotgun and a band of Ninja warriors would be fine, failing that, don't forget the hot chocolate."

Terry hugged Carrie-Anne. "That's my princess, still got a sense of humour. You'll be fine. If you hear any unusual noises while I'm away, it will probably be that mangy old ginger cat creeping around."

CHAPTER 69

Terry Heads for London to Find Mike Brindle –
Date: Wednesday 27thth April 2011

Terry pushed the Range Rover to its ear-splitting rickety limits; just about everything was juddering, including himself. Every mile seemed an eternity. The M4 was considerably generous as to its lack of heavy traffic, but the worry of the events seemed to worsen as he passed every exit on the motorway. He needed the toilet, he was bursting, but doggedly held on despite the growing discomfort, as his bladder tried to alert him of its need to be emptied.

Eventually the Hammersmith exit, he shouted "Hallelujah." This was the closest he got as far as religion was concerned. Where and how to find Mike Brindle? he thought. Was he still in the force? Was he local? More to the point, was he alive? I bloody hope so, don't you let me down Brindle, if you are dead, I'll bleeding we'll kill you.

Now what next? Where to start? What did he know? What was his reference point? Contact Lenny, of course. Although the garage would be shut, Lenny surely would be able to help, he was generally in the know, and Terry had his number.

"Lenny, thank God you answered. Now, I don't have a lot of time for chat right now, but I need to contact a DI Brindle. You remember? I told you about him. How at the time of my dad's murder he seemed to be the only one who genuinely took some interest. I need a real copper. I need Brindle. If he's around I know he can help me."

"Hey buddy, what's happened? Sounds like you've really upset somebody?"

"Please Lenny, not now! I really need to locate Brindle."

"Well, you have come to the right man; In fact, you'll never believe this, I was speaking to him recently. Funny enough, it was about you. I have his partner's card, Detective Sergeant Blakely. I'll give you the number; she's a good 'un, I can tell. She'll get Brindle for you. By the way, you must be popular, people have already been looking for you, but don't you worry, I only mentioned you were in Wales, family business etc. nothing more. They said they had some news, a possible windfall, and it could all be yours. It sounded a bit flaky if you ask me. Something didn't add up, sounded suspicious, so I passed on the news on to the old Bill, DI Brindle. I hope your OK Terry; you're not in any trouble are you?"

The plot thickened. Every step Terry took, indicated trouble ahead. The call was made, Blakely alerted Brindle, and they agreed to meet with him lunchtime.

This was going to be a long and jittery few hours for Terry, far outweighing the days he spent awaiting the army reconnaissance sorties into enemy territory. He was grateful as he reached his apartment. He let himself in, closed the door, trod over the mail and turned the television on and waited till midday.

He was relieved, glad to be home, but to unwind the coiled spring inside of him today was never going to happen. He called Carrie-Anne, no answer. That crowned the intensity of his tumult; he phoned several times, still no answer. A deep sense of helplessness swept over him, one he'd only ever felt once before, and that was when his mother died.

CHAPTER 70

Afallon Cottage. Llancayo –

Date: Thursday 28th April 2011

Terry had been away since yesterday evening. Carrie-Anne finished dressing and eased herself off the vexatious bed, wiping her eyes with the edge of the ruffled quilt. She picked up the discarded pieces of her mobile phone, recalling her dad's warning not to phone local friends for fear of inadvertently disclosing her whereabouts. She reassured herself, Sam was in France that should have been OK. "If only I'd topped up my credit on the mobile. What a complete dipstick."

The morning had taken her to the edge. Her head was throbbing, a tension evoked headache. She felt sick, queasy, and so dived into her bag for the paracetamols. "Bloody light bulb, nearly gave me a frigging heart attack. Thank you, Dad, I really appreciate you leaving me here on my lonesome. I feel about as safe as a worm in a blackbird's beak."

She started to descend the rickety stairs, entering directly into the downstairs main room. The grandfather clock registered 10.10 am. She opened the pantry door, grabbed the sliced loaf and plum jam, and then rummaged around hoping to find a toaster. Moments later she emerged with a robust, heavy metal toaster. Taking it to the sink, she upturned and shook the monster to dispose of the mouldy bread crumbs, checking it out for mice droppings at the same time. "Dad you are impossible. No TV, no land-line, lukewarm central heating, and a cupboard full of outdated appliances. You're a champion."

She plugged in a two bar electric heater that looked totally out of place set on the large fire hearth. Astounded that it worked, its elements started to glow red, letting off a scorching smell as it burnt the caked dust. There was a portable radio with a healthy reception sitting on the small bookshelf under the stairs. Radio Wales. That will do; company of a kind. It blared out, *Schools Out For Summer*.

She sat down, trying to take the sting out of the torrid night and relax. It wasn't long before she fell asleep. Weary through the lack of shut-eye, and with the pills taking effect, she was well and truly in the land of nod. Perhaps she would awake later to find it was all a dream, a disturbing one at that.

Carrie-Anne awoke; it was tea-time, 4.40pm. Nothing stirred, everything seemed quiet. She was cold, so stood with her backside facing the electric heater and wondered how she could pass the time. She thought about dusting, then changed her mind. Was Afon dead? It can't be real.

Can it? Hoping Terry would return soon, she thought about the riddle again. Hunger called, she ate baked beans on toast. "You really know how to live the high life; eat your heart out Egon Ronay." She procrastinated, but eventually washed up. After all it was quite an experience placing a kettle with a whistle on the gas stove.

A combination of cold and boredom made it a long uncomfortable night. She tucked herself up in the armchair, with the floral quilt from upstairs, banged the dust off a book and started to read, *White Fang* by Jack London. Wriggling and tossing, eight chapters in, she eventually fell asleep. Terry had not returned.

CHAPTER 71

Kensington Delicatessen, Florentina –

Date: Thursday 28th April 2011

It was midday. Terry mentioned to Brindle that he really wasn't sure where to begin, it was such a muddle.

"The best place to start is always at the beginning. Now, come on let's be having you, as the bishop said to the chorister. What's going on?"

"That's the problem; I'm not sure of where, when, or how this whole saga of crazy events began. All I know, that it's for real. It's happening, and it's happening to us. That is, my daughter and I. Talk about 'Tales of the Unexpected', It's a nightmare, so help me."

"OK, slow down, take it easy, or you'll bloody hyperventilate," replied Brindle.

"As you are now aware, I discovered only recently that I have a daughter. I first met Carrie-Anne only to discover that her mother had recently died in tragic circumstances, and the poor girl has been on an emotional roller-coaster ever since. The obvious trauma of coming to terms with losing your mother, and then finding her long lost father would be enough for anybody to cope with. But there are other unexplainable things, weird things; I can't get a handle on them. She says she has been followed, stalked for quite a while by a tall, well-dressed, Chinese gentleman; she has received mystery notes that don't make any sense, and recently an anonymous threatening phone call that may well endanger her life. It seems that either Carrie-Anne or indeed myself, have something they, whoever they are, want to get their hands on, and they're not bloody well joking.

"At Easter we found out quite by chance, that we obtained a similar Easter gift. This was a chocolate Easter bunny. We received it on the same day, and inside each there was a small folded note. Fate, call it what you may, on Easter Sunday I began to brag about my Easter gift, swanking that it was sent from some ambiguous loving admirer. I mentioned the baffling note I found within. At that point Carrie-Anne looking notably flabbergasted, confirming that she had also received a note, equally confusing.

"We returned to Primrose Pad, that's a little apartment, a drum above the hairdressers in Usk. There we gathered our notes. Upon placing them together, it became obvious they contained the same handwriting, and were from the same sheet of torn paper. They both contained a riddle, but some of the lines in each were different. We surmised rightly or wrongly, that there was a co-dependency on both the riddles before we could solve the clues. But for the life of me Mike, I cannot unravel the riddle; this has to be key to the strange events that have taken place. That's why I need your assistance. Something, somewhere, out of the past has come to haunt us, and we haven't a clue, but it's very real, and I believe dangerous."

Mike listened intently; he was intrigued, fascinated by what he just had heard. Now he needed to study this conundrum. There was nothing more energising or liberating to a man of Brindle's disposition, than to solve the clues, enter the chase, win the war against crime and 'put the bastards away'.

They sat under the low level glow of lights of the delicatessen situated in the entrance of Kensington Tube Station, Brindle tucking into a challenging large baguette, filled with Swiss cheese, roast ham, jalapeños, tomatoes, onion, black olives and mustard mayonnaise.

"I love this place, it's fantastic choosing your own fillings. Trouble is I can never make up my mind. Still, this is fabulous." He wiped his dripping mouth with his serviette and continued talking between sipping his cappuccino. "Right, let's have a gander at these notes."

Terry placed his half-eaten, smoked salmon and cream cheese bagel back on his plate, and pulled the notes out of his inside pocket, spreading them on the table.

Brindle put on a pair of heavy-rimmed spectacles that had no symmetry with his facial features whatsoever.

"Sorry about the glasses, borrowed them from the pub last week; lost mine."

He began to scrutinize the riddles, murmuring out loud and commented sarcastically, "Well it's not Jack the Ripper, that's for sure, and we won't have to contact Frederick Abberline from beyond the grave. 'When two pieces become as one, the chase for its knowledge has only begun.'"

Terry began to finish his lukewarm bagel, as Brindle continued.

"As you mentioned, Terry, let's assume that this, 'two pieces become as one', is the joining of these two notes. We now have them together as one. 'For others will follow with a mind on the prize'. Again, you confirm that your daughter has been followed or stalked, and you believe they are looking for something. That's got to be the prize. But, what's the prize? You don't have anything rare, or of special significance, nothing lately that has come into your hands that you think might be important. Something like a key, a number, antiquity or legacy?" He faced Terry. Terry just shook his head.

"'So keep your resolve bright eyes'." Brindle leant back in the chair looking up, staring at the ornate ceiling, whispering the last line several times, as if in the repetitiveness alone, somehow the answer might be dislodged from its secret chamber. "So let's assume that this is a credible warning, yes, a warning, to tell us to keep bright, alert, sharp, to be ahead of the rest. What do you think?"

"It makes sense to me, but why all the mystery, it's all gobbledegook? Couldn't the crazy bastard who sent this, just write, 'Be careful there are people after you'?"

"Get some more coffee in Blakely, that's the girl, black and strong for me. Americano please, those cappuccinos are OK as a one off, but they dunarf fill you up. What about you Terry?"

"I'll have the same again café mocha, thanks."

"Oh and get one for yourself Blakely, and don't forget the receipt."

"Sir, you're a real..."

"That's enough, Blakely, compliments will get you everywhere. Now, where were we? Where's that second note? Oh its right here under me nose. OK, the first two lines are the same in both notes then: 'A shrewd tip now, the clue's in a book.'"

Mike repeated out loud, "'The clue's in a book'. What clue? What book?"

Blakely returned.

"OK Blakely, don't make a fuss, just place them down there, that's it. Ta very much. Did you bring the sugar?"

"But I haven't been given a book, and neither has Carrie-Anne. Not even a book of bloody stamps. How can you find a clue in book if you haven't got the book? It's crazy," Terry looked exasperated.

Mike like a hyena locking its teeth on its adversary, was not going to let go. "'A shrewd tip now'. What is the tip? We don't have the book, and we don't have the tip that leads us to the book. Well, what do you think Blakely? You haven't said a word, come on, think girl, after all you went to university didn't you?"

Blakely peered at Brindle, if she had said the first words that come into her mind, she might enjoy the moment but regret it later. "Sir, I'm very good at practical stuff, pretty good at maths and science, but I am no good at puzzles, riddles or anagrams."

"Now, that's bloody typical, Blakely, maths and science, but you're not working for NASA, and you're not... Wait a minute. What did you just say?"

"I said I'm good at practical stuff..."

Brindle insisted, "No, no after that, come on."

"I'm no good at puzzles, riddles..."

"Yes, and anagrams, you said anagrams. What a smart girl, I knew all along that you were mustard Blakely." Brindle slurped his coffee extravagantly. Terry looked perplexed, and sipped his mocha, leaving a film of milk on his top lip.

"Anagram, don't you see? It has to be an anagram. 'A shrewd tip now'. That's the key to the book. Brindle tapped

287

his finger hard several times on the notepaper to emphasize his point.

"I might be thick Brindle, but I don't know of any book called, 'A Shrewd Tip Now'." Terry replied.

"That's the point, it's an anagram. Quick, get me some paper Blakely. Come on, hurry up, we haven't got all night you know."

*

The afternoon turned to evening; it was just after 9pm. Brindle was imbibing his favourite red wine and Terry a Jack Daniels and coke, he needed it. Blakely was on the fresh orange juice; if she drank any more caffeine she'd be shaking like a monkey passing razorblades.

"'A dew thorn wisp', 'wanted worship', 'withdraw pose', is that all we can come up with?" Even Brindle was beginning to flag, and the bottle of wine didn't help. He examined the attempts for the last time. "Right, I think that last effort, courtesy of Blakely, 'wish depart now', says it all, wish depart now. That's it, that's me done for the night. Come on Blakely, you better drive me home, and better get off yourself, beauty sleep and all that. Early start in the morning, my girl. Oh, and by the way, remember to keep this to yourself; we can't let this information fall into anybody's hands, can we?"

He screwed the papers up containing the riddle attempts and shoved them in his jacket pocket. "Terry, I'll be in touch. Stay local until we can sort this out. We are definitely on to something here."

CHAPTER 72

Afallon, Llancayo Mitchell Enters Cottage –

Date: Friday 29th April 2011

Carrie-Anne had decided to sleep downstairs last night, she felt safer for some reason. She awoke early morning, yawned, and briskly massaged the left side of her neck and shoulder. She had slept well, but awkwardly. Her body reacted to its overlong, cramped position, by inducing a dull ache to the offended areas. She rubbed her eyes. A little disorientated and still drowsy, focusing on her whereabouts, she mumbled, "Yes, it's real, you're still in this nightmare." She wondered when the hell her dad would be back.

She was interrupted by the rather croaky meowing, and scratching at the front door. "It's that sad old cat, bet its hungry; window's shut now, old pal, can't get in can you? Thought you were feral and looked after yourself, perhaps not then? Maybe you're a softy after all? What happened, did the last tenant bugger off, forget about you?"

She opened the door leaving it ajar, figuring the cat would enter in its own time. Then turned and walked towards the fridge, still conversing with the cat as if it understood every word. "I'll expect you'll want a drop of milk then? There's not much to eat though. I'll fry up these sausages, but don't tell my dad; you can join me for breakfast."

The skinny feline drew closer, ultimately massaging his head against Carrie-Anne's ankle, purring in anticipation. Carrie-Anne was enjoying this situation of togetherness as much as the cat. The cat was company, someone to share with, even in this limited way, it helped her.

Suddenly Carrie-Anne's attention was disturbed, the daylight from the partially open door grew brighter as the door opened wide, causing her to drop the milk bottle, which crashed heavily against the flagstone floor.

"Have we caught you at an inopportune time? I am very sorry, perhaps I should have huffed and puffed and blown the door down?"

Spider cut an intimidating figure, accentuated as his bulk filled the door, shading the brief glare of daylight. The jumpy cat with arched back and perpendicular tail hissed stridently – she had already determined this man was danger.

Two instinctive assessments simultaneously collided in that room; Spider liked what he saw, an attractive, young, defenceless female that he could torment and intimidate. Carrie-Anne's instant perception, she was in the hands of a vicious, lecherous, bully.

"Well Carrie-Anne, let me introduce to you, the big, bad wolf herself, Mitchell the Merciless, as she's better known these days; she's been gagging to meet you, and I mean gagging."

Mitchell intervened. "That's enough Harris, you're not bloody funny. Very dramatic, but don't give up your day job. I don't think you'll give Bruce Willis any sleepless nights, you cockney shit for brains."

"How did you find this place? Nobody knew… it's not possible. What do you want?" asked Carrie-Anne, hardly audible as she spoke whilst fearing for her life.

"Years being a detective taught me some things, my girl. Did you really think that you could hide from me?" Mitchell loved being in control.

CHAPTER 73

Date: Friday 29th April 2011

Brindle arrived early at the office. Indulging in a few late night glasses of red wine would instigate a heavy head for some, but not Brindle. He felt sharp, alert and ready to face the challenge set before him. He arrived at his office pre 8.30am, and sat munching a doorstop of a bacon butty. As he compressed the sandwich, the dripping sauce conjoined with hot fat ran between his fingers. His mug, a birthday present, displayed:

AT FIFTY YOU ENTERED THE STONE-AGE –

GALL, KIDNEY AND BLADDER.

This revealed Emily's typical forensic-type humour, while the congealed, sauce-stained fingerprints revealed that of a messy eater. He was engrossed, his mind on the riddle, his tongue licking his fingers, followed by loud slurps of lukewarm tea. "Bloody lovely." He affirmed his satisfaction of his greasy snack.

He planted the telling evidence of his breakfast onto the notepaper when he grabbed it from his coat pocket and straightened it out. He stared defiantly at the anagram, 'A shrewd tip now', and studied last night's efforts at the delicatessen to unravel the riddle.

Brindle began to doubt the earlier deduction; perhaps it wasn't an anagram after all. Maybe it was simply conveying the need to concentrate on finding the tip 'The clue's in a book'.

Frustration got the better of him, patience wasn't his strong point. He sprang up from his chair faster than a cynophobic in Battersea Dogs Home, releasing a barrage of choice expletives, declaring his abject annoyance of the racket rising from the courtyard below. "Is it possible, that you could keep your bloody noise down out there? Blimey, you sound like a load of cackling turkeys. Anyhow, shouldn't you lot be out on the road? You're not going to catch anybody standing there bellyaching. Now get onto it!"

He slammed the window shut, sighed out loud, finished his tea, and decided to rethink his initial responses to the clues. "Lateral thinking Brindle, something must be the key, what the hell is the answer?"

Now he was focusing on the lines: 'For others will follow with a mind on the prize, so keep your resolve bright eyes'.

"I don't know about 'bright eyes', my eyelids feel like sodding flagstones; if they shut I'll need a stonemason's chisel to open them. Mike, my old son, you need a caffeine fix." Whenever Mike felt sharp and energetic first thing in the morning, you could guarantee it was short lived; tiredness crept up on him and held him back, like someone grabbing his pyjamas bottoms as he tried to walk forwards.

He opened the office door and surveyed the corridor. "Ah, Sergeant Daniels, have you seen Blakely this morning?"

"Not yet, sir."

"Well, be sharp, fetch me a coffee, and tell Blakely when you see her, that I want a word. Thank you, officer; strong, black, two sugars."

He yawned out loud, pacing the floor, trying to energise himself from his overbearing tiredness, beginning to whistle a tune as Blakely appeared with his coffee.

"Well, you're a happy soul this morning; brought your coffee. Desk sergeant said you wanted to see me? Art Garfunkel."

Brindle blew and sipped his coffee, "Cor, that's bloody hot, Blakely. What do you think I've got, an asbestos mouth or something? Now, what in the name of God's teeth are you meandering on about?"

"Art Garfunkel, sir; you know, Simon and Garfunkel, *Bridge Over Troubled Water*, and all that?"

"Listen Blakely, what is this, Radio Two's *Popmaster*?"

"Sorry sir, I was just referring to the song you were whistling, it's Art Garfunkel."

She began to sing, "*Is it a kind of dream, floating out on the tide.* Didn't know you were a cartoon fan Guv'nor, animation and all that stuff. Thought you were more of a *Die Hard* man, action and all that?"

Brindle felt like he'd just entered Hampton Court maze and had no way out. "Blakely I'm not sure if you are aware, I'm in the middle of a serious investigation here, and you just keep harping on about cartoons and Bruce Willis. I can assure you, that neither Art Garfunkel, Bruce Willis, or for that matter, Bleedin' Mickey Mouse, are suspects in this inquiry."

Blakely smiled as she usually did, it was all harmless banter. She knew Mike well enough not to take liberties, he reciprocated with fatherly overtones, tough on the outside, but soft centred. She picked up the phone and began to make her usual morning calls, checking details etc., awaiting any further developments or new information from the administration. Without thinking she continued to sing, "*How can the light that burnt so brightly, suddenly burn so pale? Bright eyes.*"

Mike turned, staring at Blakely quicker than a startled meerkat, eyes wide in disbelief. "Blakely, *Bright Eyes*, *Bright Eyes*, don't you see, you adorable excuse for a copper, *Bright Eyes*. You've done it again."

"But I was only telling you what you were whistling, guv."

"Why would I whistle that, Blakely? What would make me whistle that?"

"I'm not sure, maybe you were studying the riddle, and subconsciously your mind latched on to the tune *Bright Eyes*. We've all done that with one thing or another. You know it's like when you buy an ice-cream, without even thinking about it, you suddenly burst into, *O Sole Mio*."

"Forgive me, maybe I am a bit slow this morning Blakely and forgotten my vitamin tablets, but what has Oh Soly Meow got to do with ice-cream?"

Blakely could not contain herself, the harder she tried the worst she became, exploding into a fit of laughter, trying desperately to cover her mouth to muffle the noise. Her stomach ached. Brindle started to laugh also, it was infectious. The only difference was that Mike didn't know why she was laughing.

The animation with the song *Bright Eyes*, what's it called, come on Blakely, the one with all those rabbits hopping about, you know…?"

"*Watership Down*, sir."

There was silence. Then Blakely went to speak.

"No Shush… Wait a minute. I've got it. For the love of Aunt Riley, I've got it! Don't you see, that's the anagram? Look, that's the anagram." Mike thumped the table in triumph.

"A shrewd tip now – Watership Down. It's *Watership Down*. That's where the clue is, in the book."

He hugged Blakely, lifting her off the floor and twirling her around. "DS Blakely, you're a one hundred carat genius."

She dispensed with Brindle's thoughtless patronisation, and warmed, with a sense of smug superiority.

"What's the time? We'd better call Terry, check that everything's OK. Can you arrange a meet as soon as possible? We'll ask him if this book means anything to him."

There was a knock on the office door, and without waiting for an invitation, the desk sergeant's head popped around the door. "Not disturbing anything, am I, guv?"

"Well if you were, it wouldn't matter now, would it, Daniels? Now what is it, I'm busy?"

"It's just that we've found this letter on the front desk, it's addressed to you. I don't think it's a letter bomb, guv," Daniels laughed.

"I'm glad you thought that was funny, Daniels, now bugger off. Go and play with your handcuffs or something."

Mike opened the letter straight away.

> *As you dwell on the riddles, and chew on the fat*
> *You'll find in the name of an elegant cat.*

Mike signalled to Blakely, "Come on, let's go. No time to waste. We must contact Terry."

CHAPTER 74

Terry Meets Mitchell at Afallon –

Date: Friday 29th April 2011

Brindle, Terry and Blakely met at some haste; Mike knew that this was dangerous territory. Together they thrashed out the possibilities concerning the riddle, agreeing that Terry needed to get back to his daughter as quick as possible.

"Think about what I've said," asserted Brindle, "*Watership Down*. Ask Carrie-Anne if it means anything to her, jog her memory. I have some things to tidy up. I'm not on duty this Easter time. I'll drive down to Wales later this afternoon. Now get going Terry, and take care, keep your eyes open."

The screech of brakes and the yanking of the hand break followed by heavy footsteps immediately alerted those inside that someone had arrived. Within seconds the door of Afallon cottage was flung open, crashing against the inside wall, causing the flaking paint to float down to the floor.

"Princess, its Dad, is everything OK? Sorry it's been a couple of days. Are you OK? Why didn't you answer the phone? I was worried about you. Good news, listen, were getting somewhere with this riddle. Bad news, Brindle reckons it's urgent, we could be in considerable danger…"

Terry calmed down and took a breath, placing a hardback book on the sink top. As he did so, Carrie-Anne appeared from out of the small auxiliary room at the rear of the main room. She shuffled out, ankles tied together, hands tied behind her back and a large hand with a web tattoo holding her mouth shut. Startled Carrie-Anne could do no more than shake her head from side to side, revealing heavy contusions on one side. Terry's initial reaction was to charge his adversary, but as he moved forward, he could see Spider's hand tightening on Carrie-Anne's mouth. He yelled aggressively, "If you hurt her you bastard, I'll rip your head off!"

"Oh, come now, calm down, there's no need to be so dramatic, Mr Mead." Mitchell continued to speak as she moved from behind Harris and Carrie-Anne. "You must be Terry? Of course, listen Terry, as long as you do as you're told, nothing will happen to your little girl. I have been waiting a long time for this moment, and nobody is going to deprive me of my right."

Terry had converted his hands into two fists; his knuckles were white as he clenched them tight with anger.

"You mentioned Brindle. A certain Mike Brindle – somehow, I knew our paths would cross again. I was anticipating it would be when I paid him the visit that I've been planning for him, but it seems he has already entered the arena." Her tone grew more assertive. "What did Brindle say?"

Terry watched as the squeeze on Carrie-Anne's mouth became heavier. She was struggling to breathe.

"Come now, Terry, you really wouldn't want anything to happen to your newly found daughter. That would be tragic. Now let's start again. What did he say?"

Terry pleaded, "OK, OK, please let go of Carrie-Anne. I'll tell you what I have, but I've got no idea about any of this, you have to believe me?"

Spider's grip of Carrie-Anne loosened, he pushed her to the kitchen table, pulled back the chair and sat her down like a rag doll. She began to breathe more easily, her heart rate slowed down; her pulse began to return to something close to normality.

"Take a seat Terry." Mitchell urged. "I must admit, it was terribly considerate of you to find such a reclusive spot, out of the way. After all we don't want to be disturbed now, do we?"

Terry spoke quietly. "*Watership Down.*"

Mitchell confronted him. "Are you taking the piss or stalling for time? What kind of answer is that? Where are the rubies? Do you have any knowledge as to the whereabouts of the blood rubies?"

Harris's grip tightened again on Carrie-Anne to amplify the point that they were not kidding.

"*Watership Down*. That's it, *Watership Down*, that's all I have. Does that mean anything to you?"

"Yes, it means that I am going to shoot your daughter through her pretty little head, as you watch, that is of course, after Harris has had his playtime with her. He doesn't like to miss a good opportunity." Mitchell produced a gun from her bag and pressed it excessively hard against Carrie-Anne's cranium. Carrie-Anne's terrified state was visible to all.

"Look, whoa, stop. Give me a chance to explain," Terry begged.

"It better be good I'm running out of patience." She pressed the gun even harder against his daughter's head.

"It's this bloody riddle; do you know anything about this riddle? All we have is this bloody puzzle. Mike Brindle was the DI. He was around at the time of my father's murder. After all the shit my daughter has faced, I reckoned this could be far more than a hoax. Only recently she received a weird phone call, stating that her stepdad had been murdered, and that I could be next. We both realised that this was not a game. Carrie-Anne disappeared from Primrose Pad to join me here. That's why I went to meet Brindle. We thought we were safe, having some breathing space to sort things out. Obviously I was wrong."

Spider Harris interrupted, "Yeah, poor old Harry Mead got in too deep. Should have kept to his cabbing and beer; got greedy see."

"The trouble with you Harris is that you don't know when to keep your big mouth shut." Harris angered Mitchell but he was necessary.

"Wait a minute; I thought your face was familiar. I'm right, I know I'm right. You're DCI Mitchell. I spoke to you at the scene of my dad's murder. You were the leading investigator. What the fuck is going on?"

"Time, time is what's going on, and you're running out of it," threatened Mitchell.

"There is this anagram within the riddle. It stressed there was a clue hidden in a book. It turns out the anagram gave us, *Watership Down*. That's as far as we got. It revealed we would be pursued, and that others would follow for a prize. What prize and where? I don't know."

"Do you have the riddle?"

"Yes I have a copy, Brindle has the original. It was he who helped me get this far."

Mitchell lifted the paper high up to her eyes, and began to read its contents. "OK, I get it. You've worked out the book, now let's proceed. 'A nut leads the way to a weed take a look'."

"It's there. It's over there on the sink top, a copy of *Watership Down*. I picked one up on the way back from

London; seems like I've played right into your hands. Please don't hurt Carrie-Anne?"

Mitchell pointed to Harris. "Fetch."

Harris obliged, handing the book over to Mitchell, who rustled through its pages, seeking earnestly any hint that would unlock the puzzle. Time passed, then an enthusiastic cry of excitement and ascendancy. "Hazel, yes Hazel… It's the name of a rabbit. 'A nut leads the way'. See, Hazel, hazelnut." She kissed the book and continued, "Come on my little beauty; reveal your secret to Vicky now. Where are you going to Hazel? Where's the weed?"

Silence prevailed, so much so that you could hear the grandfather clock ticking. All of a sudden it sprang to life, announcing the time as its chimes rang out across the room. Mitchell yelled out, abruptly and triumphantly. Hearts beat faster. They were shocked by the sudden outburst. "It's all here…! Hazel leads a group of rabbits out of the endangered warren! Here it is Chapter 5… Hazel meets Dandelion, a story teller, a buck rabbit. He's the weed. Dandelion commends Hazel for his willingness to sacrifice everything for the cause. There we have it."

They say that the eyes are the window to the soul. In Mitchell's case, her eyes exposed such an intense, almost satanic gratification as she fed her avarice, truly exalting one of the seven deadly sins. Are you willing to sacrifice everything? Your daughter perhaps, Terry? Or are you going to come clean? Now where, or who is Dandelion?"

CHAPTER 75

Mike Brindle Arrives in Wales in Pursuit –

Date: Friday 29th April 2011

Mike had conveyed to Terry that he believed part of the answer focused on a children's book by Richard Adams, called *Watership Down*. It meant nothing to Mike or Terry, but he would share the breakthrough with Carrie-Anne, see if that rang any bells. Maybe it would open up any leads as to what this was all about. Terry left London quickly; he was extremely concerned over Carrie-Anne's welfare. This may bring an end to these insalubrious events, but somehow he had his doubts. If he kept his foot down on the accelerator and no road works, he should arrive mid-afternoon.

Brindle arrived in Usk that evening. He would stay in the locality, following up on his instinctive gut reaction concerning Mitchell and company. He never pursued this as part of a routine inquiry, or for that matter in any official capacity at all. That is why he left Blakely behind, with orders to remain in touch and keep shtum. Mike was on the loose, and his first mission was to check on Carrie-Anne's father-in-law, clearing up the truth. Was he alive? Was he dead? Was the threat genuine, or just a frightener? A hoax maybe?

He parked his car opposite Afon's family farm in Nant-y-derry, climbed over the five bar gate, and tasted a long overdue experience of country life. "Bloody hell, cow dung or chicken shit? I bet that puts a hole in the ozone layer!"

Now all he had to do was negotiate with a lively border collie that was springing up, baring his teeth, and growling at the same time. This acted as the perfect alarm call. The front door of the farmhouse creaked as it slowly opened. "Shut your din for goodness sake! Calm down old gal. Who is it? Be careful, no sudden movements, she can be a spiteful bitch at times, can't you Treacle?"

"Brindle, Mike Brindle, I'm a police officer. This is not an official call; I'm just trying to gain a little more information on a gentleman called Afon, Afon Llewellyn. That's not you sir, is it?"

"Dafyyd Llewellyn, that's my name; Afon's older brother. What you after?"

Well over 6 feet tall, he stood on the doorstep with his arms angled resting on his hips. He wore corduroy trousers tucked into his mud-laden Wellington boots, thick brown leather belt, grey trouser braces and a green checked shirt, with arm sleeves rolled up exposing his muscled biceps. David's dark, tanned face was weathered and etched, as one who had experienced the worries and woes of a tough life.

The cauliflower ears and large flat nose announced years of club rugby. A roll-up cigarette in the corner of his mouth, and a mop of thick grey hair that poked out from underneath his tattered flat cap – the classic farmer's look, like generations before him.

"You're a bit late looking for Afon. Don't you read the local paper? He's gone." He turned to go back inside.

"Wait a minute, you say he's gone. What do you mean? He's left or something? Do you know where he is?"

"Oh I know where he is. His ashes are in my conservatory. Sad bugger went and killed himself. He never got over the death of his wife you know. Couldn't forgive himself. He would mope around here like a long lost soul. They reckon he just threw himself into the silage pit, became overcome by the gas fumes, and that was his lot. I'm pretty sure he meant to kill himself. After all, he'd been around the place for years, was well aware of the dangers of working on the farm. Strange though, never found his hat. Got enough information now? If so, I'll be getting on, there's lots of work to get done."

Before Mike could respond the door was shut. "So much for a welcome in the hillside. I'm obviously on the wrong bloody hill," muttered Brindle.

CHAPTER 76

Discovering Dandelion –

Date: Friday 29th April 2011

No sooner had the words 'Who is Dandelion?' left Mitchell's mouth, when a Hallelujah, Damascus Road experience hit both Terry and Carrie-Anne – a light shone, pennies dropped and jaws lowered. Mitchell had struck a chord.

"You've got to be kidding, not Dandy? That old patchwork bunny, it can't be that, can it? I don't have it. I gave it to Rhian years ago. God knows where it is now?" Terry pondered.

Carrie-Anne looked on, eager to break the silence. "Dad, I have it. Are you listening? I have it."

"Have what?"

"Dandelion."

"You have Dandelion, how?"

"You remember? You gave it to Mam when you were on holiday in Pendine."

"Yes, of course I do, but you're not telling me she kept it all those years."

"Yes, Mam kept it, it was the promise she made to you, remember? When she became sick, she asked me to look after it. It was so precious to her. It has been my little travelling companion ever since."

Mitchell interrupted. "That's all very well, very touching and all that, but I think you had better hand it over to me right now."

Spider grabbed Carrie-Anne's hair, wrenching it violently, curling his top lip. "Give it to us. Where is it you stupid bitch? I am running out of patience here. Let me tell you, that even the Archangel Gabriel himself, with all his heavenly hosts, won't stop me from cutting out your precious little tongue, and dumping your naked body in the river Usk."

"Hold off, Spider," commanded Mitchell. Then she stooped down towards Carrie-Anne. "I know you're a sensible girl. Ignore Spider; he's about as subtle as a rabid fox in a chicken coup. Now, your daddy could be about to undergo a little body surgery, sadly, with no anaesthetic. That's the problem with these out of the way cottages." Mitchell forced Carrie-Anne's chin upwards, moved closer, and peered directly into her eyes. "If you don't tell us where this rabbit is, my colleague here will begin to hone his surgical skills on your father. At the moment he's verging on the apprentice butcher status.

Carrie-Anne yelled out.

"Let's all stay calm," and slapping Carrie-Anne hard across the face demanded, "Now where is it?"

Spider turned his attention on Terry. "What have we here then?" At first glance, it looked like a primeval jousting weapon, more at home in the court of King Arthur. The closest thing to hand is this oversized steak tenderiser, or should I say, pulveriser?" He turned, holding the weapon high so that Terry could get a good glimpse of the torturous implement. Then he outstretched Terry's left hand on the kitchen table.

"That's a bit blunt for a surgical instrument, Spider. The trouble with you is that you have no class. Still, needs must. Now for the last time Carrie-Anne, where is the rabbit?"

CHAPTER 77

Collecting the Fluffy Rabbit from Usk –

Date: Friday 29th April 2011

Carrie-Anne unbuckled her seatbelt, jumped out of the car, rushed from the car-park and entered the Crosskeys Inn via the pub garden.

"Well, that's rich, it's about time you came in to explain yourself. What on earth do you think you've been doing? It's really not good enough Carrie-Anne."

Katie Williams, the pub proprietor was not impressed; she was heavily pregnant with her second child, tired and irritable. Carrie-Anne's lack of responsibility came as a big disappointment, and she prided herself at being a good judge of character. This caused her to have second thoughts."You left me high and dry the other night, with no explanation…?"

Carrie-Anne cut in; the degree of urgency in her response was tangible. She rapidly spilled out her reply. "Please forgive me, I will explain, I promise, but I really can't right now. I have just come to retrieve my little rabbit. I know it sounds daft, but I need it badly. It's above the optics in the bar, by the single malt."

"I'm afraid that tatty old rabbit got thrown out days ago. After all, we haven't heard from you. No call, no letter, we assumed you just left us. Anyhow, if you have not just left us, you have now. We can't run a business…"

"What do you mean you've thrown it away? You can't have done, it's not possible? For God's sake, please tell me you have not thrown it out?"

Katie turned to the young girl serving behind the bar. "Lauren, you did get rid of all those bits and bobs that made the bar look untidy, didn't you? What day was that? Did it all go in the bin?"

"No," replied Lauren, "I threw much of the rubbishy stuff in the waste, but the rabbit went to the Cancer Research Shop in the High Street, along with some of Rhys's old toys."

Carrie-Anne jemmied herself into the conversation. "What day was that? Please, I must get hold of that rabbit. It's vitally important."

"It was Wednesday afternoon, about 2pm."

"For goodness sake," interjected Katie, "It's only an old stuffed rabbit, you'd think it was a precious jewel or something, calm down."

Calm down! That was impossible; Carrie-Anne glanced at her watch. 3.45pm. "They're open till 4pm, I must dash."

Without any whys, or wherefores, she raced out of the bar, crossing the main road without checking the traffic.

Several ripe expletives emanated loudly from the heart pounding senior citizen in the small Fiat. But it was as if they bounced off a concrete wall, or simply evaporated into thin air. Carrie-Anne was impervious, already yards away and facing the charity shop door.

She pushed the door open, nudging past two elderly women trying to exit the shop. She leant forward on the glass counter, face to face with the assistant. "Rabbit, er… um, rabbit. Little fluffy rabbit, about this high, patchwork, placed here on Monday afternoon. Do you have it, I mean Please?" Her eyes pleaded, her body was as tense as a bowstring.

"Millie, do you know anything about a small fluffy rabbit? It appears this girl is after it, and I can't see it for toffee. Did you sell it, or put it in the back room?"

Carrie-Anne was tamping her right foot on the ground with growing impatience; she glanced at her watch and began to perspire. She wiped her brow.

"Would you believe it, it's been here a couple of days, and then all of a sudden two people want it within a few minutes! I've just sold it to a young mum with a toddler in a pushchair. The toddler, a pretty girl, looks like her mum, lovely curly hair."

"Which way?" she shouted loudly, with no regard for politeness or protocol. "Which way, which way did she go? Quickly, it's critical."

"Well, I'm not sure, but I think it was towards the supermarket opposite the post office."

Carrie-Anne moved like an escapee from a molten lava outpouring. She knocked over the stand of gent's shirts and jumpers, barging into the man viewing the paperback books who then had a very close encounter with ladies underwear.

She arrived at the shop, hope against hope. "Where's the mum with the curly-haired child?" Then, close to the delicatessen counter, passing a pot of olives into her shopping basket was a young lady. Carrie-Anne moved closer. Pushchair, yes; curly kid, yes. Albeit rather abruptly, she said, "Excuse me?"

The young mum's attention had been duly gained.

"Have you by any chance just visited the charity shop?"

Before any answer could be given, Carrie-Anne spotted the little girl holding the fluffy rabbit. "Look I'm dreadfully sorry to do this but…" Snatching the rabbit out of the toddler's hands, she speedily vacated the shop. The irate mum screamed, and the little girl bawled in ear-piercing unison. The nearby shoppers were treated to an eventful display of wilful theft, now they could gossip enthusiastically, tutting in mild disgust.

Carrie-Anne ran across the road. Within seconds she was driving the car maniacally, kicking up red clouds of dust from the drive, as she sped back onto the main road and away back to Llancayo. It was 4.18pm. She had till 5pm to return.

CHAPTER 78

Mengyao Confronts Mitchell at Afallon Cottage. Llancayo –

Date: Friday 29th April 2011

Mitchell's anticipation of Carrie-Anne's return caused her to lose concentration momentarily, and in those distracted seconds he entered the room with the furtiveness of a grey wolf. "Hello Little Tiger, you cannot imagine how long I have waited for this moment, but first let us make your stay more comfortable, and then we can talk." Spider grabbed Mitchell, forcing her into the chair.

"It was so nice of Spider to invite me, what with you in the middle of some serious negotiations. Carrie-Anne not back yet. I'm sure she won't be long. After all, think about poor Terry's fingers, squashed to pulp. She wouldn't like that. You know, you would have made a fine triad, Mitchell."

Mengyao moved menacingly towards Mitchell. She wriggled with immense force but she was bound tight to the chair. He dragged the gag down. Mitchell took deep breaths as she craved for air.

"Remember my father's saying, 'Eggs don't fight with rocks'? Little tiger, you should have learned, but your tenacity has led you right into the hands of your adversary. Speaking of rocks…" He uncovered two large ruby-red stones from a black silk handkerchief. "Does this bring back memories? You tried to trick me. Your design was to replace the genuine stones in the safe with cheap imitations. You would arrange to gain the true rubies from your thieving accomplice when it became expedient. You deviously shared damaging information with my father, Longwei. Information, which you knew would have me executed. But it went wrong, didn't it?" He grabbed her hair, twisted and tugged it with vengeful aggression. Mitchell screamed, her eyes began to water, fear and pain registered on her taunt pale face. "Unbeknown to you, your scheming collaborator had no intent of handing those jewels over. Well, not the authentic ones. You truly were double-crossed. Then, he or she profitably concluded the plan, by releasing data that would put you away for years. Tell-tale photographs."

Even in her vulnerable position, Mitchell still poured out her venom. "It's a pity you missed your own explosion, you ugly poisonous bastard. That stupid old fool Longwei allowed for the deception, fooling his own pathetic mob. Allowing you to disappear, pretending you were blown to pieces. What a pitiful masquerade. The tough, masterful,

318

Longwei, didn't even have enough guts to put his own treacherous son down."

Mengyao grimaced as he continued to expound his explanation of events. "Then the genuine rubies vanished. Where did they go? Spider here, your faithful accomplice, has been working for me for some time now, in fact, ever since your release. How on earth do you think he rose to the dizzy heights of driving a Lexus? He kept me in touch with your whereabouts, letting me know that the jewels that sat so long in your safety deposit box were also mere trinkets. How angry you must have got. Poor Soly. Today, we find we are still at a loss. These beauties before us are no more than coloured glass. But you would know that little tiger, wouldn't you? However, as you have such vociferous appetite and greed for that which was not rightfully yours…"

He grabbed her chin and started to force her mouth open, causing her bottom lip to split, releasing blood. There was nothing Mitchell could do. It was too late; the die had been cast. She tried to keep her mouth shut, but it was impossible against the powerful hands of Mengyao. She bit forcefully into his hand. "The Tiger still has teeth, but even the day of the tiger comes to an end."

The two glass stones were shoved with force into Mitchell's mouth, followed by the black silk cloth. The henchman, Tingfui, ripped the gaffer tape from off of its roll, and stuck it firmly over Mitchell's mouth. Her eyes revealed the terror she was undertaking, shaking her head violently, and then a mournful pleading noise escaped through her muffled mouth.

"What's a matter Vicky? Feel a bit Tom and Dick do you? Losing your bottle; not like you? How does it feel not to be in control? Do you think I enjoyed working for you? You greedy conniving, stuck up, toe-rag. You used me that day in Harry's flat, to do your dirty work." Spider, spat vehemently, directly into Mitchell's face, his cramped hatred at last gratified. He had waited so long for this. "No more of your swanky pretentious crap." His expelled phlegm gradually dribbled down her nose and chin.

Mitchell could not believe her own helplessness, it was as if her brain could not compute, could not allow her to grasp the situation as reality. After all, this was not how she planned things.

"Do as you say or you'd stitch me up. Hand me over to the triads on some trumped up bullshit. You bleeding coppers are all the same. You're all a bunch of self-serving, corrupt wankers. Now you'll pay."

Slowly Mitchell succumbed. Dignity and pride began to disappear, like rats on a sinking ship. Now she felt totally alone, physically and mentally spent.

Mengyao nonchalantly wiped the blood from his hands onto a handkerchief, as if he'd just been tucking into a barbecued spare rib. Then he grasped control, like a man who had waited so long to fulfil his twisted revenge; it had become darker and sweeter to his taste. He revelled in this moment, and showed no hint of compassion. He began to speak, addressing those in the room like a master would address his students.

"This is what happens when you try to cross Mengyao. It may take time. Do you know, when a scorpion has eaten everything in sight, it can disappear back under the sand lying dormant for several years before it needs to feed again? Its sting does not diminish, my friends."

His pock-marked face had become even more pronounced with his age. He turned to lecture his captive scholar. "Now Terry, do you know that when you suffocate, your body is no longer able to take in oxygen, the heart will begin beating faster, but eventually, the blood will lose oxygen and the lungs will stop working?"

With that, he faced Mitchell and squeezed her nostrils together tightly, shutting off her air supply. Mitchell jerked and twisted with great fortitude, displaying her incomparable will to live so manifestly, that she lifted the chair momentarily off the ground, snapping her left stiletto heel. But it was to no avail.

"You mad bastard! You evil, mad bastard!" cried Terry, whilst attempting a spirited attack on Mengyao.

"Come, come, Mr Mead, surely you would have a lot to admire in triad justice, swift and decisive. After all, this woman here is the orchestrator of your father's horrific murder. My colleague Harris, well you heard him for yourself, he was the reluctant executioner. I am doing you a favour."

Spider cracked Terry on the back of his skull, rendering him to the ground like a ton of bricks.

Mitchell fought hard for about an agonising three minutes. Then she lost consciousness. Her head slumped heavily to one side. Her eyes were still wide open, but she finally yielded. For her the obsessive, pernicious chase for lost treasure was over.

Mengyao spoke directly to Spider and Tingfui. "So we just wait for Carrie-Anne to arrive. What a surprise for the girl. She has experienced the tiger, now she must face the dragon."

CHAPTER 79

Afallon Cottage, Llancayo – What's in a Rabbit –
Date: Friday 29th April 2011

Terry began to come around from the heavy blow that pole-axed him to the ground. He held his concussed head, feeling for the inevitable sign of blood that confirmed the open wound. He felt sick and angry at his present state of subjugation. He tried to focus, to remember; gradually he spoke, "You honestly believe you can get away with this? You want your bloody heads read. You're bloody psychopaths, the lot of you, and that includes your gorilla bod with breath like cats' piss."

Tingfui clapped his hands and laughed; being described as a gorilla, he liked the comparison. Mitchell's lifeless body was still slumped in the chair, like a macabre trophy announcing Mengyao's revenge.

"Now, to business Terry. I am hoping your daughter is going to return with the rubies, because if she does not…"

"What in God's name are you on about; what rubies? You're all obsessed with the bloody things. What makes you think that I've got them? Do I look like a jewel thief?

All we've got is a fluffy rabbit. That is, if Carrie-Anne can get her hands on it."

Spider released a slap of such force across Terry's face that his head jolted back violently. Bruising started to appear almost immediately above his left eye. "Don't make me do that again 'cos I'm actually beginning to enjoy it. Do you get my drift, soldier boy?"

Mengyao interjected. "I'll try to put it this way, in case you don't understand. If your Carrie-Anne does not return with the goods, your newly found daughter is not only going to die, but believe me, in such a horrible way, that you would not care to witness. But you will, I assure you. You think that Mitchell's death was cruel and callous? Let me tell you, compared to what I have planned, it was simply a walk in the park. Then of course, you're next Terry. But let us leave that exciting stage for another time. So where is she, its 5pm? Where…? Wait, someone is coming."

There was an urgent knocking on the front door and a panic stricken cry. "Please, please, don't hurt my dad. I'm sorry I'm late, there were some problems, but I've got the rabbit. Mitchell, I've done what you asked." She now began banging the door with every ounce of her strength. Please tell me my dad is still alive? Dad can you hear me? Please open up, Mitchell, please? I've got the rabbit." She sobbed as she reiterated, "I've got the rabbit."

Spider opened the door and before Carrie-Anne could react she was grabbed and thrown inside. She landed hard on the floor grazing the side of her temple. "Who are you, what's happening? What have you done to my dad?" Now on her knees, Carrie-Anne gradually began to avert her gaze from the floor. She witnessed in front of her, a pair of twisted feet, one wearing a stiletto, the other without. Her eyes slowly appraised the situation, ascending towards the head of the body. She screamed in incredulity. "Oh my God, it's Mitchell, what the fucking hell is going on here?"

Just then Mengyao emerged from behind the door. His hideous face purveyed cunning and evil, not a hint of mercy or concern. "It's the little lady we've been waiting for; it's a pleasure to meet you. You've met of course Vicky Mitchell, but unfortunately she cannot say hello. Actually she became breathless with anticipation. She'd liked to have continued her little chit-chat with you; thought it would be most rewarding."

Spider nodded his head in gleeful admiration of Mengyao's sadistic humour.

"What's this little creature?" Mengyao reached to grab the fluffy rabbit. Carrie-Anne held the rabbit tightly, pulling it closer to her chest.

"Don't be shy. Why is the little bunny so precious? What secret does this little chap hold? Shall we see?" He seized the rabbit, wrenching it out of Carrie-Anne's grasp.

She turned to her father, who simply nodded his head from side to side, conveying, "Just release the rabbit. It's no use Carrie-Anne."

Mengyao spread the rabbit upon the robust kitchen table, as if he was just about to perform a post-mortem, and of course, that's exactly what was about to happen. The Stanley knife slashed into the stomach of Dandelion. A few tentative moments passed. Then withdrawn from the opened gut of the toy rabbit, was a small scarlet pouch. There was complete silence. Expectations rose to pitch-point level. Spider jostled nearer to the table, almost forgetting Terry and Carrie-Anne. "Would you Adam and Eve it? Is that the tomfoolery? Come on boss, I'm on tender hooks here. What's in the bag?" His cockney speech became more pronounced whenever he got excited, almost a cheeky-chappy conversion.

Terry's gaze was wholly on the parcel retrieved from the rabbit. Is this real? Is this what it is all about? Did his dad know? Is that why he was killed? Poor Rhian, she never had any inkling. Innocently keeping it, because she loved Terry, hoping he would return to honour his promise.

CHAPTER 80

Real Rubies Revealed at Afallon –

Date: Friday 29th April 2011

Even under the dull light of Afallon Cottage's downstairs room, you could not be anything but impressed by the incandescent glow of the blood rubies. Mengyao held the rubies in his vice like grip and turned to Mitchell's lifeless body. "Look Mitchell, look Mitchell…"

Spider looked on, simply raised his eyes. His expression said it all, "He's losing his bloody marbles".

Terry and Carrie-Anne were now perched side by side on kitchen chairs, both gagged, hands and feet bound tight. They could see everything, and do nothing. Mengyao was still wrapped up in the moment. It was worth the wait. The long wait, time only made these sparklers more valuable, desirous and gratifying.

"Right Boss, what's next? What we gonna do?"

Mengyao moved slowly towards Spider. "We've done it Spider, we've done it. Well done my loyal friend. You have played the perfect part. Listen, now we must dispose of these people. There's nothing like a blistering house fire; it seems on this celebratory occasion, the perfect send off.

You know, to finalize things…? Now, without any fuss, we need two bodies upstairs, out of my sight. They offend me. Then, we'll leave father and daughter down here. They'll enjoy the show, especially when it warms up."

Spider laughed in a pathetic, sycophantic manner that was easily readable and about as sincere as the average politician. "That's funny Boss, I'm gonna place Mitchell on the bed upstairs. She always said she was hot stuff in bed. She bloody will be now." Then it clicked. "Hang on a minute Boss, you said two upstairs?"

"Yes Spider. Two up, two down. Do you get it? You know, cottage, two up, two down."

Spider failed to notice that Mengyao was now rubbing his left index finger with his right hand, in spite of the absence of the gold ring. With no further indication, or flicker from his penetrating gape, he drove a switchblade right into the heart of Spider. "It has been a privilege my cockney china, but all good things must come to an end. Unfortunately, you will soon be, how you say, brown bread." Mengyao gloated, bordering on the psychotic.

Spider's eyes were as wide as saucers. Total disbelief of what had just occurred registered on his face, his life ebbing away by the second. He stumbled, as Mengyao removed the knife, falling onto the corpse of Mitchell, holding tightly onto her upper body and then gradually as his life drained from his body, sliding down her torso, his lips pressing against her knees, gradually arriving at her feet. Within moments it was over.

Mengyao handed his knife to his countryman, Tingfui. "Hurry, see if you can find some fuel; look in the outside shed. Our friends here deserve an efficient and cleansing send off, together to be reunited with poor Rhian, that sad, love struck alcoholic. You never know, even that excuse for a wife beater, Afon, might be waiting to say sorry. Afallon, if I'm correct means paradise? What a fitting conclusion. Let's hope your God is merciful, and accepts you, you weak, feeble, *Bai Tou's* (white heads).

CHAPTER 81

Mengyao Retreats from Afallon –

Date: Friday 29th April 2011

Mengyao became impatient and disconcerted, where was Tingfui? It had been several minutes since he left the cottage to forage for some fuel. He checked his watch, fifteen minutes had passed. He opened the front door, listening and then shouting. "If I cannot trust you with something so simple, I shall replace you with someone who can, and leave you as extra kindling. Now get a move on, do you hear?"

There was no sound at all. He became suspicious, his eyes searching the perimeter of the garden, like a periscope charting the ocean horizon, methodically absorbing all in sight. There was nothing unusual, out of place, no indication of intruders. His eyes fixed on the two captives; they were going nowhere. He began walking towards the ramshackle shed, stealthily like a cat on the prowl. Arriving at the door, he pushed it slowly open. Its hinges groaned as if begging for oil to smooth their operation. On the floor, partly covered by two heavy tarpaulins and a large plastic funnel, lay a khaki Jerry can containing petrol.

The wind had picked up, sleeting rain streamed off the corrugated iron roof making that all too familiar sound of rain with clogs on that usually heralded imminent thunder. He yelled in a whisper, as if that would convey his cry without giving himself away. There was an eerie silence. He grabbed the fuel can and moved gingerly back inside the house, closing the door, pushing his back against it, and glared directly at Terry and Carrie-Anne. Nothing must go wrong; this was his masterpiece, his master stroke, "We must not fail at this final hurdle." He didn't panic. It was not his style. Even in adverse or confusing situations, he remained adequately cool. But he knew something was not right. He speeded up his actions; his priority to make sure the scarlet pouch containing the rubies was in his grasp.

If in the finality of his plan he failed to complete the executions by incineration, the knife would have to do. He would make a decisive retreat, get out of there quickly, and disappear with his treasure. Tingfui was nowhere to be seen.

CHAPTER 82

Mengyao Planning Escape –

Date: Friday 29th April 2011

Something was evidently wrong. Tingfui had not returned. Mengyao assumed Tingfui got scared and disappeared quickly. Maybe a touch of conscience or pity, whatever, he would find him and deal with his betrayal. He checked, at least Carrie-Anne and Terry were still held captive. Fear seeped through every pore of Carrie-Anne's skin; it fed her aggressive streak, she bellowed piercingly. "Well, what are you waiting for, you madman? Come on, do your worst. I hope you rot in Hell! On second thoughts, that would be too good for you, you crazy, ugly, scumbag!"

"Your spirit does you proud little blossom. Regrettably, you know too much, and as you British would say, there is no sentiment in business. I have to concur." He ran his finger along the top of the fuel can, smiling as he delivered the verdict. "You see, one has to tidy up after oneself, it's the only way to stay ahead of the pack."

He began to pour the petrol liberally around the downstairs room, starting at the front door. Terry attempted to stand as Mengyao poured fuel everywhere. It was an admirable attempt, in spite of being bound to the chair. He strained every sinew, dragging himself forward, but Mengyao knew how to truss a captive. He delivered a rapid jab of his fist, hitting Terry full in the face, causing his nose immediately to issue blood. Terry slumped backwards, the chair toppled over, leaving him lying sideways on the floor, still bound to the chair.

"You would do your brothers-in-arms proud, fighting until the end, not giving up. One commends your father's fortitude Carrie-Anne. He has real audacity, no wonder you are so feisty, you obviously have your father's spirit." He took a breath, dramatically inhaling the overwhelming smell of petrol fumes. "Now, it is time to depart my friends. Thank you for your kind hospitality, but I really must go. Wait, there's something I nearly forgot." He pulled a cigarette lighter out of his pocket, two clicks and the flame appeared. At that moment, Mengyao was distracted by the scratching and meowing of the cat. Inquisitiveness got the better of him, he opened the door. "Well, it seems we have company."

The cat squeezed in through the door looking for a handout. What he received, was the left hand of Mengyao grabbing him by the neck and lifting him several feet of the floor. "Strange, if I were an Egyptian, I would be hailing this scabby feral as a deity. Cats were highly treasured in ancient Egypt. They were supposedly able to kill snakes."

"It's a pity it doesn't kill you then, you slimy arsehole!" screamed Carrie-Anne.

"I wonder if this scrawny mog can negotiate a deal for your swift passage into the afterlife." Upon which, Mengyao hurtled the trembling creature across the room. It bounced off a brass umbrella stand, let out a screech, and scrambled for cover behind a laundry basket. As Mengyao revelled in his knowledgeable interlude, the front door crashed open with such a hefty force that it was left just hanging on by the bent remains of the bottom hinge.

A startled Mengyao extinguished the lighter, surprised by the attack. Through the door entered Dafyyd Llewellyn. "I understand that you were responsible for my brother's death. You're going to need more than a few karate kicks to get you out of this."

He moved towards Mengyao and the dynamic fortitude of the two men came together. Dafyyd wielded brute force and immense strength. Mengyao, agility, speed, and a decisive, confident strategy on how to lay his opponent low. Dafyyd ambled forward, grabbing his opponent in a powerful bear hug, trying to crush the life out of him. Mengyao responded with forceful head butts. Dafyyd could withstand three or four, but the immense, honed power of these assaults caused him to loosen his grip. He elbowed Mengyao full in the face, causing him to reel backwards a good two meters or so, knocking over any furniture in his way. He leapt at Dafyyd, who received a flying kick that thudded into his chest. They rushed at each other again and Dafyyd let out a war cry as he smashed into Mengyao, picking him up and slamming him on to the table, crashing him down with such force that the legs duly collapsed. Mengyao stood, gained his composure and moved towards Dafyyd, demonstrating a martial art stance.

"It'll take more than that you evil bastard. This is for my brother." Dafyyd took him out like a prop forward taking out a winger, with a full tackle, hitting him like a train, felling him to the ground. Then he landed several blows on Mengyao's jaw, smacking his head hard on the stone floor, rendering him into a distinct daze.

Dafyyd turned; Carrie-Anne was pleading to be free. He rushed across trying to release her. As he began to negotiate her freedom, Mengyao grabbed his neck in a powerful headlock, squeezing it tightly, hoping that he would buckle. It was no good, the strength of the man and the size of his neck disadvantaged Mengyao, so he grabbed the left side of Dafyyd's braces, raising it from his shoulder, and in one quick movement he twisted the brace firmly around Dafyyd's neck. Mengyao placed his knee in the small of Dafyyd's back and pulled strongly, until the elastic brace thinned and began to cut deeply into his neck. It was at this point that Dafyyd threw himself backwards, forcing Mengyao back, crushing him against the wall causing him to loosen his grip. It worked. Blood was flowing from both men, but it seemed of no consequence. Life and death were at stake here, and the loser knew his fate. Like two gladiators, they exchanged blows, glances, and ridicule. Both men glared at each other, none prepared to show any weakness from the encounter. Terry and Carrie-Anne could only look on, placing their hope in Dafyyd. It was their only chance. Terry would love the chance of getting even with Mengyao, but it was out of his hands.

Mengyao realized he was facing a worthy opponent; he began to look for other ways of finishing him off. He grabbed the hefty brass lamp stand and lunged at the farmer, swinging wildly, his cool strategy turning to genuine concern. There was a real chance that Dafyyd might just get the better of him, he could not allow that.

Determined to be free, Carrie-Anne continued to wrestle against her bonds. Dafyyd's initial attempt had loosened them enough for her to wriggle, straining, until they became loose. Eventually managing to free her hands, she bent down keeping her eyes on Mengyao as she untied her ankles. Mengyao could see the inevitable happening, but engrossed as he was with Dafyyd, attempting to keep his life, he had no opportunity to deal with Carrie-Anne. She broke free, and immediately dived over to her dad who was still lying on his side on the floor. Those moments for Terry and Carrie-Anne, seemed an eternity, but now they were free, and about to enter the fray.

Mengyao quickly assessed the situation. He broke free from close battle, grabbed the lighter out of his pocket, and ignited the flame. Everything seemed to drift into slow motion. What would happen now if Mengyao's threat became active? There was petrol everywhere, including on them. Mengyao felt his pockets, to feel if the scarlet pouch was still secure. Yes, he smiled, it was still his. He moved towards the door, watching his opposition, holding the lighter up high. Dafyyd, Terry, and Carrie-Anne moved as one towards Mengyao, like three wolves slowly approaching a camp fire. They tried to talk some sense into him, pleading with him to extinguish the flame.

"Well, I have to admit, I could have done without that fierce exchange, but now I must go. For me, back to my country, for you, eternity." He held the flame aloft in a dramatic fashion, indicating the time was imminent. Just at the point of his *grand finale* the flame was distinguished. Before he had time to gather any thoughts, Brindle clubbed him on the skull with a spade he had picked up from the garden. Mengyao fell to the ground. Brindle wrenched the lighter out of his hand and placed it in his pocket.

"Now, that's what I call timing, impeccable, as always. It's OK, he's not dead, still breathing, skull like an armadillo's arse. He'll come round soon, so we better get

337

him secure." Brindle leant down, pushing Mengyao on his side, handcuffing his hands behind his back. "They don't make spades like this anymore. Good, solid, and lasting. Must be years old. I bet this degenerate didn't dig this on his loaf?"

There was a silence; nobody in the room could have believed he just said that.

"Do you get it? Dig, you know, dig this, as in spade? Of course, I could have whacked him with the hoe, but it's not Christmas." Brindle was on top form, or he thought he was. The pregnant pause was punctuated by Dafyyd, delivering a deep belly-laugh. In turn, the others began to loosen up a little from the immense tension they had just faced. Carrie-Anne and Terry began to chuckle, with relief more than anything else. They were that close to being burnt alive. They didn't find Mike's attempt to lighten the mood very funny, but the thought that Dafyyd had got the joke, penny dropping very slowly, made it worth a giggle.

Mike leant down and took the scarlet pouch out of Mengyao's pocket. "So this is what all the mystery was all about." He opened the pouch and peered in. "These are the real goodies, are they?" He let them gently slip from the pouch into his left palm. "Wow, I can see what all the fuss was about. These are worth a small fortune." He quickly returned them into the bag. "Right…"

338

Terry interrupted, "You left it late Brindle. We were nearly all toast."

"How on earth did you get Dafyyd to come along?" questioned Carrie-Anne. She wanted to give the old farmer a hug, but the awkwardness of her relationship with his brother prevented her. She bashfully looked at him, trying her best to say thank you with her eyes.

Dafyyd acknowledged her gratitude; subjected to such an ordeal, it was remarkable Carrie-Anne was still compos mentis. Dealing with the problem directly, he walked up to her, and gave her such a warm embrace.

She started to weep; emotion getting the better of her, she leant deeper into his broad chest. She joked, "Now I know what an orange feels like in a juicer." She smiled, wiping her eyes. "Terry, meet my uncle, Dafyyd Llewellyn."

Terry leant forward, smearing the blood off his busted nose onto his shirtsleeve. He shook Dafyyd's huge hand. The powerful squeeze began to hurt. No matter, Terry was determined not to flinch, but was relieved when Desperate Dan let go.

CHAPTER 83

The Leaving of Afallon Cottage –

Date: Friday 29th April

"Do you think I'll get away with reasonable force when I explain how and why I smacked this Chinaman on the head with the garden spade?" asked Brindle sarcastically.

"If it had been down to me, I'd have sliced his head clean off. They can ask all the bloody questions they want, I'm just so glad you arrived in time, albeit with not a minute to spare. Bet you couldn't do that again?" Terry challenged.

"Don't you worry I'd have got him. I was just coming up to my second breath. I'd have grabbed him by the balls and stuck that lighter so far up his arse he'd set his tongue on fire," yelled Dafyyd, with a big beaming smile, as if he'd just been in an arm wrestling competition.

"There are another two upstairs, bodies I mean." Terry informed Brindle. "In the bedroom; that lump of a henchman carried them up. Whatever happened to him?"

Brindle went to climb the stairs. "Don't touch any more than you have to. If you ever *can* forget, this is a crime scene. I'll go alone."

The bedroom door was already open. He walked in. There to his left were the bodies of Mitchell and Spider Harris. There was no affectionate laying-out of the bodies. It was clear they were simply hurled onto the bed and left without giving them a second glance. Sprawled out like two manikins awaiting disposal. No dignity or bravado now, only rest. Mike didn't expect Mitchell's life to end like this, and as for Spider, he was astounded as to how he climbed the greasy pole of criminality to become this obnoxious, callous killer. Now, it was over.

Brindle felt uncomfortable. There was something about this cottage that enhanced the uneasiness of being alone with two bodies, as if it welcomed it, embraced it. He wanted to get out, but curiosity won the day. He was on the edge. He moved towards the bed and bent over, staring into Mitchell's lifeless eyes. Just then as he began to straighten up, something grabbed his shoulder and squeezed tightly. Blood pumping overtime and ashen faced, a spooked Brindle instinctively turned around. "Bloody hell, it's you Terry, I told you to stay downstairs. You put the fear of God up me. Y-fronts nearly had a visit from Mr Browning."

"Sorry, Mr Brindle, you had been some time. I was just wondering if you were OK. What with Tingfui still on the loose."

"Look at these two," Brindle continued. "There is no fitting epitaph, unless you know of one filled with contempt,

341

or one highlighting the banality, the vanity of vanities, of a heart filled with avarice. After all, greed can never be truly satisfied, any more than a nymphomaniac can refuse her lust. There is always a drive for more, leaving a sad wake in its path as it did for Mitchell and Harris. Goodbye Mitchell, maybe at last you'll be at peace. Spider, as for you my old son, you really did get tangled in your own web of corruption. You never possessed the intelligence or strength of character to escape its lethal hold. Look at you now."

Brindle turned away, "Quickly Terry let's get out of here." They descended the stairs.

Brindle clapped his hands to rally the others. "OK, let's get going. We have to notify the local police about all of this. I for one just want to get away from here, gives me the heebie-jeebies."

"Let's get away from this creepy hellhole," Carrie-Anne shrugged her shoulders as she spoke.

Dafyyd pushed his back against the broken door, wedging it shut as they vacated the cottage. "Quite a rewarding day's work." The big farmer grinned and continued, "Haven't had a good scrap in years. I must get going; all this excitement has made me thirsty. Hope to see you soon Carrie, there is much to catch up on. I'm going to get cleaned up, down a large cold beer and then begin to put some things in order."

He winked at Carrie, got into his truck and sped away.

CHAPTER 84

Leaving Afallon Cottage; Confronted by Yun –
Date: Friday 29th April 2011

The tyres made that familiar crackling sound as they drove over the stony driveway leading out of the cottage. As they indicated to turn left on to the main road, two silver-grey BMWs edged across the driveway barring their exit. The doors of the first car opened quickly, and three Chinese men alighted, slamming their doors, simultaneously buttoning up their jackets as they walked towards Brindle. Brindle lowered the driver side window and leant out. The three men said nothing, dispersing themselves around the car like presidents' bodyguards.

Out of the second car with the shaded windows, slowly and deliberately stepped a tall, good-looking Chinese man.

Carrie-Anne spoke. "It's him, it's him, it's him. I tell you, that's the man who has been stalking me, watching me. The man I first met at the airport in Malaga. I knew I wasn't crazy."

"Would you all like to step out of the car? Please, do not try anything rash, these men are highly trained."

"Who the bloody hell are you?" Brindle asked.

"Do you remember Shanyuan, DI Brindle? I am Yun, his son. I am the guardian, commissioned by my father to let this chronicle unfold, however many years it took, until knowledge of the real rubies came to light. Please would you come with me?" He pointed to the car. "All will be revealed. We will take care of this mess; your cars will be taken from the scene. I want you to meet someone."

Carrie-Anne looked at her dad, simply raising her eyebrows and shaking her head. She didn't have a clue who this someone to meet was.

The car turned left by the white windmill onto Pontycarne Street towards Usk Town, through an impressive avenue of trees, alongside the river, turning left at the Three Salmons Hotel into Bridge Street. The car slowed down opposite the fire station, turning left into the drive of the historic Usk Castle. They vacated the car at the entrance of the castle grounds. Yun strode forward. "Here, we must climb the path. Come, come, you have nothing to be scared of."

CHAPTER 85

Yun Takes Brindle, Carrie-Anne and Terry to Usk Castle.
Date: Friday 29th April 2011

Brindle walked alongside Yun, he loved all this. Terry and Carrie-Anne followed cautiously, sticking close together, Terry's arm cosseting Carrie-Anne. The noble grounds and imposing view over Usk and beyond was quite striking. They stood inside the shell of what once was a magnificent castle. Much of the ancient walls, now covered with creeper still remained, along with a few notable towers and the remains of a banqueting hall. They walked on to the north-side, towards the open-air chapel of St. George's, followed closely by two inquisitive geese. An array of flowers and shrubbery surrounded a marked tribute of prayer.

"I guess you have many questions?" said Yun.

"I'm sure they have? Delighted to meet you all, it has been a long time." Relying heavily on an intricately carved walking stick, he walked forward, side by side with his winsome partner.

Brindle responded first. "Shanyuan, I can't believe it. You old rascal, what on earth's going on? I'd heard you were abroad, back in China? How did it come to this? Is that you Lijuan? You look great, must be the lifestyle. Still doing the Tai Chi, I bet that's what it is?"

"I will explain, but for now," replied Lijuan, "I have arranged a little light refreshment. Please…"

Shanyuan directed them to a small pagoda type shelter. "It is OK, we have arranged with the proprietors. We have these grounds all to ourselves tonight. It is getting dark, please sit. We have arranged lighting."

The pagoda was surrounded by large candles mounted on knee-high wicker pillars. The fragrance was calming. His wife Lijuan began to serve them with traditional chicken and vegetable rolls, Chinese pancakes, red bean cakes, cinnamon biscuits and raspberry cordial.

"The remains of this 13th century castle has great history. Imagine the stories it could tell, unfolding the years. Tales of intrigue and treachery, battles won and honour held. It is a fitting place, a place of romantic beauty and of grim massacres. Isn't it a wonder, how good and evil are never far away from each other? It was… Would you explain Yun?" Shanyuan gently touched his son. "Bring, Mike, up to date. I am sure he has already deduced much of this drawn out saga, we will colour in the grey."

CHAPTER 86

Usk Castle – Conclusion –
Date: Friday 29th April 2011

"Do you know, that this year between the 3rd of February 2011 and 22nd Jan 2012, is The Year of the Rabbit? You see, it had to conclude on a Year of the Rabbit. This was my father's wish. Mitchell had to be out of prison; Terry, you had to meet Carrie-Anne. The riddles were my father's test. He enjoyed bringing them to your attention. He took the risk, that you Terry, would contact Brindle. You see, your father's killers had to be brought to justice. Mitchell and Harris deserved no less.

Mengyao destroyed my father's business and took away his dignity, for that he would pay. My father's words, 'One digs a well, before one is thirsty'. Shanyuan, has now drank deep, to quench his righteous thirst, and is satisfied."

Lijuan interrupted. "Could I just ask if everybody has finished eating, or would like anymore to drink?"

"My dad and mum always spoke so highly of you Lijuan, especially you're cooking. These cinnamon biscuits are fantastic; did you make them yourself Lijuan?" Terry grabbed another. "No wonder Dad spent so much time with you guys when on his late shift. I can see why. Thank you for the lovely food. It's nice to take in something delicious, along with trying to digest all this crazy information."

"Thank you, Terry. You're very kind."

"Call me Nobby. All my friends do." He nodded his approval and winked at Lijuan, who just looked on. Kindness radiated out every pore of her diminutive body, a gentle lady, highly intelligent and extremely resilient. Quiet in nature, many would pass her by without any recognition of what a treasure she was. Shanyuan, of course, was well aware, and had been in love since the first day they met.

Yun continued. "I stood there that night, peering in from the bottom of the stairs, watching my father placing the rubies into the fluffy rabbit. How troubled he looked, how those bastards robbed him of nearly everything. But my father was smart, switching the rubies, fooling Mitchell and Mengyao. He planned ahead, he loved Harry dearly, and when later he found out about his cruel death, he was determined to revenge the brutal murder."

"You're certainly colouring in the grey, Yun; in fact, there's so much bloody colour it's more like a kaleidoscope," Brindle said, checking the effect of this sensitive news on Terry.

"Harry gave my father the photographs for safe-keeping, the evidence of Mitchell's connection with the triads. He thought that they were on to him. That night at Harry's

348

apartment, Mitchell and Spider entered, they desperately needed to find those photographs."

Brindle was taking all this in, like he was indulging in a stack of profiteroles and fresh cream. "Now hang on a minute. What you're telling me is that Mitchell and Harris were not looking for the rubies that night, but, photographs? So, that night in the Italian restaurant, Emily and I got it wrong. We were sure they were after the rubies. That seemed to be the only logical answer."

Now Shanyuan entered the conversation. "Mitchell thought she had secured the real rubies, placing them in a safe-deposit box in a UK security service in London. But my father tricked both of them. She got word somehow of the photographs and could not afford to be locked up for her dealings with the triads. Harry was brutally tortured, but still would not admit to any photos. He was a brave man. She had Spider viciously murder him, then, make it look like the Woods' doing. They searched the place from top to bottom, but there were no photographs on the premises."

"But," Mike interrupted, "Spider Harris, that day in the market, swore he had been threatened by the triads, forcing him to release Harry's address." As Brindle recalled the encounter, he simultaneously felt in his pocket, holding on to the pocket watch he took that day.

"It was fabrication, Mr Brindle. Of course, the triads would undoubtedly benefit from the Woods being put in prison for murder. But, they never threatened Spider as to the whereabouts of any of the Woods' contacts, or runners. It was Mitchell all along. With that underling Harris, they did all the dirty work. Terry, they murdered your father, now they're all dead, including Mengyao."

Terry challenged, "Wait a minute; Mengyao wasn't dead when we left him, pretty banged up, but not dead?"

There was no answer from Shanyuan or Yun.

"More cordial, Carrie-Anne?"

"Yes, thank you Lijuan, I'm so thirsty, must be my nerves."

Shanyuan continued. "So, Mr. Brindle, I deposited the photos in your car that day. That furnished you with all the evidence you needed to put Mitchell away."

Then who actually took the photographs?" questioned Brindle.

"Who took the photographs? Why, the Woods. For insurance purposes, that's why. They placed them with Harry, thus, making Harry the keeper. So if the Woods were arrested. They had the ace bargaining chip. But it all went pear-shaped. The Woods had no idea that I had obtained the photos. They had lost their insurance packet. Unfortunately for Mitchell, not obtaining the photos set her back many years."

The sky above the castle grounds was a hue of red and satin blue as the sun descended and night's blanket tucked it away.

"So, Mengyao never died in the explosion on Wardour Street," said Brindle. "It was a clever set up. The ring on the decapitated finger cleverly left as a decoy, to deceive us, men with no records, no identity. They were expendable. Mengyao and his father Longwei staged the whole thing, thus, releasing him from the ordained punishment of death. The other leaders, in turn, believing it was done by some rival faction. No problem, either way it solved their predicament, except that is, for the rubies. They were never going to recover them."

"Correct, Mr Brindle. Well done. However, the note, did you unravel the note?"

Brindle almost forgot. "Oh, well yes, I did have a quick read, but no time to investigate. Was that from you?"

Shanyuan smiled. "Just a little fun, but the direction was in the clue."

Mike pulled it out of his pocket and read it in front of the rest.

"Not another riddle, please," pleaded Carrie-Anne. But, Mike loved every minute of this.

"As you dwell on the riddles, and chew on the fat
You'll find in the name of an elegant cat."

Time passed. Everyone looked upon each other. Maybe the frightening ordeal had taken the edge off solving puzzles for now. They all shrugged their shoulders.

"OK Shanyuan, we give up, tell us please, how do we find an elegant cat?"

"That is for you to find out, maybe you already have? The rubies please, Mr. Brindle. They must be returned to their rightful owners."

Mike handed over the scarlet pouch. "If you tell me they're false, I am going to shove them so far up Longwei's arse he'll be cutting his teeth on them."

"I am afraid it is too late to fulfil that exercise. Longwei died a few years ago. Don't be upset. Justice has played itself out. The murderers of Harry Mead have finally met their end. Carrie-Anne, you are safe now and I believe things are going to improve for you, no end.

"Then who killed my stepfather?" enquired Carrie-Anne. "Was it Mengyao, Mitchell, Harris?"

"Nobody, Afon took his own life. He found the weight of losing your mother, the incessant jealousy and abuse that brought that about, too hard to live with. He could never forgive himself."

"I thought I was supposed to be the detective around here. Then what of the cap, Afon's hat, Shanyuan?" Brindle enquired.

"The cap," he giggled, almost childlike. "Sometimes you see what you want to see. I know that, and Mengyao knew that. Carrie-Anne, you were in so much of a panic, anybody's similar cap would have done, and the trick was to draw you out. Anyhow the night is upon us and there is much to do. It has been a pleasure to meet you all. Lijuan and I will always be grateful of our friendship with Harry and Jenny. Time passes on, but memories remain strong."

Shanyuan and Lijuan walked away into the night.

CHAPTER 87

Hillcrest Dairy to Nant-y-derry, Arnant Cottage –

Date: Friday 29th April 2011

Leaving the Castle, Yun drove the weary threesome to the current location of their cars. As he began to negotiate the narrow, winding road, edging towards the outskirts of Nant-y-derry, Carrie-Anne began to sit up, paying more attention to their possible destination. "Please, don't tell me, there's another episode in this bizarre saga, I am about as nervy as an alcoholic locked in a tea shop."

"Now, now, princess, take it easy, you'll be OK. It's all over, sweetheart. It's all over." Terry continued his reassurance with hugs and kisses.

They entered the village, heading towards St Peter's Church, not far from where Rhian's grave lay. Yun drove up a muddy drive and parked, facing a broad farmhouse. This was the Llewellyn's family business, Hillcrest Dairy. Brindle had already realised where he was, warning, "Mind that dog, Treacle, he doesn't take any prisoners." Terry noticed his Range Rover next to Dafyyd's truck. It was dark now, about 10.30pm. The rain had disappeared and it was quite a reasonable April night; bright stars, cool breeze and low flying bats.

"About time, what happened to you all?" Dafyyd stood there with Treacle close beside him.

Brindle replied, "It's a long story Dafyyd, I will explain later, but we are okay."

Dafyyd continued, stroking the top of Treacle's head as he did so: "It's good to see you. I was worried; I have no idea what to do now? What are we gonna do? What happened to that Mengyao and his side- kick? What about the bodies? How are we going to explain this? Who's going to believe such a complicated series of events?"

Yun stepped up, beckoning them all closer together. "Listen my friends, you do not have to worry about anything. It is enough for you that you have gone through this ordeal. We will take care of all of this. We have our own methods. If you are pursued through the legal system, trying to maintain your innocence in this affair, you will be in and out of the courts for years. Please forget this, get on with your lives. As the Chinese say, think twice, and then say nothing. What is your counsel, Mr Brindle?"

"Are you suggesting that as a law abiding, by the book, member of the constabulary, I could possibly turn a blind eye to all of this? The disappearance of a man who was already announced dead, and two obsessive, murdering scumbags who deserved their comeuppance many moons ago. I'll have to give it some serious thought." His stern look began to transform into a mischievous grin.

Yun continued, "Carrie- Anne, your grandmother and grandfather never had the joy of meeting you. It would have meant so much to Harry and Jenny. Take these." He opened a small leather holdall. "Don't worry, it's not a rabbit, just a token. He handed over Harry's beloved cherry wood pipe and taxi badge, accompanied by Jenny's book of special homemade recipes. Take care of these; memories are precious."

Terry never asked how Yun came to possess these, but was thankful that he did. Tears welled up in his eyes, as he hugged Carrie-Anne again.

Yun spoke softly to Carrie-Anne and Terry. "You must both understand that Harry knew nothing of the rubies. My father needed someone he could trust. He knew Harry would not discard the gift of the rabbit. It was a very precious time. My father would wait for an opportue time; share the truth when it became safe, rewarding him generously and returning the rubies to their rightful owners. He hadn't planned for Harry to pass the rabbit on to you Terry. That was to say, at the least, difficult. And so the story moved on, taking this long journey and eventually reaching its objective."

Carrie-Anne's mind began to wander. She was still madly in love with Sam, eager to see him again. Where was he anyway? Did he know anything about any of this, and what about her flat mate, Helen? She must be worried sick.

"We better get a move on. Carrie-Anne, you jump in the truck with me, Mike and Nobby can follow us in their cars," Dafyyd implored.

"Hey, somebody has finally called me Nobby; about bloody time. Now where are we going?"

"Good question. I'm taking Carrie-Anne home."

Dafyyd drove to the cottage that held so many memories, good and bad, hoping she would settle for a while. You never know.

"Oh, by the way, you'll never guess what?" said Dafyyd as they arrived. "I found my brother's cap after all. Daft beggar, he left it in the back of the tractor."

He handed Carrie-Anne the keys to the house. "This is yours now. It is what your mother would have wanted. Remember the precious times Carrie. Let them transcend the bad, if you can? Go on, off you go, open the door."

"Dad, will you come with me, please?" She held out her hand.

Terry grasped it firmly, looking into her eyes and said boldly, "Come on princess, let's do this together."

"Wait, the lights are on."

"Yes and the fire's made up, Carrie-Anne," shouted Dafyyd.

Brindle was just watching it all, thinking about how he was going to explain his extended Easter break. Emily had planned a few days in Weston-super-Mare with her sister.

"Sam, what are you doing here? Dad, Sam is here."

Sam hobbled up to cuddle Carrie-Anne. "How I've missed you. Remember you owe me a *tout a l'heure*. Come here chick, what have you been up to?"

Carrie-Anne was lifted completely off her feet. They cuddled tightly, imparting all the love they felt for each other, in that long, warm embrace. "Talk about, absence makes the heart grow, well, you know the rest." She kissed him like she tried to impart a month's love into one day. Then it began to sink in that all eyes were firmly set on the passionate embrace. Carrie-Anne fanned her face with her hand.

Terry's princess was indeed all grown up. If he was in any doubt, it had become clear now. It might be his little girl, but it was Sam's whole lotta woman.

She noticed the small photo on the mantelpiece. There she was, in her primary school uniform, sitting on her mam's knee. How proud her mam looked. "I love you, Mam," she whispered.

Just then, breaking the intensity of the moment, a skinny, ginger cat rubbed his head against her shin. She picked him up. "How did you get here? Still hungry you little darling?" She kissed him on the head, "That makes three ginger knobs in the family." Turning to Sam she answered, "What have I been up to, Sam? What have I been up to?" Smiling at her dad she continued, "Nothing much; nothing much at all. Let's all have a glass of wine, I think we could all use one. Dad, no ifs or buts, you're staying tonight, and Mike, you're welcome."

"Oh, I'd love to, but I have a beautiful, and I expect, somewhat angry woman waiting for me. A hellish Celtic temper when roused! I hear Weston-super-Mare is lovely this time of the year. Good food and everything. There's nothing like a stroll up the Grand Pier with sand on your toffee-apple."

All of a sudden Brindle began to laugh out loud, as if he had just uncovered some fiendish plot. "You wily old fox Shanyuan. You haven't beaten me. You haven't beaten me. *You'll find in the name of an elegant cat.*" He looked to the heavens, and shouted out, "an elegant cat. Of course, Elegant-Dandy and Cat-Lion – the fluffy rabbit, Dandelion!" He was just about to exploit his mastery of the puzzle when his mobile phone rang.

"Hello is that you guv'nor?"

"Thank God it's you, Blakely. I was preparing myself for a blitzkrieg from my loving other half."

"A murder, sir, there's a body of a semi-naked male, mid-thirties, found with what seems to be ritualistic damage to his chest. And get this, he's wearing a dog disc attached to his left ear lobe, like an earring, some strange inscription, can't make it out, it's not English, possibly Arabic. The victim has been unceremoniously dumped in the car park of the Duke of Wellington, Nottinghill, Portobello Road, W11."

"Well, Blakely, looks like I can't be away for more than two minutes! Call Emily, we need a forensic report and post mortem immediately. No holiday now; what great timing." That cheered up Brindle, he'd managed to escape the caustic tongue of Emily's sister, and there was no love lost there. "I am on my return now."

Brindle's eyes lit up, it was what he craved, what he lived for. The hunt was on.

Lightning Source UK Ltd.
Milton Keynes UK
UKHW01f1704010918
328164UK00001B/1/P